I0676124

Setanta
The Warped One

Sean Doyle

Copyright © 2011 by Sean Doyle

An Aon Epic
P.O. Box 1071,
Easthampton, New York 11937

ISBN: 978-0-9835604-0-1

Library of Congress Control Number: 2011912727

Design and Typesetting by
Geoff Benge at
Silver Fern Bookworks

Printed in the United States

Contents

Note Bene   *1011, Anno Domini*

This is a trial of my pen here, by Mael Moró, son of the son of Conn.

I am a monk, an artist, a scribe, and a scholar, living on a rocky isle off the coast of Ireland.

At the bequest of my order, I live alone in a beehive shelter of slate and stone. At the request of my order, I have recorded tales of Setanta the Warped One, from ancient books and elders skilled in oral lore. In tower tall and cottage small, Setanta survives as the soul and spirit of our pagan past.

Inscribed with golden letters on a calfskin from my order. is the legend:

SETANTA THE WARPED ONE

On a lonely isle, in a restless ocean, these tales of Celtic Gods and immortal heroes occupy my attention.

> O, My Lord Divine,
> O, This day so fine,
> My prayer is still.
> Granl me words at will.

Mael Moró

One

O NCE UPON A time, in the beginning, when Old God made the world and whiskey, Old God had a piece left over. This piece puzzled Old God. It did not belong among the stars above or the earth below.

When no one but himself was looking, Old God dropped this spare piece into the sea. Old God then inhaled the clouds in the sky through his left nostril, and exhaled them through his right nostril. Thus did Old God conceal his odd isle with mist, myths, and mystery.

Old God called it Éire, his Garden of Eden. Others named it Ireland, some say as a nod to the disposition of its inhabitants. This Old God of the Gaels doted on tales of heroes and harlots, and all he could put into the making of them.

The following is one story of the begetting of the immortal hero, Setanta. It is as true as the next tale or the one after that.

As usual, Briar MacMalice the Satirist got out of the wrong side of his bed on a cold spring morn. Briar was a man inclined to dark cloaks and black thoughts. He was a long, horse-faced man with one raised and one lowered eyebrow; long in the tooth, short on wisdom, bald on the pate, and loose on the nape, he was sharp with the tongue and blunt with the thought.

The long and short of Briar MacMalice? Briar of the poisoned tongue had an ability to talk out of both sides of his mouth at the same time.

Wrapped in his dark cloak, Briar stood beside his chariot driver and said, "To the Red Branch House of King Connor, driver, and don't spare the horses."

Briar's pithy statements became the vernacular of the multitudes. He sucked on the juice of his abiding jealousy of King Connor until they reached the plain outside the Red Branch House. His chalice of malice overflowing, Briar was pissing vinegar behind his chariot. His raised eye focused on the virgin sister of King Connor, picking a bouquet of spring flowers. Dectain the Delectable. "Go to the Red Branch, driver. I'll follow on foot." Briar shook his staff and girded his loins. He lusted after Dectain, as he had for years. Fearing his cold eyes and caustic tongue, Dectain kept enough distance from Briar MacMalice to draw attention to her aversion. Briar's vicious invectives raised blisters on the face and boils on the bum of his victims.

"Luck of the Irish to you, my dearest Dectain." Briar laid his hand on the startled girl. Dectain sucked in her breasts, feeling the chill of his dead eyes on the curving calves of her legs. The tight grip of his fingers on her elbow froze her heart. She felt like the last rose of summer on the first day of winter.

Then, as now, men who survived on their baser instincts sought to intimidate by strength and fear. "It is time we discussed our future, pet." Briar cupped her firm rear. Dectain looked above and about for aid. Then, as now, help came from the heavens above; flocks of gorgeous birds descended from the sky to land on the meadow around the tense couple.

Soon enough the voracious birds ate the roots of the plants, flowers, and grass on the plain. The birds left naught alive but Dectain and Briar MacMalice. To fight off the birds pecking at his ankles, Briar released Dectain.

"We must tell the king about the birds before they ruin the province," Dectain said, backing away from Briar.

"The king can wait; we must settle what is between us, Dectain, before it dies like the land." Briar moved toward Dectain.

The birds advanced, pecking at the large feet of Briar MacMalice. Blood spurting from his calves, Briar ran after the fleet Dectain to the house of her brother, the King of Ulster.

King Connor MacNessa called for nine chariots to chase the birds away from his land. His heroes were adept at hunting birds, and he picked the best of them for the task.

"Where is Ibor the Driver?" King Connor called for his charioteer.

"Connor, my brother, let me drive your chariot," Dectain said, wishing to escape the attentions of Briar and see the beautiful birds again. Connor nodded his assent. He loved his lovely sister. Dectain ran to ready the king's chariot.

Among the Ulster warriors picked by Connor were Conall Carny and Laire. His thoughts on the king's sister, Briar offered his aid to the king.

Across the green fields of ancient Ulster, the nine chariots led by King Connor followed the flight of the birds. The beauty of the birds was excelled only by their song. Each coupling of birds was linked by a silver chain, making nine score pairs in all.

Two birds flew to guide each flight, connected by a yoke of silver and a song of golden notes. The flight of the birds above the nine chariots ceased when night brought a heavy fall of snow. Losing sight of the birds, King Connor ordered his men to unyoke their chariots. Before his heroes, he praised his brave and beautiful sister for her aid. Only then did Connor send Conall and Briar to seek shelter from the inclement weather.

After a search in the thick snow near the River Boann, Briar stumbled upon a solitary house of modest size. The bold Conall knocked on the door of the lonely house.

The door opened to disclose a tall, broad man, with closely curled blond hair and a green cloak wrapped about him. Beneath the cloak, he wore a short tunic embroidered with red thread, pulled tight against his white skin. A knob of yellow gold glinted on the black shield slung on his shoulder.

Gauging the small size of the house, Briar MacMalice ignored king and comrades outside in the foul weather.

"Would you have food and shelter for two bird lovers adrift in the snow, kind friend?" Briar asked, kept in his place by the presence of the host. Looking sharply at Briar, the man of the house greeted his night visitors. "You are more than welcome to my hospitality. If there are others abroad on this blessed night, especially any women, bring them hither. We have much to celebrate."

Thanking the stately stranger, Conall Carney returned to King Connor's camp in the storm.

The reluctant Briar followed; sharing was not in his character.

"King Connor, comrades, we are welcomed to a house of blessed events—especially Dectain."

Conall had their full attention as he spoke. "I have a feeling that a birth is imminent. Our host is a man of extraordinary grace—tall as a god from the other side."

King Connor hugged his sister at the news. All looked at Briar, awaiting his remarks. As usual, Briar's mouth outran his mind. "The house is so small, you'd have to shift the walls to set the table. As for sleeping, it is tight enough—for discomfort and discontent."

Once more, they yoked their chariots. They made their way to the small house through the thick snow. The man of the house bid them enter, and they crowded into his storeroom in the cellar at his suggestion.

Soon these hunters of birds were in rare good form. Fueled by food and strong, strange drink, the house seemed to expand with their good humor.

King Connor and his sister were much impressed with the manner and style of their host. They followed him into a small, well-appointed room.

"Welcome to my house on this side of the river. I am known as Lugh." The tall stranger did not tell them his place of birth or pedigree, the custom of introduction in the province of Ulster.

"I am King Connor MacNessa from the province of Ulster, and this is my sister, Dectain," said Connor.

Lugh looked deep into Dectain's green-flecked eyes. She felt her soul swoon under his gaze and love enter her heart. Never had she experienced such joy from another's glance. Her eyelashes quivered with an ecstasy of expectation. A single tear from her right eye acknowledged her enthrallment to the handsome stranger.

"I have to see to the birth of a hero." Lugh took his leave, glancing at Dectain. King Connor felt a kinship with the elegant Lugh. He sensed they were both from the other side, since Lugh bypassed the custom of reciting birth and pedigree.

From the way Lugh had looked at her, Dectain knew this was an enchanted evening.

When Lugh returned, he asked permission of Connor to address his blushing sister. "There is no other woman in my house but yourself on this snowbound night. My home needs a woman's touch," Lugh said. King Connor nodded his assent. Dectain followed the stately stranger and Connor drank deep of Lugh's strong ale.

Briar MacMalice stayed close to King Connor, plying him with the strong ale of Lugh of the Narrow House. Once again, his meanness of spirit overwhelmed Briar's sense of obligation to his king.

"Are there any women here for the king's pleasure?" asked Briar in a sharp tone.

"There are no other women here," said King Connor. Dectain appeared as he said this. Spite and malice overcame Briar as he observed Dectain glowing with love from her encounter with Lugh. She had never reacted to his advances as she did to this dark stranger. Briar handed Connor another goblet of foaming ale, and set his malice in motion.

"Dectain," Briar spoke so that it seemed the name Dectain came from the voice of Lugh. Surprised, Dectain fell, with a slight push from Briar, into the arms of her brother.

"Help the king, assaulted by his sister!" Briar spoke from the other side of his mouth in the tone of King Connor's voice, with an emphasis on the word "assaulted." The bird hunters rushed to the aid of King Connor. They stopped at the sight of an inebriated king holding tight to his sister. Because of the high regard of his subjects, King Connor had first rights to any woman in his kingdom. With the promise of passion and the presence of youth, Dectain was one of the most desirable women at the court of the King of Ulster. The satirist in Briar knew that a salacious detail, true or false, could demean Dectain with infamy—forever.

After a last glass of ale poured for the king by the demonic Briar, Connor and his Ulster heroes fell into a long, dreamless sleep. Nine full months and nine long days passed. Enough time to conceive and birth a child.

They woke to the lusty cry of a newborn babe. All was gone. The fresh snow, the tiny house, the stately host named Lugh. All that remained of that enchanted evening was a bonny baby boy in Dectain's arms.

Close by, tied to an oak tree, stood two newborn foals, one black and one white. King Connor untied the foals. They made their way on unsteady legs to where Dectain cuddled her baby. They were bound to the newborn babe for life. A gift from Lugh? All were awed by the long sleep, the new babe, the memory of Lugh, and the mean mouth of Briar.

And so they returned to the Red Branch House of King Connor. Shortly afterwards, King Connor married his sister Dectain to an older warrior named Sualtáin MacRoigh, who adored both the boy and Dectain.

Dectain called the boy Setanta, as named by his father, Lugh. To distract the people of Ulster from the truth, Briar MacMalice spread the rumor that a drunken King Connor was the father of Setanta. It was Dectain's custom to sleep in the king's bed for protection when traveling, and many believed the lie.

Setanta was reared on the plains of Muirtaine by his mother, Dectain, and his foster father, Sualtáin. Because of the caustic tongue of Briar MacMalice, Dectain kept her son far from the court of her brother, King Connor.

Setanta was a fretful babe, ever seeking the unavailable. It was not until Dectain used a shield of her husband as a cradle that Setanta slept like a baby.

King Connor had his smith, Cullen, forge tiny weapons for his sister's son. A short javelin, a round shield, a gold- handled sword, and a barbed spear arrived at Dectain's house, delivered by Katbad, the king's Druid. From the finest ash, Sualtáin carved a boy-sized hurley stick for his foster son. These, and a silver ball called a sliotar, used in the sport of hurling, were the toys that soothed the boy Setanta in his early years.

Setanta grew up strong and strange on the plains of Muirtaine. Each day he went alone to practice with his warrior weapons until they became part of his being.

In his mind, he saw his spear hit his target before he threw it. Thus, his arm and aim welded with his weapons. Setanta could throw his spear through the eye of an eagle and catch both before they hit the ground. Alone and unaided, he wrestled with wolves and wild boars, building his strength by learning their weaknesses.

For speed and stamina, Setanta ran with the two horses born on the same day as him. Over time, he could outrun his horses. They followed him at every opportunity. So savage a nature in so young a boy made him as one with all who survived the times that were in it.

At home, Setanta listened closely to the tales told of King Connor and his court. The sister of Connor cherished the king. When his mother Dectain told him of her life with King Connor, Setanta was filled with excitement. In her stories, much was made of the doings of a boy named Ferdia, first among the youth of consequence at the Red Branch court. When members of the court paid a visit to the house of his mother, Setanta crept under the feast table to hear of Ferdia and his mastery of the feats of a warrior.

When Setanta heard of the warrior's sport of speed as perfected by Ferdia, he asked his mother for guidance on this feat. Dectain told him that if he could dream vividly of performing it, a warrior's skill in arms would accrue to him.

So Setanta learned at a young age how to channel his dreams for success in his adventures. And, always in his dreams, the long arm of Lugh his father came to show him the way and save the day.

Alone by day on the plains of Muirtaine with his two horses, Setanta knit together the contents of his doings and dreams until he made one garment of both. Since there were none to tell him of the impossible, he combined feats that made him unique in the annals of warriors.

Setanta could hurl his spear straight from his shoulder, chase it with a spurt of speed, leap on to it, and guide its point with his bare feet until he reached his destination. Many black and blue bruises decorated his young body in pursuit of his learning this skill. Always, in his dreams, the long hand of his father Lugh balanced the boy Setanta in all his endeavors.

By the time he reached the age of reason, Setanta was enamored of the glamour of the Red Branch. He could not wait to test his deeds against those of Ferdia, the esteemed boy hero of Ulster's Court.

Two

THE PROVINCE OF Ulster grew to adore and adorn their king, Connor MacNessa. To the people of Ulster, there was none in the wide world with his wisdom and judgment. It became the custom that every man who married in Ulster urged his bride to spend the first night with Connor the King. This made Connor the first in affection of the new family and an ally for life. And whosoever welcomed Connor for a feast or festival offered his wife for the king's pleasure. The heroes of his Red Branch court went before him in every battle to protect Connor from harm.

The king owned three households of great distinction. The house named The Twinkling Hoard stored the javelins, shields, swords, and daggers of the Red Branch court. Among its treasures, the hacking sword of Fergus stood tall beside the savage sword of King Nuada. The shield of Connor had a surround of four gold borders. The glimmer and glitter of gold and silver lit the many rooms of The Twinkling Hoard from the plates, cups, goblets, and drinking utensils of the king.

The spoils of war and the severed heads of enemies were kept in a house named The Red Branch.

Connor kept court in his House of the Red Branch. Red reflecting royalty, the walls, floors, and ceilings of this house—all one-hundred and fifty rooms—were paneled with red yew. Connor's regal room of welcome occupied the center of the Red Branch. Large screens of solid copper held carvings of gold birds with priceless jewels for eyes. On top of one screen lay a wand of silver attached to three golden apples. This wand was used to maintain order and discipline. If Connor the King shook it or raised his voice, silence ruled.

For hospitality beyond reproach, King Connor kept full the Vat of Gerg, with its coal-dark beer. It held more than enough for the thirst of thirty heroes.

Connor so favored Druids, musicians, and bards that a reaction set in among the people against the number of youths dawdling at poetry and its assorted lascivious pleasures.

Thrice one fifty boys of consequence were fostered in the way of the warrior at the court of Connor. Here they played the ancient game of hurling; learned the art of sword, spear, and shield; and grew strong under the watchful eyes of the Ulster warriors.

This is how King Connor ordered his day. At the first light, Connor rose to pass judgment on problems vexing his province of Ulster. Then he reviewed the personal distribution of land and animals of his subjects. A woman could obtain her husband's property if he did not perform his spousal duties or neglected his family. Druids and bards were confirmed or denied access to the king according to ability or misfortune. The rest of the day, King Connor encouraged his boys of consequence in the age-old games of hurling and war. Then the king played board games with his warriors of the Red Branch.

To conclude his day, King Connor often feasted and drank with his guests until he fell asleep. Of the four provinces of Ireland, there was no king with the quality of Connor MacNessa.

Fedlim MacDall, one of Ulster's beloved storytellers, created a tale for the appreciation of King Connor. Because Fedlim's wife was very pregnant, he invited King Connor and his inner court to his house to secure the king's blessing on his child. Before he began his story for the king's ear, he brought Connor, Katbad the Druid, and Fergus of the Long Sword into the birth chamber to meet the wife. As they left, Fedlim's wife began her birth pangs.

The heroes with King Connor crowded into the room to hear Fedlim's story. Alert and attentive, they were content in the company of king and storyteller.

As Fedlim began his story, the babe in the womb of his wife screamed a screech out of her that none who heard would ever forget. It slowed the hearts and chilled the blood of Fedlim's audience. Each reached for a sword to protect King Connor and himself. Fedlim ran to his wife. Again, the babe in the womb screamed. A blood mist filled the eyes of the armed heroes. They formed a circle around Connor, prepared to die for the king. All eyes were on Katbad the Druid, who could read the meaning of wails and winds.

Katbad did not move, but stood as one stricken by the immediate. For the third time, the child screamed in her mother's womb. The Druid clutched his staff and rolled his eyes. A cold wind and hailstones shivered the people and province of Ulster. The natural world turned unnatural. Dogs fought, cats scratched, bulls charged at anything in their path, lightning flashed, blasting open graves of the forgotten and hidden ways to the other side.

A time to pay heed to the future. None but the unknown reigned. None but the unknown ruled. None but the unknown screamed death to thousands from the womb of the innocent.

On the plains of Muirtaine, a small boy named Setanta crossed swords with the lightning bolts flashing around him.

King Connor took his wand of silver with its three gold apples from his foster father, Fergus of the Long Sword. He held the wand over the head of Katbad the Druid. Connor spoke softly to Katbad. "There is a warning in the babe's cry. Tell its meaning, Druid."

Katbad answered in his voice of prophecy. "Her name shall be Deirdre, and she shall be the most beautiful woman in Ireland. Perfection beyond conception, beauty without blemish— and yet a daughter of sorrow."

The heroes sensed a moment of truth. Swords and daggers drawn, they circled King Connor. Katbad spoke again.

"Her name shall be Deirdre, the most beautiful woman in Ireland, of form and grace to die for—and thousands of Ulster's warriors shall die with the name of Deirdre on their lips."

Murmurs of anger emerged from the heroes surrounding King Connor. He shook his wand for silence. Katbad continued his prophecy.

"Her name shall be Deirdre, the most beautiful woman in Ireland. All who see her shall love her. Skin like fresh snow in moonlight. Lips like crimson blood on white flax. Hair as gold glinting in sunlight. Deirdre—the fall of the House of the Red Branch."

At this, the heroes of the Red Branch erupted in anger. It was one life for many.

"Kill the babe."

"Save the king."

"Protect Ulster."

"Remove the cause."

"Kill the effect."

King Connor shook his wand of silver. Silence ruled the unruly. Order and discipline returned. Connor slipped from the room and went to the birth chamber. Here he found an old friend, Biddy Bentbook, attending to the newborn babe.

"Take the babe Deirdre away from here, and raise her far from the eyes of men. Let none see her ever. The men of Ulster will kill her to save themselves. Take Deirdre now, dear Biddy, to a place known only to me. Listen close."

And so, the wise King Connor saved the babe Deirdre from the fear of the heroes of the Red Branch.

Over and often, the seven-year-old Setanta asked of his mother, Dectain, permission to go to the Red Branch court of her brother, King Connor.

"Setanta, you are too young to travel alone. Wait, my boy, for the escort of some Ulster warriors," Dectain said. She knew Setanta was very different from other boys.

Setanta moved close to his beautiful mother. Dectain bit her berry-red lips. He looked deep into her green-flecked eyes, stroked her silken hair, and kissed her three times on her white neck.

"Point out to me the direction of Connor's Court, the Red Branch, mother." Setanta spoke as a man coming into his own.

A single tear escaped Dectain's right eye. "It's a long, hard journey to the north; around the mountains. Wait, Setanta, wait," she pleaded.

Setanta kept his own council. That night when Dectain fell asleep, Setanta set off on the first of what would be his one hundred adventures.

These are the accoutrements Setanta took with him the night he left home to seek his fortune at the Red Branch of King Connor MacNessa. He took his hurley stick of ash and a silver ball called a sliotar. On his shoulder a shield with his short javelin attached, and in his hand his long spear with its killing point. This is how Setanta made his way from his mother to her brother.

An indifferent moon lit a boy followed by two curious horses, Ban and Dub, on the journey of his life. He walked through the night, daring the world of darkness to impede his passage. First comes courage and then what may.

Three

T HE FIRST DAY: "Tell me of my father, that I may know my future," Setanta had asked often of his mother when he reached the age of reason.

"His name is Lugh. He is more than a god to me, and so are you, Setanta." Dectain told this to her son.

To measure the length of his journey, Setanta hit his silver ball with his hurley stick high in the clear air. He leaped upon the back of his black horse Dub and chased the ball across the plains of Muirtaine. Bent double in the charioteer's crouch, he guided the horse with his bare feet and charged into the legend of his life. Half a day later, he caught the ball before it hit the ground at a ford of clear water. Here he stopped to attend to his noble steeds. They drank deep at the ford, and then munched on the rich green grass on a sloping meadow. His jet-black horse Dub sported a plaited mane woven by Dectain for the delight of her son. Dub had a high, stepping gait, was broad in the rump, slim in the flanks, with chestnut brown eyes that glowed in the dark. A tongue of crimson between teeth of coral, and a fearless heart. This was Setanta's jet-black horse.

Setanta's white horse, Ban, had a float of white mane blowing in the wind, long ears, a broad chest, smooth belly, and coal-black eyes. An elegant rump on broad flanks and a strong and violent heart.

The two horses, born on the same day as Setanta, had no fear or favor of any but Him. A gift from his father, Lugh of the Long Hand, they were bound to Setanta for his lifespan. He tied his hurley stick and shield to the white mane of his horse, Ban.

Setanta refreshed himself at the clear crystal waters of the ford and ate well of wild berries, nuts, sloes, and acorns. When content, he flung his spear straight before him. He jumped onto the back of his white horse. Guiding Ban with his strong toes, crouched low on her elegant rump; he chased his spear into the long afternoon. Dub and Ban ran nose-to-nose, eager to please the seven-year-old Setanta.

The pale moon was rising and the sun declining when Setanta glimpsed his flying spear ahead of him. Straddling his two horses, one bare foot on each animal's back, he urged them forwards until the spear was between them, then he jumped from the horses onto the shaft of his spear. Balancing his strong young body on the spear, he flew toward the rising mountains. Setanta gripped the point of the spear between his toes to direct his flight, his green-mantled cloak blew in the wind, and his horses galloped behind him.

Setanta leapt from his spear before it sliced into a tree at the base of the mountain. Over and over, Setanta rolled until he stopped at the lip of a still lake in a small clearing. Overhead, a half moon reflected itself in the lake. Excited and awed, his two horses nudged him to his feet. The black horse cantered off and returned with Setanta's spear in his strong mouth. The white horse rubbed against Setanta until the boy removed his hurley stick from the animal's mane. Armed with his spear and hurley stick, Setanta faced the lake.

A push from the black horse at his elbow raised high Setanta's spear. The spear's reflection spread slowly across the lake. A nudge from the white horse raised high his hurley stick. It seemed to Setanta that his hurley's reflection increased in size and heft until it reached the middle of the lake.

An owl hooted in surprise as the reflection of Setanta's hurley stick assumed reality. A massive hurley stick rose up from its reflection in the lake. A great long arm emerged from the water, holding aloft the hurley stick. This vision of the hand arising from the moonlit water awed young Setanta. The long hand of his father Lugh waved his hurley stick toward Setanta as if seeking a player for a moonlit game. Ripples of water caressed Setanta's feet.

Straight and true, Setanta pucked his slioter ball toward the hand in the lake. The powerful hurley whacked the ball upward. The sliotar flew toward the mountaintop, faster than any object Setanta had seen in his young life. Dropping his hurley stick, Lugh's long finger pointed at his son's spear.

Setanta threw his spear across the lake. Lugh's long hand caught and pointed the spear toward the top of the mountain. Setanta looked up, watching a tiny object strike the rim of the mountains, bounce sideways, and slam into the half moon. The sliotar ball fell from the moon like a falling star, lighting the night until it impaled the tip of the spear in Lugh's long hand. Like a white flame of lightning, the silver sliotar lit the small clearing.

Lugh's hand dipped the silver sliotar into the lake, turning it into a white sheet of brilliant color. Setanta blinked as his father's hand flung the spear into the night. Straight and true, the spear blazed forward. A comet of awesome intensity. Lugh's finger pointed toward Setanta, indicating the boy's next move.

Hurley stick in hand, Setanta performed his salmon leap onto the palm of Lugh's hand in the center of the lake. His father's fingers closed around Setanta. It was the best the boy had ever felt in his life. A quick flick of Lugh's wrist sent Setanta flying through the air after his blazing spear. Fierce with pride from Lugh's aid, Setanta landed neatly on the spear's shaft. And so he flew through the night, a young boy on a flaming spear, followed by two horses, one black and one white.

Setanta's clothes were well aired when his spear touched the fields of the Red Branch court. The hand of Lugh his father had a long reach.

Setanta pulled his silver sliotar from the tip of his spear. Followed by his faithful horses, Setanta set off toward the excited shouts of boys starting the day's first game of hurley.

Near the court of the Red Branch of King Connor MacNessa, thrice fifty boys played hurley on his meadows. Each group had a hurling field to practice on, bounded on both ends by wooden goal posts. The boys were divided into twenty-five hurlers on opposing teams. To indicate their allegiance and identify their opponents, the boys wore the colored jerseys of opposing teams.

Hurling was a game played by young boys of consequence with a hurley stick and a small leather ball called a sliotar. The object of the game was to hit the leather ball with a hurley stick along a field and score by pucking the ball between the wooden goal uprights. It took balls to play hurley.

Setanta knew from listening to the tales of King Connor at his home of the way of the hurley games. A challenge from a team of hurlers from elsewhere was treated with respect and arranged at short notice. Holding high his hurley stick, Setanta walked between the two teams on the first field. Twenty-five boys in blue jerseys faced twenty-five boys in black jerseys.

"Where is Ferdia, the Fearless One?" asked Setanta.

"Be gone, small one." So spoke Moroco, the tallest hurley boy in black.

"I challenge the best you can muster to a game of hurley," said Setanta.

"Who do you represent, midget?" asked Moroco.

"I am from the plains of Murtaine, the home of immortal hurlers." Setanta turned his back and walked to the goal post. The blue team left the field. Moroco marched toward Setanta, scanning the meadows for the small boy's team. Nothing did he see but a pair of horses, one black and one white.

"Where is the rest of your team, sparrow fart?" Moroco pointed his hurley stick at Setanta.

"*I* am the team. To even the field, you skinny malink, I offer you a penalty," said Setanta.

Moroco turned and ran back to his team.

"Listen close, lads. The wee scut insults us. He—himself alone—is the team," yelled the angry Moroco.

The boys in black jerseys looked at Setanta and then at each other. None were at ease.

"Are you ready?" yelled Moroco. "Take your penalty, dog's vomit," answered Setanta.

Moroco held his hurley stick as he would a spear. He ran three steps and flung his stick at Setanta. This was not allowed in the hurley games. Not ever. Moroco turned his angry eyes on his team. One by one, they ran, aimed, and flung their hurley sticks at Setanta, who stood between the goal posts.

One by one, Setanta caught the hurling sticks in his quick hand as they flew at his head. One by one, he threw them back. One after another, a hurley struck a boy. One by one, they collapsed, until only Setanta stood erect on the field. The game was over.

Setanta walked over to the next hurling field where the boys were gathering their balls. He appeared under the goal post, watched by a pair of fine horses.

"Be gone, tadpole. A boy with no jersey is not welcome here." The leader of the red jersey team said.

"I challenge the best of Ulster to a hurley game." Setanta stood still until the boys stopped laughing at him.

"To level the field, I offer a penalty. A goal puck to start the game," said Setanta.

"We accept your challenge. Bring on your team." So spoke the leader of the red team.

"*I* am the team. Take your pentalty," said Setanta.

One team left the field but stayed to watch the downfall of the strange boy. Twenty-five boys stood in front of Setanta. Each had a round hard leather ball in one hand. At a signal from the leader, one by one each boy flung his ball straight and true at Setanta. One by one, Setanta struck the hurling balls with his hurley stick. One by one, a ball struck the hurler who'd tossed it at Setanta. One by one, the red team fell to the ground until only Setanta remained standing. The boys on the sideline huddled together. The horses behind Setanta snickered and snorted.

"Stay and play—or run away." Setanta tapped his sliver sliotar on the base of his hurley stick.

The spectators ran from the field to warn their comrades of the arrival of a hero in the making, and of the toll he was taking. Setanta strode to the third hurley field. Informed of his feats, a team of twenty-five of the best that Ulster could muster stood strong in two lines in front of a goal post. They were ready for him. Both sidelines of the hurley field were alive with boys who witnessed or heard of his deeds. Setanta strode to the center of the hurley field. This team wore orange jerseys.

"I challenge you to a game of hurley," Setanta said.

"If you tell your name, we accept your challenge," the leader of the orange team said.

"My name is Setanta, from the plains of Murtaine. The home of immortal hurlers," said Setanta, to honor his mother.

"The game begins when your team arrives," the leader said.

"*I* am the team. I claim a penalty because you did not meet me at the center of the field," said Setanta.

The leader of the orange team arranged his boys in two lines in front of his goal posts.

"Take your penalty. Let the game begin," said he.

Setanta struck his silver sliotar straight and true. It hit the leader of the team on his forehead, bounced onto the goal post, and rebounded into Setanta's raised hand. The boy lay prone on the field. Setanta turned his left side toward the boys and yawned. Boredom was the final insult.

The boys in orange jerseys put down their hurley sticks. Each pulled forth a short spear strapped to his back. Straight and true, they hurled their sharp spears at Setanta.

Swiftly Setanta detached his gifted shield from his shoulder. The spears flung at Setanta were so fast they appeared as one long spear aimed at his heart. He caught each spear on his sturdy shield. One by one, he detached each spear from his shield. Straight and true, he threw back the spears, embedding them deep in the goal posts behind the boys. Setanta dropped his shield and pucked his silver sliotar with his hurley stick. The sliotar struck the cross piece of the goal post and rebounded into his hand.

The goal post shuddered and shook loose the spears embedded therein. It shattered into lengths of lumber that fell on the heads of the boys in orange. None remained standing. Only Setanta stood erect on the field of play. Setanta addressed the boys on the sidelines.

"Where is Ferdia, the Fearless One?" he yelled.

None dared reply to the fierce wee warrior. He ran at them and knocked down nine boys with his hurley stick. The rest ran for their lives. Setanta chased a dozen scared hurlers into the Red Branch House of King Connor MacNessa.

The king was playing chess with his foster father, Fergus of the Long Sword. The frightened boys sought the king's protection by hiding behind his back. Without breaking stride, Setanta leapt across the chessboard to harass his opponents. King Connor seized Setanta by his forearm and held him tight.

"You are not treating the boys with respect," said the king.

"They did not respect my challenge," answered Setanta.

"What is your name?" asked the king.

"I am called Setanta, the son of your sister, Dectain."

The king looked at Fergus.

"The custom here is to ask protection when you issue a challenge," so spoke the impressive Fergus to Setanta.

"I will protect them, if needed," said Setanta.

"And if not?" asked Fergus.

"I will destroy them," said Setanta.

King Connor looked from Setanta to Fergus.

"Setanta is a boy of rare consequence. He will be fostered by all with courage to spare here in the Red Branch. Katbad, the king of the Druids, will inform his intellect; Fergus will form his manhood as a warrior; oratory and eloquence will be absorbed from Amargin the Poet and Senca the Sage. In return, Setanta will protect our province of Ulster from evil." This was the judgment of Connor, a king in thought, word, deed, and image.

Setanta took his place between King Connor of the Red Branch and Fergus of the Long Sword.

"Where is Ferdia, the Fearless One?" he asked of them.

"Ferdia left today to learn the craft of arms from Scatach the Shadowy One," said King Connor.

"If he survives her training, across the sea in Alba, he could kill any hero in Europe," said Fergus of the Long Sword.

"What Ferdia can do in Europe, I can do better in Ulster," said Setanta.

The king and Fergus shook with laughter as they resumed their chess game.

Still alone on a rocky island off the coast of Ireland, I await news of my first volume of slim vellum about Setanta. Has my order ordained the saga of Setanta as my life's work?

Above all, let God's will prevail.

For long days and nights, I have labored over an ancient manuscript preserved for centuries in a bog hole in the north of Ireland. This rare volume contains eyewitness accounts of the youthful deeds of Setanta from those who survived him.

Here I beg indulgence to advance to a later era in Ulster's epic age. Setanta is now in his prime as a warrior hero. Fergus the Virile, foster father to King Connor and Setanta, has defected from the Red Branch with three thousand seasoned troops. On the border of Ulster, Fergus joins forces with Queen Maeve and King Aillil, who have assembled the largest army ever seen in Ireland.

On the eve of their invasion of Ulster, Fergus tells his royal audience of the boyhood deeds of the legendary Setanta. It is a wonder and a warning that these vivid characters have survived hundreds of years on parchment in a bog near the Mountains of Mourne, and even longer in the tales of bards and poets.

> God, light of my heart,
> Consummate my will,
> Bid my pride depart,
> Consecrate my quill.
> So be it.

Mael Moró

ᚠOUR

O N THE EVE of the epic battle, on the border of the
Kingdom of Ulster, two kings and a queen sat before a
blazing oak fire. King Aillil touched his golden crown.
This king of the province of Connacht poked the fire with his
short spear and looked at his wife. Queen Maeve smiled at
Aillil and touched an identical crown on her regal red head.
This couple thought as one about the power and privilege of
royalty, and agreed on nothing else.

They turned their royal attention to their guest at the fire.
A former king in exile, without a crown on his brown hair.
Yet still a man of majesty in a green cloak and a red hooded
tunic. Polished and perfect, Fergus the Virile poked the fire
with his long gold-tinted sword. The fire flamed a reception
to the famed sword of Fergus.

That afternoon, Fergus had marched three thousand exiled
warriors from the province of Ulster into the camp of the
Connacht army. The first company of a thousand warriors
caught Maeve's fancy in their cloaks of funeral black, curved
shields as tall as themselves, and short bristles of hair.

The second company of a thousand Ulster exiles in dark grey cloaks and red embroidered tunics reassured King Aillil. Exiles fought the hardest and knew the terrain.

For Fergus, the third company of a thousand men were hard nobs from the true north, dark and bitter in combat. Troops of heroes in purple cloaks, with curved scallop-edged shields on their backs.

"Is Setanta the best they have in Ulster?" asked Queen Maeve of Fergus.

"Yes. No warrior more ferocious, none wilder in the wide world. There is none of his stature for flame and fury in battle, for swiftness in slaughter, for splendor in valor, for youth and strength. None now. None ever approaches the heroic Setanta."

The flame from the oak logs leapt high at the name of Setanta. Fergus continued his story.

"I will tell you one deed of Setanta when yet a boy of seven. Some I witnessed, some I heard from Ibor, King Connor's chariot driver.

"It began when Katbad the Druid brought ten of his pupils to visit his son, Connor, the famed King of the Red Branch court of Ulster. My interest in the boys was to which one I would foster as a warrior. This being the custom of the court. To this end, I listened to Katbad lecture his new students in the courtyard of Connor's compound on the three parts of Ulster society.

"As was his custom, Katbad spoke first of the Druids to his pupils. He told them that it takes twenty long years of learning law, science, and religion to become a Druid. Druids are guides to the king and his warriors who rule the province. If a king is virile and without blemish, as is Connor, the land will rebound with fertility, the sea with fish, and the people will reap ripe harvests. Most of all, a Druid must absorb knowledge of the other side, the land of eternal sunshine without shadow. The land of the ever young.

"This is done to ensure tranquility for the men and women of the province of Ulster. These are the audience for the authority of Druids, the audacity of kings, and the tales of bards and poets.

"A tall student raised his hand and asked, 'What is the luck of the Irish for this day?' This is the question most asked of and ignored by Druids. Not so by Katbad. 'If a young warrior takes arms for the first time today, his name is immortal as long as Gaels tell tales,' replied Katbad, or words to that effect as I recall them."

Fergus paused for a glass of foaming ale proffered by the pale hand of Queen Maeve. After a long swallow, Fergus returned to his story. "A young boy new to Katbad's school slipped away upon hearing that today was blessed for the taking of arms. He was called Setanta the Squinter by the other boys, due to his habit of focusing his right eye. Setanta did not stay to hear Katbad finish his prophecy. I quote from memory: 'Today's young warrior will become immortal in memory but brief in mortality,' said Katbad. Setanta ran to claim his weapons from his uncle, King Connor. I followed the boy, aroused by his passion.

"Amused by the spirit of his nephew, King Connor gave Setanta access to the swords, spears, and shields stored for new warriors. Excited and exalted, Setanta bent, rent, and brandished these weapons until all remained in fragments at his feet. At last, King Connor gave him his own weapons, forged by Cullen the Smith. These king's weapons survived Setanta's assault, much to Connor's relief. On or about this time, Katbad the Druid arrived to visit with his son, King Connor. Here he saw the boy Setanta armed and able.

"'Do I behold a new warrior fully armed?' Katbad asked.

"'Yes, our little Demon of Death,' King Connor laughed.

"'This merits attention; whoever arms for a warrior today will live long in deeds, but short in days,' said Katbad.

"'If I secure fame, I am content though I survive for one day on this earth,' swore the boy Setanta to his Druid and king.

"Katbad looked at Setanta and said, 'Whoever boards his first chariot today will leave his name to fame forever.'

"'King Connor, my chariot, I beg you!' implored Setanta.

"Fearing for the destruction of his warrior chariots at the assault of Setanta, King Connor called for Ibor, his own charioteer.

"'Now boy, mount my chariot for your first adventure in arms,' said King Connor. Setanta slung his weapons into the chariot and stood beside Ibor the king's driver.

"'Now unyoke these horses and replace them with my swift steeds, driver,' ordered the small boy. Ibor looked at the king. Connor laughed and nodded assent. Ibor did as ordered, much impressed by the strength of the black and white horses. He smiled and drove the chariot in a small circle, returning to where he started.

"'Now you have had your adventure, lad, get out of my chariot.'

"'You will lose no fame today if you take me to the end of the road.' Setanta pointed the king's sword at Ibor's guts. They drove forth for Setanta's adventure until they reached the end of the road, at the ford of the watchman on the Faw's mountain."

Fergus the Virile wet his whistle with another glass of ale, and resumed his story of the young Setanta to the king and queen of Connacht.

"What follows was told to me by Ibor, the king's charioteer," said Fergus.

"Each day a warrior of Ulster guarded the province at this ford to welcome bards and poets, and repulse those with evil intentions. None entered Ulster without a challenge to purpose and passage. They met the hero Conall Carney at the ford of the watchman. This warrior of the day greeted Setanta.

"'I welcome you, young son of Ulster. Are they the arms you have taken today?' said the bold Conall Carney.

"'Return to King Connor, watchman, and I will remain here for the protection of the province,' replied the boy Setanta. Checking his weapons, Ibor shook his head and rolled his eyes to Conall Carney.

"'However you handle bards and poets, you are light in years and strength to deal with men of action,' said Conall and smiled.

"'I have heard that warriors are found close to Lake Ectra. We will continue our quest to redden my hands with the blood of my enemies today,' said Setanta.

"'I will be your foster guardian until you reach the lake,' said Conall, and he leaped into his yoked chariot. They set off together, much to the chagrin of the young Setanta. He did not appreciate a protector on his first adventure. He set a stone in his sling and slung it fast and true at the shaft of Conall Carney's chariot. The shaft smashed and the chariot departed from the horses.

"'How dare you break my chariot, boy?' cried Conall.

"'I dare alone and armed to kill the enemies of Ulster,' said Setanta. They left Conall Carney in the dust from their chariot. Upon reaching the lake, they found neither friend nor foe there.

"'It is time to return to King Connor's house for food and not to forget the strong drink and good company there,' said Ibor the Charioteer.

"Setanta pointed a spear at Ibor and asked, 'Are we near any enemies of Ulster?'

"'There, past that mound, is the fort of the MacNegtiv clan. They say his three sons have killed as many Ulstermen as are now living.' Ibor presumed these tidings would change the mind of Setanta.

"If they left now, they would be back at King Connor's feast before the ale ran out. After a day with a boy like Setanta, Ibor craved the company of jesters, jostlers, and drivers like himself, men who appreciated the humanity of the moment.

"'Let us go meet them at their stronghold,' said Setanta, arranging sharp-edged marble stones for his sling.

"'You are looking at death,' swore Ibor.

"'I'll not avoid it wherever it is,' said Setanta.

"Those who see seldom lead, those who lead seldom see.

"Ibor drove the king's chariot to the stronghold and Setanta jumped onto the green. He ran to a pillar stone on the green. A round hoop of bogwood encircled the pillar. On the wood was carved the dire deeds of the three sons of MacNegtiv in their destruction of the Ulster men."

Fergus paused to see the effect of this on King Aillil and Queen Maeve. His royal captors, entranced by his story, listened close to every word. The flames in the fire flickered in anticipation of Setanta's first adventure as a warrior of the Red Branch. Fergus the Virile stretched and resumed his tale.

"Setanta seized the bogwood and cut his name across their deeds with the king's dirk. Then he flung it far and deep into the upstream of Ulster's enemies. The current passed it along toward the Fort of MacNegtiv. Setanta yawned and stretched his seven-year-old body. A boy's best friend is his bed.

"'Pay heed, Ibor; arrange the rugs and coverlets of this chariot that I may sleep for a while. If one son or two sons of MacNegtiv come, do not awake me, but if all three sons come, rouse me to glory.'

"So Setanta lay himself down to sleep on the rugs in the chariot. Meanwhile, the bogwood ring with his name on it crashed against the moat of the fort of MacNegtiv. The youngest son of MacNegtiv, named Kilseer, heard the thumping of the bog oak and brought it back to his brothers.

"Ibor the chariot driver knew well the terror of close encounters with death and destruction. He fussed with horses and the rugs of the chariot, hoping to awake the sleeping boy. And yet, there was something, a squint in Setanta's eye when he touched a weapon, that scorched the heart of the first among Ulster's charioteers.

"Courage is as contagious as cowardice, if not as common.

"Then the three sons of MacNegtiv arrived on the green, each in his own chariot, and with their weapons beside them. They tied their chariots to the post of the green. Kilseer, the youngest, left his brothers watching, and approached the chariot of King Connor on foot and unarmed. 'Do not graze your horses on our land, driver. Do not unyoke them,' warned Kilseer the Deceitful.

"'These are just the reins I hold ready to leave as soon as the babe in the chariot awakens.'

"'I recognize the chariot of King Connor, but not these brave steeds. Who dares to trespass on our land?' demanded Kilseer.

"'A sweet wee lad who took up arms today and raced to the border to display them,' said Ibor.

"'If he were a man instead of a boy, it is dead instead of alive he would be,' boasted Kilseer.

"'Indeed, he has just reached his seventh year of life and knows naught of nothing.' Ibor knew well the conceit of champions like Kilseer. Brute force and ignorance were ever twins.

"'The soft lad needs to return to his cradle. Take him home to his mother, driver,' Kilseer ordered, hoping to impress his brothers.

"Setanta heard this as he awoke. He passed his hands over his face for shame, blushing crimson from head to toe. Anger precedes action in children and heroes.

"'Arm yourself, slut of scoundrels, enemy of Ulster. There is no fame in killing a fool,' Setanta said. Kilseer the Deceitful cursed the boy. He ran back to his brothers. They helped Kilseer arrange his weapons and board his chariot.

"'Be wary of Kilseer the False,' warned Ibor.

"'Why so is that?' asked Setanta as the chariot shook with his anger.

"'No points of spear, no thrust of sword, no sharp-edged shield can harm Kilseer,' said Ibor.

"'None, not even Kilseer, can escape a stone from the sling of Setanta. Forward the chariot, driver.' Setanta pointed his sling toward Kilseer's chariot.

"The brothers of Kilseer the False struck his horses with the flat of their swords. Across the green, the two chariots charged toward each other. It was then, as Ibor goaded his horses forward, that he saw the first warrior spasm seize Setanta. On

Setanta's head, each hair shot upright, as if hammered in. A firespark tipped and flickered on each hair. Setanta squinted his right eye narrower than the eye of a needle. Setanta the Squinter! His other eye opened wider than the mouth of an ale goblet. Shaking, twisting, turning, weaving, and wailing, Setanta grew in stature until Ibor shivered in his shadow. Malignant mists and spurts of smoke formed vaporous clouds boiling over Setanta's head, obscuring his form and figure from Ibor's view.

"The chariots thundered closer over the green grass. Ibor clutched the side of his carriage for support, unsure of what was happening before his very eyes. Under the mist, the small hand of Setanta snapped, cracked, and warped into a killing hand with seven fingers and iron nails. Setanta's seven-digit hand grasped his sling. He whirled it until it spun faster than the wheels of Katbad the Druid's chariot on one of his midnight runs to the other side. Now Ibor could see the demonic smile of the deceitful Kilseer as he aimed his spear at Setanta's smoky outline. The chariots were closing fast when Setanta released his slingshot of Connemara marble. With a screech like a banshee about her business, the marble found its target. It slammed through the skull of Kilseer and out of the back of his head, taking blood, brains, and bones with it. Ibor glimpsed the brothers of Kilseer through the hole in Kilseer's skull, a bloody pair, indeed.

"'Swing left, Ibor,' yelled Setanta.

"The chariots passed so close that sparks flew when their wheels touched, scorching Ibor's hands. Setanta's hand with its seven fingers grasped the bloody hair of Kilseer. His other hand swung a sword and sliced the head of Kilseer from his body. Setanta dropped the head with the hole through it into the back of Ibor's chariot. The bloody head swished from side to side. Kilseer's headless body, still upright in his chariot and spouting blood, vanished into the woods as his terrified horses ran for their lives. Afraid to look at Setanta, Ibor licked the blisters on his hands, smelling the bloody head behind him in the chariot. From the white post, Kilseer's older brother, Tuball, began a stiff-leg march toward them. Biting his lips with rage, he confronted Setanta and Ibor in their chariot.

"'You will die by my hands before you can boast of your kill today, smoke hound.' Tuball spat blood and hate at Setanta.

"'I care not a snap of my fingers for the enemies of Ulster.' Setanta snapped his fingers. Sparks flew from his iron fingernails and set afire the red hair of Tuball MacNegtiv. Tuball flung his cloak over his burning hair. Cursing and vowing vengeance, he ran back to his chariot, his brother, and his cunning weapons.

"'Heed my warning about Tuball yonder, Setanta. Unless you kill him with your first blow, he will overcome you with weapons, skill, and cunning,' said Ibor.

"'Why do you doubt me, Ibor? Hand me the weapon of venom, King Connor's spear. Stand fast until I return.' The warped warrior that was Setanta the boy stepped from the chariot, his head and shoulders in a cloud of malignant smoke. In one seven- fingered hand, Setanta held Connor's famous venomous spear. In the other hand, he held King Connor's sword, stained with the blood of Kilseer the False. Tuball clanged his weapons on his stout round shield, bidding farewell to his brother fondly. Roaring his warrior's cry, Tuball began a crooked run toward the fearsome Setanta. Hefting his heavy spear, Setanta took aim at his running target. Tuball stopped, dropped, rolled, sprang to his feet, and threw his short spear at Setanta. Before Tuball's spear passed six sword lengths, Setanta cast his heavy spear. It split Tuball's spear, slammed through his shield, and pierced his heart. With a ferocious swing of Connor's sword, Setanta sliced Tuball's head from his shoulders before his body hit the ground.

"With an overhead throw, Setanta flung the severed head of Tuball past the startled head of Ibor onto the rear of his chariot. Here it lay in a bloody state beside the head of his brother, Kilseer, which had a hole through its forehead. Blood wove a sticky carpet on the floor of Ibor's chariot. Placing a warped foot with seven iron toenails on the heaving chest of the headless Tuball, Setanta pulled his spear from Tuball's heart."

King Fergus the Exile smiled as he told of Setanta's second kill. King Aillil handed Fergus another glass of ale. The making of a warrior such as Setanta held primary concern upon the pagans of Old Ireland. Queen Maeve held tight to herself. It was said of her that she never had one man without the shadow of another behind him. King Fergus the Virile cast the largest shadow in the camp.

"How old is this Setanta now?" asked Queen Maeve.

"He is in the prime of his first manhood." Fergus stood, stretching tall, still talking.

"There are rumors of suffocation among the Ulstermen when Setanta shows."

"How so?" asked King Aillil.

"By the tight legs of the women of Ulster. They sit on the men's shoulders to see the elegant form of their high hero Setanta." Fergus noticed desire on the queen's lips when he mentioned the name Setanta. Maeve had a monarch's appetite for amorous adventure. Her friendly thighs widened as Fergus poked the fire. Fergus knew women.

"It is only out of Setanta that a warrior like himself will come," said Fergus. "His seed and breed come from the other side."

"I have a daughter, a beauty without blemish, if Setanta prefers younger women," said Maeve.

"Is Setanta here for fighting or fornication?" demanded King Aillil. He spat in the fire.

"Here is a man who can tell you about Setanta. Meet Ibor, my chariot driver, the king of charioteers and the charioteer of kings." King Fergus waved at a tall man in a dark cloak walking a pair of splendid horses. At the invitation of Queen Maeve, Ibor tied his horses to a tree and joined them at the fire.

Ibor told the royal company that he contacted a bard named Sceál Galore to shape his life as a chariot driver into an epic poem. Ibor's plan was to tour the provinces of Ireland, exchanging his tales of gods and Gaels for gold and ale. With relish, Ibor continued the story of Setanta where Fergus had left off.

Five

Setanta the Warped One returned to my chariot, covered with Tuball's blood. I watched the third brother called Fondle prepare for his encounter with Setanta. As if his brothers were still alive, Fondle made ready to kill Ulstermen as he always had. He brandished, and then buckled two sharp swords on each hip. On the shield on his shoulder were fastened six short spears, shorter than his arms. Four sharp knives were strapped to his calves. Fondle removed all the armor from his body, including his bronze sandals.

"'Setanta, listen to me while I tell you about Fondle.' The Warped One did not reply. Fondle entered his chariot and drove slowly toward them.

"'Setanta, do not fight Fondle yonder in the water. Fondle is named after the swallow, because of his prowess in skimming across the water.' I forced myself to turn around to seek Setanta.

"The two heads on the lake of blood in the back of my chariot had their eyes on me. No sign of the Warped One. Perhaps he was washing Tuball's blood off himself in the upstream of the green. No sign of him in the stream. At least he would avoid an attack in the water by Fondle the Swallow. Where was Setanta? No true warrior ever deserted his charioteer, but who knows what captures the attention of a seven-year-old boy? I could hear the wheels of Fondle's chariot passing slowly over the green, the creaking of his harness, the snorting of his black horse, the clank of his weapons.

"I felt Fondle's cold eyes on the back of my neck. I turned to face him. Fondle took a short sword from his hip and pointed it at my heart. He stopped his chariot and stood down.

"'Setanta, where are you?' I whispered as loud as I dared.

"'I am here behind the chariot, Ibor.'

"It was the voice of Setanta the seven-year-old boy that answered me! Gone was the warped monster warrior of Ulster.

"'What are you doing boy?' I whispered. Fondle strode toward me, following his outstretched sword.

"'So be it. I die as I lived in battle on the king's chariot.'

"'Let Fondle the Swallow skim across my water because now I have to piss,' said the boy Setanta. The water passed by Setanta flowed under the chariot. It soaked the bare feet of Fondle. His toes spread wide, digging into the green. Fondle's body shook and his eyes rolled up into his head. With a thirsty cry, he vaulted into my chariot. Fondle's cry turned into a scream of rage when he saw the heads of Tuball and Kilseer. The horses of Setanta raced for the stream bordering the green.

"I have always feared a watery grave. Now I was approaching one at an incredible gait. Before I could rip the life from his throat with my bare hands, Fondle clubbed me with the flat of his sword. Soon I lay prone with his piss-soaked bare foot on my neck. Cross-eyed, I watched the two severed heads skid across the bloody bottom of my chariot. The hole in the head of Kilseer MacNegtiv proved most distracting as I tried to collect my wits. Looking away, I believe I glimpsed two small hands hanging on to the back of my chariot. Suddenly, I was jerked to my feet by the rough hands of Fondle the Sparrow. Nostrils streaming, tails erect, ears flat, the black and white steeds charged alongside the stream.

"Lifting me high over his head, Fondle flung me deep into the stream. I thought I glimpsed a small hand waving farewell from behind the back of the chariot. The splash of the cold water in the stream restored what remained of my senses. I saw Fondle, whistling like a swallow, swoop across the stream and land on my chest with his bare feet. Before going under water, I gulped as much air as possible for what I presumed would be my last breath. Beneath the clear stream, I watched the duck feet of Fondle seek and find my throat and belly. In a dance of death, Fondle pumped the air from my lungs with practiced feet. I dug my nails into his legs and pulled free a dagger strapped to the calf of Fondle. I aimed to plunge it into his kneecap. My failing strength translated into a flailing attack. A red mist covered my eyes. The dagger bounced from Fondle's kneecap and floated away. I was a drowning man.

"It seemed to me that the legs of Fondle trembled on my body. A sudden stiffness followed by a shudder forced bubbles from my mouth. A ball of gloopy matter floated down. Fondle's bloody head, severed at the neck, spread a red stain as it floated toward my belly. His open mouth, rotten teeth, bulging eyes, and seaweed-coated hair increased my fear of drowning.

"A powerful foot with seven iron toenails appeared and kicked Fondle's head toward my face. Just as its swollen tongue reached my bubbling lips, a hand with seven fingers grabbed the twisted hair on Fondle's head. I was a drowning man. My eyes closed.

"I awoke face down on the floor of my chariot. A relentless foot on my back pumped streams of water from my mouth onto the dirty faces of the three severed heads sliding before my eyes on a slake of sticky blood. A big foot with seven toes alongside my left ear announced the return of Setanta the Warped One. The pressure on my back lifted. Another foot with seven toes landed beside my right ear.

"A warped right hand with seven fingers poked one through the hole in the head of Kilseer the False, one of the three heads slip-sliding along the floor of the chariot. A warped left hand with seven fingers grabbed my shoulder and pulled me erect. I stood side by side with Setanta the Warped One on King Connor's chariot. Again and again, I sucked in what pure air survived under the malignant mists of Setanta.

"Along a flowing stream, the Warped One drove his flawless horses toward the fort of the MacNegtiv family. I'd have much preferred the opposite direction. Finally, Setanta slowed his horses to a walk. Ahead stood the chariot of Kilseer the False, while his horse drank deep in the stream. The headless body of Kilseer held tight the chariot's frame while the headless body of his brother Fondle the Sparrow floated downstream. Setanta strode toward the chariot containing the body of the head with the hole that he tossed from one seven-fingered hand to the other. Setanta pushed this head, hole and all, under the nostrils of Kilseer's chariot horse. The horse snorted and galloped away alongside the stream. The Warped One laughed like the demon he was as the headless body in the chariot passed the headless body in the stream. Leaping from where he stood into my chariot, Setanta dropped Kilseer's head between those of his brothers.

"'Follow that chariot, Ibor,' Setanta commanded.

"Against my better judgment, we charged after the runaway steed with the headless driver. I swore never to venture forth with Setanta again as long as I lived. The day was still young, the grass never so green, the water never so clear, and the sky never so blue. Before we reached the fort, Setanta had me drive around the surrounding buildings and with a snap of his iron fingernails, sent sparks flying into the hay stored for the horses. Blowing softly, he scattered the flaming hay until the buildings flamed and smoked. The farmers and their families ran screaming to the fort for protection.

"'To the stream, Ibor,' Setanta said, satisfied that he had laid waste to all that surrounded the fort of the MacNegtivs. The headless body of Fondle the Swallow thumped against the moat of the fort, courtesy of the rushing stream. Setanta hefted Connor's heavy spear and plunged it into the chest of Fondle. He held the dripping, headless body on the tip of his spear, high over the heads of the horses. Thus, we crossed the long moat and stopped beside the chariot and steaming horse of Kilseer. Setanta swung the body of Fondle on his spear and dropped it beside the headless body of his brother Kilseer. The two chariots stopped close to the barred gate of the fort, one with the headless bodies and the other which held a warped warrior with a smoking head, and a half-drowned charioteer.

"Then came a roar from Setanta. It was his challenge call to conflict, a prophesy of the death of champions, a cry to the goblins, spirits, and demons above, beyond, and about him. Aroused and alarmed, Nesta, the mother of the sons of MacNegtiv, ran to the tower of her fort. Below her, Setanta held high the severed heads of her three sons. Nesta's screams of anguish aroused his wrath.

"'Thus die the enemies of Ulster, now and forever, at the hands of Setanta.' Waving the heads as trophies, Setanta signaled me to turn and depart from the screaming mother of the MacNevtig's. Demonic with energy, Setanta goaded his horses as we returned to the house of King Connor of Ulster.

"The Red Branch was the most elegant of Connor's many homes. It had over one hundred and fifty rooms built of red yew. A third of the day was spent in feasting and friendship, gold and silver glinting on goblets, cups, and drinking horns. The king's charioteer is an honored guest from the kitchen to the king's couch. My musings were rudely interrupted by Setanta the Warped One. He stopped the horses on the heather to Slieve Furt, host to the hidden ways. A herd of wild deer watched the battle of two stags for which would rule the herd. The crash of their antlers echoed in the demented attitude of Setanta. 'Are they tame or are they wild deer?' asked Setanta.

"'That is a herd of wild deer from the hills,' I said. My images of ale in goblets were fading fast.

"'Which could most impress King Connor, a live or a dead deer?' Setanta checked his weapon.

"'None has ever captured a live stag from here,' I said, hoping to discourage the Warped One.

"'Take the reins, Gilly,' was his reply. Setanta hefted his heavy spear, and from the top of his head, he pulled seven fire-tipped hairs, which seemed to have no end to their length, from his pate. Before my awed eyes, he turned the spiked hairs into a neat ball of rope at his feet. Setanta tied the hair securely to the shaft of his spear; the flame-tipped hair smoked as he flung the spear toward the battling stags, passing through both antlers as they clashed for supremacy.

"'Forward the chariot, Ibor.' Setanta unreeled the ball of hair. I guided my horses after the smoking spear, and so the chase began; Setanta's horses after the spear flung by the Warped One.

"'Faster, Ibor, faster,' yelled Setanta, spitting hot gobs at the rumps of the galloping steeds. He let loose his roar of conflict, stampeding the horses and the herd of wild deer. My horse's feet left the ground. It seemed to me I was steering two flaming comets pulling a fiery chariot, burning through a herd of terrified deer. Setanta reached high and grasped his smoking spear, whooping with delight.

"'Slow the chariot, Ibor.' Setanta untied his fire-tipped hair from the shaft of his spear. Slowly he reeled in his line to the entangled stags, pulling them closer to the halted chariot. When the stags were tight behind the chariot, Setanta stood before them. He stared directly into their animal eyes until they bowed before him. Setanta tied the wild stags to the rear shafts of the chariot with his flame-tipped hair. To the Warped, all things are warped.

"A flock of white swans with lovely necks and curious eyes circled the stags. 'Are these swans wild or tame, Ibor?' asked Setanta, reaching for his sling.

"'Wild swans from the islands out in the ocean.'

"The boy Setanta knew little of nature and the Warped One even less. 'Which would most impress King Connor, a live or dead swan?' asked Setanta.

"'No one has ever captured a live, wild swan from the ocean isles,' I told him.

"'So be it,' said Setanta.

"The chariot shook with another warp spasm, and from beneath the malignant mists covering his features came his swan song of infinite intimacy, whistled on the wind. From the sweet spot of infants, the dead center of Setanta's skull, arose a dark spout of scarlet blood. A plaintive whistle from the Warped One's mouth turned the pumping blood into a placid lake of clear water above the chariot. The wild swans settled on the floating lake. Thus he made his head bleed out, blood that became a lake in the air.

"Enchanted by Setanta's melody, they plunged their long necks beneath this lake to see his curious chariot. Setanta wove his rope of hair into a seductive string of submission. This he tied to his missile of arrow-shaped Connemara marble. With a slow, sure swirl of his sling, he swung his stunning shot at the swans. His necklace looped around the lovely necks of sixteen wild swans before returning to his seven-fingered hand. Setanta tied the captive swans to the shafts of my chariot, and dissolved the floating lake into a golden summer shower.

"'Home, Ibor, and spare the four-legged beasts and long-necked birds,' said Setanta.

"Amazed by his perversity and perseverance, I obeyed the smoke-hound.

"It was thus that we returned to the Red Branch House of King Connor of Ulster with eight wild swans, with long white necks, flying high on each side of Setanta's horses, and two splendid wild stags running between the rear shafts of the chariot. A warrior possessed by the wildest warp-spasm ever witnessed, alongside what remained of the king's charioteer, in the front of the chariot. Behind them the red lake of blood on which swam the three severed heads of Ulster's worst enemies.

"'Beware the king's chariot, an ugly warrior is approaching who will spill the blood of the whole court,' cried the watcher of The House of the Red Branch. Upon hearing this, Setanta turned the left side of the chariot toward the king's house. The left side is known as the sinister insult of charioteers.

"'I swear by Old God above that if nine nimble warriors will not fight me, I will spill blood in every one of the one hundred and fifty rooms of this house,' yelled Setanta. Then the warped warrior let loose his challenge cry to conflict, a call to the goblins, demons, and spirits above, beyond, and about. Alarmed, Katbad the Druid turned to King Connor. I listened closely.

"'Naked women to him. Naked women to the boy or he will slay us all,' Katbad warned.

"'Naked women to him,' the Druid repeated.

"'It is my sister's son who went to redden his hands. Setanta has not had his fill of combat,' King Connor said.

"'Naked women to him, naked women to the boy, naked women to him. Save our lives.' So the cry went around the women in the king's court, from an alarm to a lament.

"'Naked women to him.'

"'Naked women to the boy.'

"'Naked women.'

"And so, one hundred and fifty young women, one for each room in the king's house, danced forward to charm and disarm the Warped One.

"All disclosed their nakedness without shame to Setanta. 'These are the warriors you must overcome,' I said, enjoying the excitement and the view. The wild swans settled on the antlers of the stags to watch the proceedings. Shaking, warping, wailing, Setanta shrank in stature. The malignant mists and spurts of smoke covering his upper parts spun into smoke rings and drifted away. Setanta's series of contortions aroused his naked audience and shook the chariot. I held on bravely, gentling the horses, watching the women, ready to throw my body between the boy and them.

"While this warping was evolving, Katbad the Druid had the warriors fill three large vats with cold water from icy streams. The boy Setanta hid his face against the side of the chariot for shame at seeing the nakedness of the women. A minstrel struck a wild chord on his harp. The boldest of the naked women seized the boy Setanta from beside me in the chariot. The women formed two straight lines from my chariot to the first vat of water.

"With a cheer of abandon, fifty naked females flung the boy Setanta high over the wooden vat. Crimson from head to feet, for all to see, Setanta was plunged into the icy water. Clouds of steam arose from the vat and silenced the naked women. Hot waves of water splashed over its top. There was no sight or sound from the bold Setanta, only the bubbling of boiling water, the hissing of steam, the protest of heated wood, the inhalation of one hundred and fifty naked females.

"With a crack like a branch breaking off a tree in midwinter, the staves of the vat burst asunder. Laughing and screaming, the naked women scattered from the boiling water. Alone, standing among the hoops of the vat, the small boy Setanta surveyed his surroundings. Still crimson from head to foot, his stance and form proclaimed the warrior he would become if he survived the day and what was in it.

"'Naked women to him. Naked women to him.' The voice of Katbad rallied the running women and they reformed into two straight lines from the naked wee lad to the second vat of icy water.

"This time they handled Setanta with care, passing him gently from one to the next. Setanta averted his eyes from the naked women, earning their respect and admiration. Katbad ordered an oak bench from the dining hall to be placed beside the second vat. Two comely women stood on the bench and lifted Setanta into the cold water. Once again, the water bubbled and boiled, hissed and steamed, evaporating from the heat of Setanta's mind and body. When only his ankles were covered by the water, the women lifted Setanta from the second vat and, placing the still-crimson boy on their shoulders, two women carried Setanta to the third vat.

"Standing on the oak bench, they left him sitting on the side of the vat. Setanta dipped his feet into the cold water and let the temperature adjust to his needs and then, and only then, did he drop into the vat and let his anger abate in the cooling water. His crimson skin and averted eyes returned to normal. King Connor dispatched two women from his house with garments to cover Setanta's nakedness.

"The women lifted Setanta from the third vat, placed him on the oaken bench, and dressed him in a gold-threaded blue tunic, covered by a soft green cloak and held in place by a silver brooch from the forge of Cullen the Smith. On his feet they tied high-laced sandals of supple bullhide, and carefully they combed his hair until it looked as if a cow had licked it. I followed Setanta into the king's house between the lines of naked women, carrying the king's heavy spear and fabled sword. I can say that no charioteer ever experienced such a welcome from one hundred and fifty women, naked and glorious. This I owe to Setanta.

"King Connor welcomed his nephew Setanta. He sat Setanta on his knee and stroked his shining hair. This became Setanta's favorite seat at the court of King Connor forever after."

Ibor the driver finished the tale of his first adventure with Setanta the Warped One. King Fergus thanked Ibor for the skillful telling of his story. Queen Maeve returned from the royal tent to present Ibor with a silver-handled whip from her private collection, and King Aillil's reward was a gift of gold reserved for bards and poets. Thus, the delighted Ibor returned to his horses, confirmed in his future career as a touring bard of chariot lore. The two kings and the queen stood around the oaken fire. "What now of Setanta?" asked Queen Maeve.

"It is a privilege long held by the kings and queens of Ireland to protect their borders by the use of one warrior," said Fergus.

"Setanta claims the right of single combat against all comers until the arrival of King Connor and his chariot warriors." Then Fergus the Virile concluded his tale with the following:

"It is a small wonder that a boy who did these deeds when he was seven should triumph against all comers in his young manhood."

The royal trio looked deep into the fire, wondering what tomorrow would bring.

Today I row my small boat through a swelling ocean to reach a lonely isle. I walk through the damp grass to my stone sanctuary. Here I stand at a wooden lectern and open a package from my order.

Embossed in gold letters on a calfskin cover is the legend, "Setanta the Warped One." Inside the cover is my volume on vellum of Setanta.

Young Setanta's deeds on one afternoon captured the hearts of the superiors of my order. His warping as a warrior, beheading of three enemies of Ulster, and befriending one hundred and fifty women has met with their utter approval.

The birth of Connor MacNessa and his ascent to the throne of the Red Branch is pertinent to the story of Setanta's immortality.

To display the characters and condition of this pagan province, I return to an earlier time in its history, twenty years before the birth of Setanta.

These tales of Celtic gods and immortal heroes occupy my attention on a lonely isle in a restless ocean.

O, My Lord Divine,
My prayer is still;
On this day so fine,
Grant me words at will.
So be it.

Mael Moró

Six

THE FOLLOWING IS one story of the birth of Connor, the future King of Ulster, on a night like none before and none since.

Connor's conception signaled the end of the world of Old God and the start of a story that is still unfolding. These are the details of the tale that caught Old God's ear and tormented his heart. When Caesar Augustus was emperor of Rome and Herod the great king of Judea, Fergus the Virile ascended the throne of the province of Ulster in Ireland. Then, as now, all Ireland was divided into the four provinces of Ulster, Munster, Leinster, and Connacht. Each province had a king or queen responsible for the wealth and well being of its subjects. For reasons lost in legend and loved in lore, the oracular throne of Ulster, the famed Stone of Fál, lay in state in the center of the courtyard of Katbad the Fair of Face, King of the Druids of Ireland.

From its height, Katbad could see the handsome house of King Fergus, known in glory as the Crave Rua, the Red Branch. Inside this house of kings were one hundred and fifty inner rooms paneled with red yew, red for blood and royalty. Which came first, blood or royalty, may be argued, but that one begat the other is a bloody fact none can deny.

Once upon a blue moon, as was his want, King Fergus liked to sit on the oracular throne of Ulster and review his standing as an upright member of his fabled kingdom. Tonight was such a night. It was also the night when Genann, the son of Katbad, arrived at the age of reason upon his seventh year. On this occasion, Genann of the Brow of Light was allowed the privilege of following in the footsteps of his father for a day and a night. And there never was such a night as this for Genann! Tonight his father would take him to the top of the tower for the first time. No boy of his age had reached so high so soon. No boy in the school for Druids in Katbad's house had Genann's gifts for magic and healing. Genann shivered with delight at the night that was in it, the moon of the blue above and the stars of gold around it.

Katbad the Druid sighed as he stood outside the round tower, the top of which disappeared into the mists of May. The legs were the first to go, even for the First Druid of Ireland. A small tug on his fingers brought Katbad's attention back to earth and son. Katbad patted the head of his son and bent to look into his eyes. In silence, they bonded as father and son, Druid and human. Each had a foot in this world and a big toe in the next.

A study in grey from the hair curled around his shoulders to the seven folds of his full cloak, Katbad was known as the Druid of the Fair Face. Around his high forehead curved a gold headband. Set in the center of his headband, a dark green emerald covered Katbad's fabled third eye. He touched this emerald with his finger of knowledge and then traced its outline on the forehead of his son. Genann closed his eyes, a golden glow of light and love massaging the ridges of his brain. All of his being flowed into the eye slowly forming in the middle of his mind. Not for nothing was he called Genann of the Brow of Light.

Katbad lifted his son onto his broad shoulders and stepped inside the tower of the throne of Ulster. He began his ascent up the circular stone steps cut into the grey limestone. Around and around, higher and higher, the stone whispered of his ascent, his long cloak caressing each step. Genann lit the way up the dark tower by holding high Katbad's short three-pronged javelin. Each prong of the javelin had a ray of the blue moon embedded in its curved point. Upward, ever higher, climbed the Druid with his son on his shoulder.

On this climb up endless stairs, Katbad blessed the rarity of a blue moon that drew kings to thrones and aches to his knees and joints. Even for Druids, mortality proclaimed its presence with sharp pricks and long pains. Finally, the three-forked lightning bolts of the javelin dimmed and died as they stood on the top of the round tower. Nothing higher than them to cast a shadow, except for an occasional cloud lonely for the light of the moon.

Now Genann saw with his inner eye what he'd never seen before. Buried within the walls of the tower he witnessed the heads of ancestral heroes famed for strength and wisdom. Katbad the Druid lifted his son from his shoulder and placed him in front of the fabulous throne of Fál.

"Behold the throne of golden stone,
source and scourge of Ulster's Own."

Genann touched the cold oracular throne of gold-veined Connemara marble set on a slab of blackest slate. Above the throne stood a shield of startling clarity. Over all, like a hero's halo, hung the moon.

"Can only a king sit on the throne?" Genann asked his father.

"A king *or* a queen. Listen closely, my bright boy. Whoever would seek to reign in Ulster must sit and submit to the throne."

Genann stared at the huge throne, cold and indifferent, except to the plight of kings and queens.

"Tell me," he urged his father, tugging at his hand.

> *The man who would be king*
> *must mount this throne before the throng*
> *and wake a single harp to song."*

"And if a pretender?" Genann wondered.

> *"A banshee's wail of desolation*
> *Will denounce his coronation.*
> *Who defiles this sacred throne*
> *Within a year will die—alone!"*

Katbad walked to the parapet of the tower and stared at the faint outline of the king's house in the far distance.

"See there, my wide-eyed boy." He pointed. In the still of the night, a small shadow detached from the house and moved slowly across the plain toward the tall tower.

"The king is on his way to us, Genann. The shield must be clean."

Genann followed his father to the shield above the throne. Two small ladders were fastened to each side of the shield. A snow-white lambskin hung on the bottom rung of the ladder. Katbad lifted his son to the top of the ladder and handed him the lambskin.

"Now, Genann, wipe tonight from the shield of the past."

Genann rubbed the lambskin across the shield. The shades of night vanished under his quick round strokes.

"Tell me," Genann said.

"There are veins of memory in marble, especially from Connemara. Who sits on the throne leaves impressions of his past, indelible and eternal."

Genann rubbed harder with his lambskin, staring deeper into the shield. Suddenly, the naked breast of a beautiful young woman appeared on the shield. Astonished, Genann clung to the ladder. Slowly, he caressed the image of the woman's breast as if in a dream, his mouth and eyes wide open.

"Tell me," he gasped.

"These are the loves of Fergus the Virile. Tonight he will revisit his past to endow his future. It is the way of kings. Close your mouth, Genann, and open your ears."

Katbad lifted his son from the ladder and left him facing the king's house.

"Watch for the king's chariot. Tell me when it arrives." Katbad turned his attention to the shield of the past. A parade of long-legged beauties floated across the shield. The loves of the youthful Fergus, downy, dreamy, delicious. Katbad rubbed the green emerald in his headband.

From the early manhood of Fergus, visions of naked girls morphed into round, firm-fleshed, warm-buttocked young women. A sight to please a prince and pleasure a king.

Katbad blinked. The shield glowed bright and the women vanished. A tall, naked, blood-eyed regal rossy appeared, queen of all queens, Maeve of the Appetites, future lover and equal of Fergus the Virile. Maeve of the Three Round Spears, one at hand and two on her breast. Maeve of the red hair and friendly thighs. The throne groaned with desire. For shame, the moon hid behind a snowy-breasted cloud. Genann of the Brow of Light risked a backward glance at the naked queen on the shield. Maeve of the Immortals. Fiery, fearless, ferocious, Maeve winked at Genann.

"Yoho the Tower, Fergus is here!"

The lusty voice of Fergus brought Katbad to the side of his son. Maeve vanished from the shield and the cloud from the moon. Fergus the Virile, King of Ulster, cast a tall shadow, like a tree with foliage, as he waved to Katbad on the tower.

Poised, polished, and perfect, King Fergus sat on his throne and smiled down on his kingdom. Dressed in a green cloak, a red embroidered and hooded tunic, and bronze blunt sandals, Fergus of the Brown Hair and Arching Eyebrows was a figure of fierce and immaculate majesty. His gold-hilted sword, long as a boat's rudder, stood tall between his thighs. For Fergus, his throne was also his phallic stone.

"Katbad, my Druid, this king needs a queen, and your aid in finding one."

"What queen in Ireland exists that Fergus has not known already?" Katbad asked.

"I have heard of a queen called Nessa who lives where the Mountains of Mourne sweep down to the sea; you will seek her out for me."

Genann watched his father move closer to King Fergus. They both glanced at Genann then Fergus changed the subject.

"Before we talk of queens and crowns, my Druid, I want you to interpret a dream I had last night—a dream of a queen and a crown." As King Fergus told of his dream, the shield above the throne glowed bright in the still of the night. It reveled in the details of the king's dream.

"It seemed to me, in my dream state, that I was alone in my chariot. I was on my way through the Giant's Causeway on the coast of my kingdom in Antrim."

Entranced, Genann watched the dream drama unfold on the shield.

"The sun was at its height; the sea green and gorgeous. Suddenly, a deep bull's roar bellowed through the rocky road of the Giant's Causeway. Boulders and stones crashed above and about me. I pulled to a halt my frightened horse. From a gap in the Giant's Causeway, a massive bull, brawny and brazen, charged at my chariot. It was not the bull so frantic as the bitch so antic astride him that froze my heart. It was Queen Maeve with her friendly thighs wrapped around the backbone of the ivory-horned beast.

"Queen Maeve, nude and naked, with her round spear in hand, at one with the animal and elements. The brown bull ploughed to a halt. Then, with a savage hook, it sank its ivory horn into the heart of my noble horse. A jet of dark blood from my horse's heart splashed onto my face. Jerking backwards, I dropped my sword to retrieve the crown knocked from my head. The bull upended my chariot with another savage hook of its horn. The crown sailed from my grasp. It landed on the upturned horn of the bull. I was flung clear of the chariot. Framed by the smoke from his flaring nostrils, the baleful eyes of the beast glared at me. This monster of Ulster scalded the sultry air with a scorching breath that set the heather blazing.

"Thunder roared. Lightning flashed. Ancient graves gaped open. The dead arose to witness the disturbance. I found my long sword amid the blazing heather. A round-tipped spear flashed before my eyes. On the spear's tip dangled my gold crown. Before me, Queen Maeve rode back and forth on the bull.

"I climbed on a rock for the advantage of height. The duel for my crown began. Sword versus spear. King versus bull and queen. The crown spun down my long sword. Maeve's spear slammed the hilt of my sword. The crown spun free between us. The bones of the dead rattled with applause. Maeve's tip captured the crown. The crown on the spear. The crown in the air. The crown on the sword.

"The naked queen wrapped her friendly thighs around the arched backbone of the brazen bull, and with its haunches heaving, hooves flailing, the excited animal reared high. Queen Maeve grabbed the bull by the horn. Demented, the bull sprang toward me. Hot snot balls from its nostrils singed my beard. Maeve laughed. The bull's hooves crashed between my feet, cleaving in two the rock on which I stood.

"I fell sideways. Queen Maeve spun my crown on the tip of her spear, and quickly I scrambled to my feet. Suddenly, the bull snorted flames and farewell and headed for the hills.

"So ends my dream of a warrior queen with a whore's backside, with my crown dancing on her spear. Tell me what means the Brown Bull?"

Katbad assumed his Druid's stance. "It appears to me, King Fergus, that Queen Maeve rode the Brazen Bull away to save your life."

Once more, the throne groaned with desire as Fergus imagined future love encounters with Queen Maeve.

"What of Maeve and my crown on her spear?" asked Fergus.

"Queen Maeve is your equal and opposite. She rode away with your heart, which she claims for her own." Katbad had knowledge of Queen Maeve and her wanton ways.

From this night on, Genann's dreams were in vivid color. As Katbad and Fergus did, he wore red when traveling as protection from predators.

Seven

QUEEN NESSA, THE daughter of Eoin of the Yellow Heel, sat with her royal women where the Mountains of Mourne sweep down to the sea. Even the birds of the air acknowledged the beauty and character of this queen. Queen Nessa had a female curiosity that matched her civility, and an ambition equal to her lineage. After a swift frolic in the cold ocean, Nessa's maidens adorned her fabulous form with a tunic of regal red that clung to her as the foggy dew on a spider's web. They combed her long black hair until it hung straight down her back. After washing her feet with the first milk of the day, they laced high gold sandals on her comely calves. Old God himself lounged on a fleecy cloud, enjoying the beauty of Nessa beneath him. He blew a warm breeze toward her that warmed her nipples and relaxed her cherry red lips. Every woman has a soft spot that brings her woe and wonder.

The sight of a tall stranger approaching on a wondrous chariot drawn by two jet-black bulls stopped the gossip of the women in front of Queen Nessa. When talk stops, trouble enters.

Just a passing glance between the stranger and Queen Nessa cast a fascination between them, as ordained by Old God himself. The stranger stopped his chariot, bowed, and smiled at Nessa. Mystic symbols and ivory accoutrements decorated the tall man's chariot. Between shafts of polished silver, the two black bulls looked slyly at Nessa, then at each other. They licked their drooling lips, as did Old God above. The bulls twisted their tails together, and one scratched another notch on the shaft with his polished horn. Queen Nessa studied the stranger in queenly silence. Nessa noted his grey traveling cloak, held fast by a gold brooch. She noted his long grey hair, curled softly around his shoulders as if a magician from the mound world. She noted no spears or swords in his chariot, but a short three-pronged javelin in his hands, and a black raven on his broad shoulders. Looking only at Nessa, the stranger walked to her side. He waved his three-pronged javelin in a circle about them. The seagulls ceased swooping and formed a wall of wings between them and Nessa's royal maidens. A Druid's fog of invisibility settled about this handsome couple, alone in the land of promise, seen only by Old God on his cloud on high, and Katbad's black raven.

"Luck of the Irish to you, Queen of the Day." The tall stranger stared deep into Nessa's eyes. Queen Nessa knew by his greeting that this was Katbad, first among the Druids of Ireland, sage and seer, counselor to kings, comforter to queens, diviner of dreams. Katbad the Druid, whose clear eyes and healing hands sustained his friends and devastated his foes.

"What is the luck of the Irish this fine afternoon?" Nessa asked.

"To conceive a king," Katbad said, letting the world and his conscience recede. Fergus could wait for this queen. Nessa

looked back, under her black eyelashes, amused at his insolence, her skin like virgin snow, the hue of the foxglove on her
cheeks, beautiful without blemish. Nessa was indeed a queen
among women.

"It takes a king to conceive a king. I know not your kingdom or name," Queen Nessa said.

"I am king of my tribe. The first of the Druids in Ireland.
My name is Katbad the Druid."

Katbad the Druid took Nessa's hand. They stood silent
and straight, untouched by the world, casting no shadows,
and they became as one.

"Is this the luck of the Irish for this queen?" asked Nessa.

"Indeed, Queen Nessa will conceive an immortal king."
Katbad bowed and released her hand. Flaven the Raven
hopped from Katbad's shoulder to the palm of his hand.
Flaven swiftly plucked a gold ring from Katbad's finger.
Fascinated, Nessa watched the raven perch on the gold
headband in the middle of Katbad's forehead. Suspended
by a thin silver bracelet from Flaven's beak, the gold ring
hung between the deep green eyes of Katbad the Druid.
Slowly and surely, Flaven the Raven swung the gold ring in
a gentle pendulum before the rapt gaze of Nessa. Deeper
and deeper into the hypnotic green eyes of Katbad did the
queenly Nessa stare. The trees leaned forward, the waves
on the shore leaped high, and Nessa, as in a dream, recalled
a tale told of Katbad by one of her royal maidens. If Nessa
blinked before Katbad did, he would overcome her will and
have his way with her. Nessa fingered the gold brooch that
held her red tunic tight to her breasts. If Katbad blinked
before Nessa did, he would be under an obligation to tell
her future. Flaven warbled a seductive air. Katbad reached

forward to touch Nessa. The world waited. Nessa dropped her tunic. Katbad blinked at the perfection of her breasts. Nessa smiled. Flaven whistled.

"Is there a king of Ulster in my future, Druid?"

"A king—the greatest king ever of Ulster," swore Katbad. He moved closer. The world hushed. Not a berry fell from a bush.

"A Druid who would lie is a Druid who would die."

Knowing this, and seeing no other kings in her vicinity, Queen Nessa braced herself for this offering from Katbad, the Royal Druid of Ulster. These coming events cast more than a shadow. The frenzy and fury of Katbad's and Nessa's embrace moved the earth and shook the heavens; waves crashed, winds roared, trees cracked, lightning flashed, bulls bellowed, stallions stomped, the seagulls scattered, the royal women wailed and wept. Flaven the Black Raven flew between the lovers and the sun, an augury of slaughter. Old God roared with laughter, thunder rolled down from the top of the Mountains of Mourne.

For three years and three months, Katbad's seed lay in Nessa's womb. Neither hide nor hair did she see of Katbad the Druid or his bulls during her time in waiting. On the darkest night in the midst of winter, a thunderous battering on the door of Nessa's abode awoke all within. Nessa's dogs howled and ran circles around her at the night that was in it. Nessa watched as her door opened and two black bulls charged into her courtyard. No charioteer stood in the bronze car with the silver shafts. The bull reins were tied to a three-pronged javelin inside the chariot. A golden ring glittered on the point of the middle prong. Nessa knew that her time had come, and her birth pangs began.

Wrapping herself in her warmest cloak of supple black bull skin, Nessa approached the chariot. The black bulls bowed before her as she entered the car. The golden ring on the javelin's prong was fashioned in the shape of the crown of Ulster. Nessa slipped the ring on her finger and took the javelin in her hand. Nessa waved the javelin in a circle about her as Katbad had done three long years and three full months ago.

Darkness fled the sky, replaced by multitudes of stars assembled to celebrate this holy night. Nessa shook the reins at the black bulls. Snorting plumes of white smoke, the bulls turned to look at Nessa and beat a farewell to the earth with hooves. Flakes of snow anointed Nessa's eyelashes, and over the plains of Ulster, under the whitest snow, the bulls flew. Faster than the winter wind, the chariot blazed a path through the driven snow.

The snow ceased when the chariot reached the fort of Katbad the Druid. A bronze door opened wide and the bulls plowed to a halt inside. As the door closed, a sweet perfumed mist enclosed all within. Katbad stood splendid before Nessa. Dramatic in a cloak of deep purple and a tunic of red silk, with a gold helmet on his head and silver buckles on his shoes, Katbad bowed deeply to Queen Nessa. Still and grave, Katbad escorted Nessa through the rooms of his stately mansion. As in a dream, Nessa followed Katbad through the marble halls into rooms of ivory, with walls of gold that turned night into day, through silver curtains into an ebony bedchamber. In a sacred space within the Druid's dwelling place a hundred harps tuned the music that whispered in the night.

Tonight Katbad reigned as the King of the Druids. He removed Queen Nessa's cloak and sat her before a blazing fire of oak logs, and gently, with his healing hands, he brushed the soft snowflakes from her face and form. A fine young boy brought Queen Nessa a gold goblet filled with foaming red ale.

"This is my son, Genann of the Brow of Light. He is the bright love of my life," Katbad said.

Queen Nessa looked with approval upon Genann's strong, ten-year-old body, his jet-black hair, and his broad, bright forehead. Katbad and Nessa drank deep from the golden goblet, gazing into each other's eyes.

"Genann will be to your son as I am to the King of Ulster," Katbad said.

"He will be a protector to his brother, a Druid to a king?" Nessa asked.

Katbad flung the remains of his goblet into the fire.

"Tonight, two kings will be born—one called Connor, one called Christ." Nessa watched the form of a kingly man blaze among the hissing flames. Lifting the queen into his arms, Katbad carried her through his house to the throne on top of his tower. Gently, Katbad placed Nessa on the throne of Fál, beneath a mantle of snow. Sweet music from a solitary harp magnified all that flowed toward the heavens. Transfixed by the stars, Katbad pointed his javelin upward.

"Tonight, the Son of God will be born where sand covers the land and carpets fly through the sky." All the stars but one fled the sky. Nessa by starlight looked at Katbad.

"When the star of the East reaches heaven, Christ the King will be born in a stable." The lone star above glowed brighter.

"Sit tight on the throne, Nessa, bind the birth until the star expires." Brighter glowed the star as Katbad handed his javelin to Nessa. On the center prong of the javelin, Nessa placed Katbad's ring. She shook the javelin for the soothing of her unborn babe, and to prepare him for a king's walk through the world. Higher toward the dome of heaven sailed the star. The harp stilled.

In a stable in Bethlehem, the Christ child was born, and on the throne of Ulster, the Stone of Fál, a boy was born to a queen named Nessa. Katbad, his father, wrapped the babe in a cloth of red linen and held him high. A final blaze of light extinguished the one star above.

A hundred harps sang the birth of a true king of Ulster. None who heard that music ever forgot it. As Queen Nessa cuddled deep into the marble throne, a vision of Fergus appeared on the shield above the throne. Poised and perfect in his emerald-green cloak and bronze sandals, Fergus the Virile smiled down at Nessa. For the throne of Ulster was also the phallus stone of Fergus, King of Ulster. Splashes of Queen Nessa's blood formed a scarlet pool that dripped from the marble throne onto the black slate beneath. A gush, a rush, a river of blood disfigured the shield above the seat of kings. The blazing blood-shot eyes of Old God burned through the blood on the shield. Old gods do not die easily.

Ennobled by the birth of his son, Katbad considered himself the first man in Ireland. Nessa the queen gave over to dreams of her son Connor on the throne of Ulster. Connor MacNessa, King Connor the son born of Nessa, as long as Gaels told tales.

The boy Connor was fostered by his father, Katbad. Seven years passed before Connor ascended the throne. Here is the narrative of how this occurred.

Katbad the Druid reared Connor in his house of enchanted chambers. He kept Connor close to home, away from the keen eyes of King Fergus the Virile. Rumors are the currency of royalty. Another small boy of consequence around a Druid aroused small concern at the House of the Red Branch. For a Druid, knowledge is attained through the senses. The natural world yielded to those who studied long and dear. This also applied to the human race. At night, Katbad taught Connor to divine coming events by reading the stars. By daylight, Katbad showed Connor how to read passing clouds, reflecting events beneath them.

Because of his treachery to King Fergus, Katbad kept his distance from Queen Nessa. Katbad sent news of Connor to Nessa by means of his black raven. The raven Flaven flew on nightly missions to the abode of Queen Nessa. Here he reported on the aspects and ascensions of her son Connor.

By nature a fly-by-night bird, Flaven was a nestling when picked by Katbad. In a Druid ceremony under a yew tree, Katbad slit the raven's tongue thrice. He then sewed Flaven's tongue with golden string. Flaven went everywhere with Katbad from his perch of privilege on the Druid's shoulder. He learned to whistle words in a musical manner.

The presence of Connor in Katbad's house magnified a touch of malice in Flaven. No more was he the bird of note on Katbad's shoulder. He was relegated to aerial surveillance and domestic eavesdropping; a fall from grace for a Druid's raven.

One night after Nessa fell asleep listening to his talk of her son, Flaven had an urge to monitor her dreams. He settled snugly between her perfect breasts and blew softly on them. The memory of the Phallus Stone of Fergus on the throne had haunted Nessa's dreams since the birth of Connor. Tossing and turning, she cried out for Fergus in her dreams, over and over: "Oh, Fergus, my love, my jewel, my darling." On this note, Flaven flew back to the throne in Katbad's courtyard. King Fergus sat on his throne, dreaming on his Phallus Stone. With his beady eyes, Flaven studied the sleeping king Fergus the Virile. The King of Ulster earned his reputation for virility the hard way. Fergus lived his life at the gallop. None complained of his riding skills. Since manhood, Fergus had satisfied seven women a night and eight on a feast day. The origins of Leap Year lay in his carnal delight at one extra night in the calendar. In over six years of dreaming, Queen Nessa had replaced his visions of Queen Maeve. Nights of nocturnal excursions with Nessa by starlight changed the life of King Fergus. A dream of Nessa caressing his gold crown with her pale hands released his heart from the snares of Queen Maeve. Flaven hopped with delight with the king's dream speech.

"Oh, my Queen Nessa, my love, my darling, my jewel." Fergus turned and tossed. The top of the tip of the Phallus of Fergus cracked and fell on the black slate beneath. In dreams lie solutions that escape the awake. Fluttering his feathers, Flaven dropped down to the black slate to steal the tip of the top of the Phallus of King Fergus.

If Flaven could drop this under the bed of Nessa, it might replace the need for his nightly flights to her with news of Connor. If Nessa cast her lot with Fergus, she surely would arrange for her son Connor to live in the Red Branch as a prince. This could return Flaven to his preferred perch on the shoulder of Katbad, the King of the Druids.

Fergus awoke and stretched. The sight of a black raven hopping between his feet brought Fergus back to the reality of the year seven, anno domini. With a flick of his finger, Fergus knocked Flaven on his backside. He swept the Phallus segment into his king's grasp.

Flaven forced himself onto his shaky feet and flew a shaky course through the house to Katbad's bedchamber. Taking a deep breath, Flaven squeezed his ruffled feathers through the wee raven's hole cut in the bedroom's door. Inside, Flaven confessed his transgressions into the sleeping ear of the Druid.

Aroused and alarmed, Katbad waited at the bottom of the throne for the descent of King Fergus. A chastened raven clung to his shoulder. In royal good humor, Fergus swaggered toward Katbad.

"It's well you are looking, King Fergus," Katbad said.

Fergus eyed the shrinking raven on Katbad's shoulder.

"What news of Nessa, Druid?" asked Fergus.

"The same; content in her condition," said Katbad.

"I wish to change her condition," Fergus said.

"Send Queen Nessa a king's gift," suggested Katbad. "At your command, Fergus, I will approach the queen with your offering."

"No, not you, Katbad; not this time." Fergus smiled to show his teeth. "This time, I will send an equerry with an inquiry, the way of a king with a queen."

Flaven the Raven ventured a soft whistle as Fergus departed.

Katbad sensed that Fergus no longer had implicit trust in the Druid's ability to secure whichever female pleased the king's eye. At least where Nessa was concerned, Fergus might forgive a human impulse, but he would not forget the hint of a need above his own—the King of Ulster. The ways of kings are the woes of advisers.

eight

T HIS IS HOW King Fergus pursued and married Queen Nessa in a glamour of dreams. In the time and place of the Red Branch court in Ulster, words and music ruled. The imaginative tellers of tales and musicians were regally welcomed in the abodes of the affluent and influential. For his pursuit of Queen Nessa, King Fergus began by sending an equerry with an inquiry.

For this romantic adventure, he picked as his equerry, Sceál Galore, the foremost teller of tales at the court of the Red Branch. Sceál means "tales," Galore means "abundance." The first of the king's gifts was music, the language of love. Fergus had Malachy the Minstrel compose a love song called "Nessa's Dream." At the king's request, he accompanied Sceál Galore to play it for Queen Nessa.

The arrival of Sceál Galore and Malachy the Minstrel caused a sensation among the royal ladies in Nessa's house. Due to his scandalous reputation, the name of Fergus the Virile warmed more than the hearts of the women as they set the tables for a royal feast in the welcome hall. Queen

Nessa, as usual, stayed aloof and alone. When Malachy played "Nessa's Dream" on his harp, the queen knew that her world was changing.

Thanking Sceál for tales and Malachy for melody, Nessa departed the party. Later, in her bedchamber, Nessa listened to the raven tell of her son Connor's character and condition in the house of Katbad the Druid. How Connor was fed on the immortal food of the Gaels, nuts, apples, and sloes. In public, her son Connor appeared on a speckled horse of great height.

Katbad built a platform on his chariot and taught Connor to drive the dashing black bulls. As Connor passed along the plain, the people of Ulster grew accustomed to looking up at him. The small boy on the great chariot warmed their hearts. Queen Nessa smiled and settled for sleep.

At the same time in another place, a harpist plucked "Nessa's Dream" on his harp for the dreaming king on his throne. A love conceived in dreams continued in melody. King Fergus had a notion to visit Cullen the Blacksmith. It was time for another gift of love for Queen Nessa. When a king proclaims passion, the world stirs in wonder.

The foremost artisan in Ulster, Cullen was renowned for his genius and talent. Among heroes seeking immortality, Cullen's gift for forging weapons of destruction in his swords, spears, and sharpened shields rendered him unique. In the kingdom of Ulster, Cullen lived on an estate equal to his artistic endeavors. To protect his property, Cullen kept an enormous wolfhound of extraordinary savagery.

"Good day to you, Cullen," said Fergus as he strode into the smithy of Cullen on a bright spring day.

"Good day to yourself, King Fergus," said Cullen, emerging from a cloud of crimson smoke. The hound of Cullen barked a welcome. Cullen's mighty frame and giant dog bespoke a world warm from creation.

"I need a man who can put a shape on a dream," said Fergus. "I need a king's gift to woo a queen's heart."

"Tell me of your dream," said Cullen. He pulled a bark of charcoal from a bundle of faggots and, listening to the king's dream, Cullen sketched a rough design on the stone outside his forge with his charcoal stick.

Fergus stayed as a guest at Cullen's house. The presence of a king raised the value of an artisan to mythic heights, and so Cullen called upon his cunning to please King Fergus. Cullen formed the refined fingers of Nessa's two hands in the finest gold at his disposal. Fergus expressed his approval. Cullen split in two with his sharpest chisel the top of the tip of the Phallus of Fergus. He perfected each stone until they fit between the gold fingers of the queen. One stone he formed into the heart of Nessa; the other he formed into the Phallus of Fergus. In a golden burst of exuberance, Cullen made the replicas of the crown of Ulster.

These he affixed to each stone. Cullen made a measure of the royal ring finger of King Fergus. From this, he assembled a gold ring that looked as if it grew on the finger of Fergus— two hands holding his phallus, topped by the crown of Ulster. That night, with Cullen's ring on his finger, Fergus experienced the most vivid of his dreams of Queen Nessa.

When dreams exceed reality, reality recedes. Each dream of Fergus the King ended with the elegant hands of Nessa holding his gold crown.

As for Queen Nessa, each night's dream began with her son Connor on the throne of Ulster, protected by the doughty warrior King Fergus. At the request of Cullen, Fergus sent a messenger to Sceál Galore. When Sceál took a measure of Nessa's ring finger, the messenger returned it to Cullen.

By this time, both Sceál and Malachy were entranced with Nessa to the dismay of her ladies in waiting. The more aloof she remained, the more enamored they became. Two days later, Sceál Galore arrived at the forge of Cullen the Smith. Nessa's ring, finished in all details, awaited its return to the queen.

"When you tell the tale of the rings, Sceál, tell the truth," Cullen said. His massive hound growled in agreement.

"Words are temporal; art is immortal," Sceál said. Neither Cullen nor Sceál noticed the black raven perched above them. Flaven was back to domestic surveillance for Katbad the Druid. The raven hopped closer. Cullen dropped the royal ring into Sceál's soft hand—a ring of polish and promise.

Flaven studied the ring so he could describe it to Katbad the Druid in all its powerful persuasion. Sceál, a tall man with a reflective air, studied the ring. The great hound of Cullen barked and leapt high, catching a tail feather of the raven in its powerful jaws. Flaven flew from the forge, seeking the comfort of Katbad's shoulder and the privacy of his ear.

"Beware, storyteller; Druids know more than mortals," Cullen said.

Sceál thanked the smith and put the queen's ring in his pouch. He rode back slowly toward the house of Fergus. His thoughts on Druids and queens, rings and kings, love and glory, truth and story, Sceál came to a fork in the road. To the left lay the house of Katbad, and to the right the road to the one hundred and fifty rooms in the house of Fergus the King. Love won the day. Sceál turned his horse left.

After a savory supper, Katbad poured a yard of red ale for his guest, the storyteller Sceál Galore. Thus began the conflict between the Druid and the teller of tales. The magic of words versus the magic of magic.

Both were aware that after thirteen years on the throne, Fergus was a master of shifting alliances. All of them were in love with Queen Nessa. Sceál downed a foot of ale for courage and comfort.

"I love a woman whose heart belongs to the son of a king," he told Katbad.

"Is that what she told you?" Katbad asked.

"Yes, I have a gift from Fergus for her."

"Fergus is not the son of a king. Is the gift a ring with hands, heart, and crown?" asked Katbad.

"Yes. I need a love potion to even the field."

Sceál placed the ring between them and said, "Fergus has the twin of this ring to color his dreams."

"At his request, I have endowed the rings with passion," lied the King of the Druids.

Katbad had to appear at the beck and call of the king, whatever the occasion. For the sake of survival, Katbad was a master of deceit. Confusion of friend and foe was as necessary to a Druid as food and drink. Besides, storytellers like Sceál have access to the ears of kings.

"If Fergus finds out I helped someone seduce his intended queen?" asked Katbad.

"Would I cut my throat with my tongue?" answered Sceál.

Katbad looked deep into the eyes of Sceál Galore.

"I will make you immortal in song and story if you advance my cause," swore Sceál, and drank eight more inches of ale.

"Immortal as a Druid?" asked Katbad.

"Immortal as the King of the Druids," said Sceál.

"If Fergus finds out?"

"Would I cut my throat with my tongue?" replied Sceál.

"If I help you, Sceál, will you swear by Old God never to tell what you see in the forest with me?"

Katbad's eyes did not blink. Sceál nodded. Katbad's eyes and ale were a lethal mix.

"It must be done before Fergus arrives," said Katbad.

Katbad picked up his three-pronged javelin and reached for the ring. Sceál grabbed his hand. They stared at the ring between them.

Sceál Galore held tight to the queen's ring in his right hand. His left clutched the embossed side of Katbad the Druid's chariot. The sight of the black bulls in front, tearing through the night and the forest, unsettled his story-telling mind. The sight of Katbad the Druid beside him unsettled his rumbling, tumbling stomach. Maybe it was the other way round. Magic muddles certainties.

Katbad had wrapped himself in a dun grey hornless bull-hide that transformed his form from human to Druid. A white-speckled bird headpiece held by a golden torque hid his face from creatures of the mound, such as himself. Things of the night whiffed, swooped, barked, brayed, harked, strayed, bumped, thumped, cursed, and prayed at the wild flight of the black bulls.

Into the heart of the forest where few had gone, and none returned, Sceál held tight to his sanity and the queen's ring. Three times around the king of the forest, the oldest oak in Ireland, flew the Druid's black bulls. They stopped. All was still. Katbad picked up his three-pronged javelin. As he spoke, each spear burned with an illuminating fire.

"Spears of hawthorn, rowan and yew make my spell both sharp and true."

Katbad threw his javelin at the giant oak. It flamed through the night and sank deep into the ancient oak. Katbad strode toward the tree.

He stopped opposite the smoldering javelin. Eyes and mouth open, this is what Sceál Galore witnessed in the woods that night.

Katbad, balanced on one leg, one arm outstretched, both eyes closed, spoke of Druidic charms and spells. Like the smoke hissing from the wounds inflicted by the javelin, smoke and fire issued from the mouth of Katbad. Excited, the black bulls snorted fire and smoke. A hot, smoky night in the old forest.

The ring in Sceál's hand glowed hot and burned its imprint into his palm. Sceál screamed and dropped the ring. The black bulls bellowed.

The ring of fire rolled from the chariot and along the ground to land at the foot of the fire-breathing Druid. Katbad broke his one-legged pose and marched to the ancient oak. What Sceál witnessed next drove the pain from his mind. Katbad pulled the javelin from the oak tree, leaving three burning wounds in the bark of the wood.

He flung the flaming javelin high in the air. It flared across the dark sky as a comet in flight, and plunged to the ground on top of the ring of fire. The middle spear of rowan wood pierced the center of the ring. The bull-Druid with the bird's headpiece grasped his javelin and pointed it at the sky. The ring of fire burned bright on the middle spear as he intoned:

"O, ring of magic, flame and fire,
Anoint your point with love's desire."

Katbad marched back to the oak tree. He pushed the spear tops back into their still-smoldering holes. The middle spear with the ring burned with a purple glow and the ancient branches of the tree waved in the dark. A gush of sap spat the javelin from the oak. It landed beside Sceál in the chariot. The queen's ring spun through the air and fell into Katbad's open hand. He placed the ring between two sprigs of mistletoe, the all-healing Druid's weed.

nine

BACK IN THE abode of Queen Nessa, Sceál made ready in his room for his return to the feast hall. Tonight he would tell a love story before approaching the queen with the gift of the ring. Sceál practiced with the ring, slipping it on his left finger, fitting his words to the gesture.

That afternoon, Malachy entertained the queen and her ladies at a picnic. To harp her to sleep, the minstrel moved to a room next to the queen. Most distressful to Sceál, Malachy occupied the favored seat at the evening feast, to the left of the queen, nearest her heart. The former seat of Sceál Galore.

Tonight Sceál sat in silence in the former seat of Malachy the Minstrel. In the absence of words, music had conquered the queen and her cohorts. Queen Nessa raised her hand. The festivities began. Sceál rose to his feet. Tonight he would begin a tale of love with a dramatic pause to ensure attention. Before he spoke, the strings of Malachy's harp filled the hall with heavenly resonance. Shocked, Sceál slunk from the feast. None noted his departure because all the attention was on the queen, the minstrel, and his music. To salve his pride and solve his problem, Sceál planned his assault on the queen.

Love in a teller of tales takes place in the mind. The body is more reliable, but less rewarding. Sceál bribed a steward at the feast to arrange a meeting with Queen Nessa for that evening. Over and over that afternoon, he repeated the mantra impressed on him by Katbad the Druid. If the crown of the ring points toward Fergus, Nessa's heart will follow the ring. If the crown of the ring points toward Nessa, this signified that Nessa's heart was occupied. If the crown of the ring points toward Sceál Galore, then...

Sceál checked the image of the ring burned in the palm of his hand. The crown of the ring pointed to Sceál. A good omen in the eyes of this teller of tales.

At the feast that evening, Sceál consumed a yard and a half of ale before the steward tapped him on his shoulder. Sceál followed him to the seat on the right side of Queen Nessa. On the left side of the queen, Malachy tuned his harp, and turned his eyes toward Sceál Galore.

"Welcome back, Sceál Galore. When did you return?"

Nessa's eyelashes were a scourge to Sceál's heart.

"Queen Nessa, I bring you a gift from King Fergus. If I may see your hand?"

The touch of Nessa's pale and perfect hand moved Sceál's center of gravity. Flustered, awkward, off center, he dropped the gold ring on the table. The queen took the ring into her hands and passed it to Sceál. Sceál wiped his sweaty hand on his tunic. Again, he touched the queen's hand. Carefully, he centered the ring on the tip of Nessa's finger with the crown pointing toward Sceál's heart. His moment was here. Malachy strummed his harp. The ring hopped from Sceál's hand and rolled toward the queen. This ring had a life of its own. Nessa smiled and examined the ring. Sceál recovered his speech.

"King Fergus invites you to share a dream or two," he said.

"Where would the dreaming occur?" asked Nessa.

"On his throne—you by his side."

"And the ring?" Nessa stroked the crown of the ring.

"He has the match of it on his finger."

"Is this a betrothal ring?" asked the queen.

"You may ask King Fergus; I am to escort you to him."

Queen Nessa prepared to slip the elegant elements of the ring onto her middle finger.

"No—no—o, no. The crown must point outward, toward me, please," Sceál begged.

The concern in Sceál's voice alarmed Queen Nessa. She noted his shaking hands, his eyes focused on the ring. Kings and storytellers changed the world to suit their purpose. So did queens in distress.

Nessa unclasped her necklace, watched by the shocked eyes of Sceál Galore. She smiled at Sceál, slipped the ring on the necklace, and closed the clasp. Now the king's ring dangled between her perfect breasts. Forgetting himself, Sceál stood to stare down Nessa's bosom to ascertain the direction of the crown on the ring. If the crown pointed upward, did this mean Nessa's heart was occupied? And by whom? If the crown pointed downward, what then was occupied? And by whom? Not him!

On top of Katbad's tower, King Fergus pointed his ring finger toward the approaching chariot. He felt his blood thicken. The power of the ring enriched more than his dreams. Tonight he would share the dreaming of the first sleep with Queen Nessa on his throne beside him.

In the open door of his courtyard, Katbad the Druid awaited the arrival of the approaching chariot, with Sceál Galore and Queen Nessa aboard. After thoughts of rings, kings, and the mother of his son, Connor, Katbad summoned his Druid power. Fergus might kill Katbad for his betrayal with Queen Nessa. Then what of his son Connor? Katbad hid Connor deep in his house. He did not wish the king to see Connor and his mother Nessa together. Fergus might make the connection between them.

The chariot with Sceál Galore, Queen Nessa, and Malachy the Minstrel charged through the door held open by Katbad. He closed it as Malachy finished his music for Nessa's chariot ride through the night. Sceál stood down from the chariot and asked, "Would Queen Nessa appreciate a love story before bed?"

Mired in her adventure and the music, Nessa replied, "No; tonight is for the ring, the king, and the music."

Lost and lonely, Sceál stood aloof.

"Welcome. There is quail and ale inside, Sceál. My son Genann will tend to your needs," said Katbad. Stiff of neck and legs, Sceál made for the ale. Katbad held both perfect hands of Nessa to assist her from the chariot. No rings on her fingers. Malachy the Minstrel paid heed.

"Welcome to the Queen Mother," said Katbad.

Nessa kissed Katbad on his lips until he pushed her away.

"How is Connor? I need to see him," Queen Nessa said.

"Where is the ring, Nessa?"

"Next to my heart, Katbad."

"Fergus wants to see it on your finger."

"Whenever he is ready."

"The king before Connor!" exclaimed Katbad.

"The king, and then Connor, Katbad." Nessa turned and walked toward the dark stairway to the tower. Malachy slung his wild harp behind him and followed the queen. Katbad stood and watched. Nessa began her ascent up the pitch-black stairway. A light charged with her love for Connor lit the ring between her breasts, escorting the queen and her minstrel to the top of the tower.

Malachy the Minstrel had become the music of Queen Nessa's life. Kings and queens used minstrels at feasts and occasions of state to add credence to ceremony. To Malachy, Nessa was his muse, inspiring him to compose music for her many moods and movements. This rare blending of the heart and harp fulfilled a need in both. It also allowed Malachy the privilege of Queen Nessa's most intimate moments.

Malachy stood tall and thin, a skinny malink topped with bright red hair, who followed his muse wherever she allowed.

Love assumes immortal aspects when assimilated by the arts. Katbad unlocked the dark chamber where he had hidden his son Connor in case King Fergus noted Connor's resemblance to Nessa. Flaven the Raven flew from the room before Katbad could command him. Upon hearing of the arrival of King Fergus, Flaven chose to make himself scarce. Fergus had tipped Flaven arse over beak on the tower. Not to mention the feathers missing from his tail, courtesy of Cullen's watchdog. Enough of kings, thought Flaven the Raven. Kings had power as lightning in a storm. None questioned where or when or whom they struck.

"Stay here, Connor. I wanted Flaven on the tower with the king and queen."

Katbad had much on his mind. Connor loved Katbad, his father and mentor. If Katbad needed an eye on the roof, Connor could help him. Taking a deep breath and his three-pronged javelin, Connor set out on the adventure of his young life. Softly he crept through Katbad's house, crossed the courtyard, and climbed the dark, twisting stairway.

Up, up, and away the stairs stretched to the stars. Never so dark a passage for Connor. Never so forever a climb. Blackness above. Darkness below. Endless and unforgiving night. Even Katbad would not climb the stairs tonight. First comes courage. This Connor learned from his brother Genann. Both reared in a world of men. Warriors bred in the bone and honed in the head for honor and courage.

Connor was a small boy alone in the dark. Very much alone. Connor sat and closed his eyes. Katbad's counsel: close one sense to strengthen the other senses. In an hour of need, follow your star. Be a man. Eyes closed, hugging the wall, Connor restarted his ascent to the top of the tower. Higher and higher up the spiral staircase he went, keeping the vision of his star before his closed eyes. Upward, ever upward, Connor's sense of time and place floated away.

So long and so lost seemed Connor that the harp music he heard could only be from Old God's heaven. And the music— haunting, evocative. The same song Flaven the Raven whistled and sang until Katbad approved his performance of it.

And the nearer to heaven the closer to his star. Could a breeze on high be ruffling his hair? Connor raised his head and opened his eyes. The image of one star vanished, replaced by the reality of the canopy of heaven. On top of the tower, Connor pointed his javelin at the brightest star in the sky. Standing in the shadow of an arched doorway, Connor recovered his courage. It is soon told what the young hero Connor saw on the throne of Fál that changed his life in a most dramatic fashion.

In the shadow of the throne, Malachy the Minstrel played the music of "Nessa's Dream." The shield above the throne reflected the heat of their passion, lighting the night with a golden glow. King Fergus spun the ring from Nessa high in the air.

Snug on the marble throne sat King Fergus and Queen Nessa. A king and queen who loved as royally as they lived.

"To love and glory, Nessa," Fergus caught the ring and placed it on the queen's finger. They held hands. The rings touched. Crown to Crown. The circle of love complete between them. Connor's star danced in the sky. An image of the ring finger of Queen Nessa appeared on the left of the shield above the throne, and from the crown of the ring of the queen, a rainbow of radiant colors soared toward the middle of the shield. An image of the ring finger of Fergus appeared on the right of the shield. From the crown of the ring of King Fergus a rainbow of radiant colors soared toward the middle of the shield.

The throne glowed, lit by a hectic multitude of lights. Love has many delights before it dims and dies.

Released from earthly constraints, Fergus and Nessa rose slowly above the throne. Balanced atop the meeting of the rainbow, they danced a stately jig of regal delight. Stalwart stewards of the throne, they danced into creation the epic epoch of the court of the Red Branch of Ulster.

They danced a conspiracy of ecstasy, shaking a swirling storm of multi-hued flakes from the rainbow onto the throne. The flakes spilled from the throne, a stream of dancing lights flowing toward Connor in the doorway. Connor tingled from his toes to the top of his head as it washed over his feet and splashed down the stairs. The rainbow stream lit every twist and turn of the interior of the tower.

Whirling, twirling, turning, burning. The flying feet of Fergus and Nessa kicked rainbow dust onto Malachy and his harp. Malachy changed his tune. He struck up a reel of riotous abandon. The wild reel enchanted Connor's feet and set him dancing toward the throne. Nessa's form and figure enchanted Connor's eyes. Her hair dark as pitch, her posture perfect, the queen of the dance. Bright eyes that opened wide when she saw the small boy dancing toward her and Fergus. She clutched her heart and stopped dancing. At last her son Connor, born on the throne of Fál, now dancing toward the throne. Connor with the same black hair, same bright eyes, strong and straight. Connor MacNessa. Connor, son of Nessa. At that moment, Queen Nessa swore to see her son Connor seated on the throne of Ulster.

Beside Nessa on the rainbow, Fergus looked from Nessa to Connor, and back. Both the boy and the queen were so involved that neither noticed the king's inspection. It was long and thorough. Once again, Malachy's music quickened the feet of the boy Connor, clouding his mind. Connor only had eyes for the marble seat of his birth. He danced on toward his destiny.

Holding hands on the rainbow, the king and queen watched the small boy claim the throne as his own.

Crowned by a rainbow, ordained by a queen, Connor sat on the throne of Fál.

Now and forever, as long as Gaels tell tales of King Fergus the Virile, and of Queen Nessa and her son Connor, the legend of the Red Branch endures.

"I dream of a son on my throne," King Fergus said.

"As do I, Fergus."

"A son with Nessa's hair—and Katbad's nose."

Executing a quick two-step backwards, Fergus danced a two-handed reel, alone. Nessa touched the brooch on her tunic. Connor savored his seat on the throne, his feet dangling over the province of Ulster. He touched his hair and rubbed his nose. Above him, Fergus danced alone and made a gesture toward the queen. "I will foster Connor in courage and kinship," he offered.

"I will foster Fergus in love and loyalty," Nessa said.

The minstrel changed his tune. Love filled the air. Closer came the dancing feet of Fergus the Virile. With grace and elegance, they renewed their dance of love atop the rainbow, and the small boy on the throne.

The prize: a crown. The price: a heart. The dream: immortality in memory.

"Give Connor the throne for one year. The first year of our coming together," Nessa asked.

"Why would I do that?"

"So that Connor can tell his son his father was a king." Nessa kissed Fergus on his lips.

"What gift for a crown?" Fergus kissed Nessa on her eyelids.

"My loyalty and love."

Nessa kissed Fergus on his ring finger.

"For a year?"

"Forever."

"Let us sleep on this tonight."

Nessa touched her brooch, glowing with love. With a queen's hair and a Druid's nose, six-year-old King Connor ruled the night and all the stars in the sky.

Queen Nessa prevailed upon King Fergus to accord Connor the honor of ascending the throne of Ulster for a year. Then Fergus would return as king. The sons of Connor could call their father a king. Fergus gave his blessing and agreed to foster the young king. He stayed close to the throne and the people of Ulster, assuring them of his concern. Amused and tolerant, Fergus loved Connor and Nessa. Both returned his love. It was a very good year for Fergus the Virile, full of clarity and comfort.

Queen Nessa became the perfect wife to her husband, giving no cause for complaint in public or private. From the beginning, Nessa raised Fergus above all. From the beginning, she obsessed on her vision of Connor on the throne. This she hid from Fergus, although Nessa suspected that he knew much more about her motives than he pretended.

During Connor's reign as king, Queen Nessa's advice to Katbad's household was closely adhered to. Through the summer and autumn, Katbad and Nessa arranged fairs, feasts, and festivals to honor Connor's prowess. Nessa gave of her own wealth in Connor's name to the warriors of the Red Branch. This embellished their opinion of Connor as golden.

Connor's public appearances were carefully choreographed. Nessa designed rare apparel for her son, fit for a king. Bards and poets sang of Connor's humor and vitality. On the front of his silver-shafted chariot, Katbad placed a magic harp, played by the wind. Malachy the Minstrel composed a coronation theme for his golden-stringed harp. This ensured an enduring image of Connor when he drove his black bulls among the plain people of Ulster. His scepter: a three-pronged javelin. His court: seven comely women in his train. Connor became the darling son of Ulster.

Under the auspices of Nessa, art and its endeavors flourished. The likeness of King Connor appeared on shields, spears, and swords, forged by Cullen the Blacksmith. Objects of interest to a warrior race carried Connor's form and features. The sea filled with fish. All harvests were abundant. Peace and prosperity prevailed.

As adviser to the king, Katbad the Druid stayed close to Connor. All his Druidic powers were focused on his young son in pursuit of a kingdom. To regain his prestige as a master of intrigue, Flaven the Raven conceived another bird-brained scheme that he revealed to Katbad. This is how Flaven returned to his favored perch on Katbad's shoulder. On a night when the moon was full, Flaven summoned the birds of the air to the top of the round tower. Silent and still, in a circle, the birds perched on the stones. On the throne of Fál, Flaven surveyed his fine feathered friends. He whistled his introduction to Katbad, King of the Druids, standing in the arched doorway. Bowing to honor Flaven and the birds, Katbad cast an enchantment of music and magic.

Accompanied by Malachy the Minstrel in the shadow of the throne, Flaven whistled and sang "Connor is king" to the birds of the night. From the wee wren to the mighty eagle, the chorus of birds whistled "Connor is king." From then on, from dawn to dusk, from night to morn, the birds of the air whistled "Connor is king" to the people of Ulster.

As the year progressed, so did Connor in bearing and being. By winter, Connor possessed the trappings of royalty expected by his subjects, large and small. Music and magic in place of words and deeds. Appearance over performance. Dramatic arrivals and departures, courtesy of his silver-shafted chariot and the titanic black bulls.

At the command of my order, I am instructed to interrupt Queen Nessa's plot to secure the throne of Ulster for Connor with further adventures of Setanta the Warped One.

Standing at my wooden lectern, I contemplate a calfskin with the legend "Setanta the Warped One" embossed in gold letters.

I ponder my predicament. As a scribe and scholar, these tales were hard won from old books and older bards and poets.

So I return to the Isle of the Blest, in the time of a seven-year-old hero who traded life for immortality in memory. With aid and inspiration from God, I continue the saga of Setanta, with the tale of how his name, but not his nature, was changed.

> God, light of my heart,
> Consummate my will,
> Bid my pride depart,
> Consecrate my quill.
> So be it.

> Mael Moró

Ten

I T IS SOON told how Setanta changed his name, but not his nature, at the estate of Cullen the Blacksmith.

Cullen the Smith was known as the smith of kings and the king of smiths at the Red Branch court of King Connor MacNessa. It was his custom to entertain the king at a royal feast at the end of the summer. None had his skill and cunning in the forging of weapons of vast destruction for warriors who could afford his wares.

On the morn of Cullen's feast, Setanta had a private audience with his foster father and teacher, Katbad the Druid. They sat in the sun outside Connor's house on a stone seat. A small boy with a squint in one eye looked at the imposing figure of the king of the Druids. Both came from the other side. Both had immortality in memory as a goal in this world and the reward of Tír na nÓg in the next.

"You are foremost among the boys of consequence here in skill and savagery," pronounced Katbad, fixing his unblinking stare on Setanta.

"But not in regard and leadership," said Setanta.

"Heroes walk alone. Others follow," Katbad said.

"Before you judge me, tell me of my father."

Setanta moved closer to Katbad to avoid his eyes.

"What did your mother say of your father?"

"Dectain told me Lugh of the Long Hand was more than a god," Setanta said.

"When King Connor was your age, he made a journey to the other side to meet Sreng the Strong." Looking around to ensure they were secure from listeners, Katbad continued his story.

"Sreng survives in a mushroom mound with the last of the Firbolgs, the bag men with the bulging bellies. Our Druids of Dana arrived on this blessed isle shortly after Sreng's tribe. We hoped to share the fertile land with Sreng and his ilk, but this was not to be. Sreng joined forces with Balor of the Baleful Eye, the most formidable of the Fomorian monsters." Katbad paused for breath.

"Tell me of my father," said Setanta.

"Balor of the Baleful Eye heard a Druid's prophesy that he could only be killed by his grandson. So Balor saw to it with his good eye that his daughter Eitne should stay away from men."

"And what of his other eye, his baleful one?" asked the boy with the squinting eye.

"Balor's baleful eyelid was so heavy it took nine able men with iron eye-hooks to open. All caught in its glare expired immediately. This eye was only opened on a battle field."

"Tell me of my father," said Setanta.

"In time, Balor's beautiful daughter Eitne was seduced by Cian, and gave birth to Lugh of the Long Hand, a god of light and a paragon of the arts. Lugh was the first great god warrior from Dana's people in Ireland—young, handsome, and wise."

Setanta smiled at this portrait of his father.

"Before the final battle with Balor and Sreng, Lugh came to Tara to aid and abet Dana's people. King Nuada was gathering his army at Tara to attack the enemies of Dana and secure a kingdom for us in Ireland." Katbad said. He watched with relief as a messenger from his son, King Connor, approached. Katbad was never at ease with Setanta. Few were.

"Tell me of my father," said Setanta.

"Lugh was stopped by King Nuada's soldiers and asked to identify himself before meeting this king. This is how Lugh described himself: 'I am a builder; a blacksmith; a poet; a seer; a harper; a historian; a cup bearer; a magician; a craftsman of metal; an inventor of horse racing, the sport of kings; an inventor of Fidkill, the board game of kings.'"

Katbad stood to acknowledge the arrival of the king's messenger. "King Connor would appreciate your presence before the court leaves for Cullen's feast," the messenger told Katbad, looking at Setanta. The Warped One had replaced Ferdia as the most talked about of the boys of consequence.

"You will tell me more of my father?" asked Setanta, standing in front of Katbad.

"When we meet again." Katbad gave Setanta a Druid's blessing and stepped around him. Thinking of his father Lugh, Setanta watched the king of the Druids depart.

Later that day, a restless Setanta set forth with his two horses to seek peace in motion. As usual, he took his curved ash hurley stick and silver sliotar along. He paid small heed to the direction his horses took, day dreaming of his father, Lugh of the Long Hand. The black and white horses of Setanta followed the ruts and droppings from the chariots of King Connor and his heroes of the Red Branch.

When King Connor arrived at Cullen's abode, he was welcomed in style by the giant smith. Soon the ale feast began, to the delight of all. Cullen plunged a white-hot rod of steel into the red ale, sparking laughter and good fellowship.

"Are all your men here, King Connor?" asked the redfaced Smith.

"Indeed, who'd be late for an ale feast?" said the king.

"Then I'll loose my bloodhound and lock my door. He's a gift from the king of Spain to protect my land, my cattle, and my guests."

They followed Cullen the Smith for the unleashing of the hound. Cullen stood by the door of his fort and whistled three times. Three times three strong men held a massive mastiff by three iron chains. The beast dragged them to Cullen's open door. Cullen patted his hound on the head. At a signal from the smith, the dog handler released the iron chains. The dog bounded through the door and Cullen slammed it closed behind him.

"We will sleep safely tonight, King Connor. Man or beast, none has survived the stewardship of my great hound." Cullen beamed at the king.

Deep in thoughts of his father, Setanta sat on the back of his black horse, Dub. His white horse circled slowly in front of Setanta, watching for danger as they neared the fort of Cullen the Smith. It was how they always traveled together, one horse under Setanta, the other horse on guard for the boy. They were now deep into the territories of the Black Hound of Cullen. Mouth open, tongue drooling, eyes glinting, the hound stood high on a sharp-edged boulder overlooking the two horses and the small boy.

When they were beneath him, the hound announced his intentions. He bayed his challenge to Setanta and the horses.

So loud and raucous was his howling barks, all who slept awoke in fear and trembling. Babes awoke and wailed; old men moaned with fear; old women sighed and died. The animal kingdom howled in unison; the birds fled for shelter; men turned from love to lust; women from angels to harlots; children from play to passion. Old God roared with laughter.

The hound of Cullen launched himself from the top of the boulder. Paws outstretched, jaws open, a mass of muscle and massacre, the animal flew straight for the small boy on the black horse. The horse reared high, front hooves flailing, Setanta slid off the rump of Dub and rolled beneath the protective flanks of his white horse. And so the battle began.

The black horse and black dog smashed together, rolling over and over in a snarling, snapping tangle of teeth, claws, and hooves. Ban, the white horse, rained down kicks on the head of the hound, as he circled the savage pair. Ripping skin, tearing hairs, chomping at bloody bits of grizzle, slashing claws, howls, growls, gnashing teeth, hell dust and hatred unto death clouded the air around this slaughterhouse of hound and horses.

When the air cleared, Setanta thought he felt the long hand of Lugh help him to his feet, shivering and shaking; his two horses stood over the prone hound, slamming it with vicious kicks. Slowly they returned to Setanta. Dub and Ban cuddled together, licking each other's wounds.

All Setanta had at hand was his silver sliotar and hurley stick. He'd left his spear, shield, and sword back at the Red Branch. He checked the state of his horses. Dub had the most wounds, back and front. Leaving Ban on guard, Setanta led Dub back to a small stream of clear water. Here he tended the wounds of his black horse, kissing Dub three times on the neck.

A loud whinny from the white horse alerted Setanta. Dub bolted from his healing hands and galloped toward his brother, Ban. The black hound was back, standing on its four wicked paws. Slavering and slobbering, the hound bayed defiance to the world. Dub and Ban ploughed the earth, looking hard at the approaching hound. Ears erect, tails high, bodies bunched, they charged the hellhound in front of them. Setanta held his hurley stick and waited.

Within spitting distance of the hound, Dub and Ban bunched together. Hooves curled and cruel, they leaped high into the air to crush the hound's head. In a burst of demonic speed, the hound flew under the horses. Dub and Ban landed in a tangle of hooves and horseflesh, all fight knocked out of them.

The hound and Setanta took measure of each other. A small boy tapping a silver ball on his hurley stick. A pony-sized hound with marble teeth, bloodshot eyes, and gouged body. Now came a rumble of thunder from Old God.

The mouth of the hound opened wide enough to swallow the head of Setanta. Before his charge, he renewed his red guts challenge, this time with the teeth of death in it. Setanta waited until the hound finished, then let loose his warrior's challenge, loud enough for the ears of his father on the other side.

Those in the fort and forge of Cullen the Smith clutched tight their ale goblets. Setanta and the hound! Could the hound and boy survive each other? They moved closer to comfort King Connor, pale at the peril to his sister's son.

His open jaws still slavering and slobbering, the hound advanced on the small boy. Straight and true, Setanta struck his sliotar a powerful blow as the hound leaped at him. The silver sliotar rammed the hound's tongue down its throat, and slammed its guts and gizzards through its arsehole. Nothing daunted, Setanta dropped to one knee and struck the brute flying over his head a shrewd blow with the edge of his hurley stick. This changed the direction of the hound so its neck slashed against the sharp edge of a standing boulder. A spatter of blood, tissue, and teeth and the head of the hound split from its body.

Sword and spear in hand, King Connor led his cohorts through the open door of Cullen's fort. Fergus the Virile was the first to see his foster son leading two hobbling horses behind him.

Cullen stood aside, watching King Connor slam his sword on his shield in a royal display of pleasure. Setanta was a boy of consequence at his court and his sister's son. None at Setanta's age had his grace and renown. The heroes of the Red Branch clustered close to the small boy. The shadows of these men would never grow less if they stayed close to Setanta. Personal or as part of another's destiny, eternity is the dream of those without God's grace.

Lost and lonely for his dog, Cullen whistled three times. The third whistle was a final farewell to his beloved hound. Its plaintive sadness affected all who heard it. King Connor patted Setanta's head and approached the grieving blacksmith.

"I will send you three royal wolfhounds to replace your hound, Cullen, plus two heroes to guard you from harm," said the King.

"None can replace my one true hound. Yonder boy has two horses bound to him, as was my hound to me. Setanta is not welcome in my house," Cullen said.

"If the boy is not welcome, then I cannot stay here. Cullen, you are my friend." Connor clasped hands with Cullen.

"Fret not, Cullen, I will be your hound and guardian until I raise a whelp from the same litter. My two horses and I are now bound to your protection," so said Setanta to the king and blacksmith.

"Well spoken, Setanta; you have saved the day," said the grateful king.

"My dog had the strength of a hundred," declared the smith.

"Then we were well matched," said Setanta.

"Let the offer stand, Cullen. You will never get one as good," said Katbad.

"Let the boy change his name to Cucullen, the Hound of Cullen, so all may know his function, said Briar MacMalice. He hated Setanta because he'd loved and lost the boy's mother.

"Cucullen has a ring to it. Well, so be it—if Setanta will change his name," said Cullen, who knew well the power of a name in legend. "Cucullen, Cucullen—the Hound of Cullen. Yes, it is a strong name to grow with, Setanta," said King Connor.

"Cucullen."

"Cucullen."

"Cucullen."

The heroes of the Red Branch baptized the name by saying it to each other.

Setanta looked to Katbad, who looked away. Setanta did not want to dishonor the name given to him by his father. How would his mother Dectain react to the changing of his name?

"Setanta—I mean Cucullen—let the name stand as long as you remain with Cullen. When you have trained a new dog, you can reclaim your father's name." This was the judgment of King Connor MacNessa and accepted by all. Cucullen, The Hound of Cullen. The boy warrior. Cucullen, The Hound of Ulster. Cucullen, a name for the age—and ever since.

eleven

ELEVEN MONTHS INTO the year of Connor's reign, Queen Nessa had an audacious idea. Nessa told Katbad to steal the wealth from the half who had it and give it to the half who needed it. This was to secure the throne for Connor. Katbad set about Nessa's scheme with dispatch and daring. He had Raven the Flaven contact Jack and Jane Daw. These birds of prey knew of Katbad's gold galore storeroom in the depths of his dungeons.

Jack and Jane were old codgers who had spent their honeymoon on Noah's Ark. Rescued by Old God from a floating log, Jack and Jane landed in Ireland. Here they became the father and mother of all the Daws in the four provinces.

Far gone in thievery and chicanery, the Daws helped Katbad amass a fortune in return for protection and increase in progeny. In his gold galore storeroom, Katbad poured a tot of ale for the bold Jack of the Daws.

"Luck of the Irish to you both, friends of my inmost heart." Katbad knew flattery worked wonders with birds.

"Luck of the Irish to you, Katbad," chirped Jack Daw. "And to your golden boy, Connor the King."

Jane sipped at Jack's ale. These three were birds of a feather and thick as thieves.

"Sweet old friends, Connor's fortune is in your beaks and claws," Katbad said. "In one month, plan to steal wealth from one half of the people and give it to the other half."

In Katbad's den of thieves, Jack and Jane Daw fluttered their feathers. Jane Daw hopped along a gold bar. Jack Daw slid down a shaft of silver. Wealth has its own weight.

To celebrate the end of Connor's reign, Katbad announced a great hurley hooley for two days and one night. At the finish of this father and mother of a pucking fair, Fergus the Virile would resume his monarchy, Connor would return to his father Katbad, and Nessa's plans were up in the air with Jack and Jane Daw.

Two days of hurley; two days of feasting; two nights of drinking. Two days of music and dancing. Two nights of excess, courtesy of Katbad the Druid to honor his son King Connor's last days on the throne.

Jack and Jane Daw whistled a family meeting on top of Katbad's round tower. The Daws are a large and alert family of birds, with beady eyes and thieving claws. Jack Daw ventured a bird count of his extended family. Thirty one thousand and two feathered offspring, and six hundred and seventy six eggs in the nests. Jane Daw whistled for attention. The extended Daw family whistled their love for Jack Daw. He whistled for silence. The assembled Daws applauded by whistling and fluttering their feathers when Jack Daw finished his tale. A day of thievery in empty houses. A night of moving wealth from the haves to the have-nots.

Whistling "Connor is king," they flew into the night. Alone again, Jack and Jane Daw nestled together.

For these perfidious avians, progeny approaches perfection. Connor the boy-king knew well the Druid light that illuminated his life with Katbad the Druid. Before sunup on the first day of the Hurley Hooley, Connor awoke to a swift shake from his half-brother, Genann, and the Druid light from the three-pronged javelin in Katbad's hand. Connor dressed, grabbing his ashwood hurley stick and round pigskin ball. He ran through the long halls to the courtyard of the Druid's house. Genann of the Brow of Light drove the two black bulls around the dark courtyard.

Lit by the three prongs of the javelin, Katbad stood behind his son on the chariot of mystic symbols. At a gesture from this King of the Druids, the door to the courtyard swung open. Connor ran for the door, holding high his hurley stick by both ends. As the bulls charged through the door, Katbad reached down from his chariot, grabbed the hurley stick, and swung the dangling Connor up and onto a space beside his smiling brother.

Thus they ventured forth upon another Druid escapade while this world slept and the next world went about its business. By the flattened ears, rolling eyes, and sweating flanks of the black bulls, Connor deduced that this was a dangerous assignment into unchartered lands. Genann clapped him on his shoulder. The Druid life had its rewards if one survived temporal and immortal powers.

And so, they dashed for the border between this world and the next, across a darkling plain concealing hidden and sudden dangers. Sinister bogs sucked at their flying feet, the black bulls flew alongside blood pools of endless depths. Without breaking stride, they flew through the most ancient of Ireland's forbidden forests. Here no birds nested, no deer roved, no wolves or foxes hunted, and nothing green grew to freshen the fetid air. And out of the foreboding forest onto a rutted path, through a barren burren, onward toward a toad-shaped mountain of desolate granite.

The flight of the frightened bulls ended at two enormous stone pillars. A sun without heat rose on top of a great slab of stone perched precariously on top of the pillars. Carved on these columns curled spirals and circles of Celtic infinity. This doorway of death lay at the bottom of the toad-like mountain. Connor looked through the doorway at a lush green meadow alive with red flowers and a multitude of bright white mushrooms. Then he looked to each side of the stone columns.

A wild bramble of blackthorn and briar trees with wicked thorns presented an impassable circle around the base of the mountain. Entangled in these barbed branches lay skeleton hands, arms, and skulls, bleached by nature—human and other. The bulls knelt flat before the columns, laying down their heads in abject fear. Connor clutched Genann's hand and held it tight. Neither brother would show fear before their father. Both knew the columns were a passage to the other world of Druids and departed souls. Without the right guide and the luck of the Irish, those who passed through might never return.

Katbad the Druid stepped from his enchanted chariot and boldly walked to the right column. He ran his healing hands over the mystic carvings, absorbing knowledge and power. Overhead, the stone slab groaned a protest against the rigid columns. Katbad repeated this process with the left column. With a clap like thunder, the earth moved. The granite slab lurched forward, cracked, and a jagged edge fell at Katbad's feet. He carried the fragment of granite toward the prone bulls and petrified boys, and placed it at the feet of the animals.

Connor leaned forward. A carving on the granite looked to him as an imprint of a beast, a cloven hoof emitting elements of fire and smoke. Katbad touched both bulls with his hands, raising them on their trembling legs. When bulls show fear, beware.

Stroking the left hoof of one bull, Katbad placed it slowly into the imprint of the smoking cloven hoof. The left pillar shifted on its base, shaking the chariot and bulls. The entrance between the pillars widened, and smoke from the cloven hoof formed a fog about the doorway and the three Druids.

The massive stone slab ground harshly against the moving pillar. Sparks of angry friction rained down on the entrance to the meadow of mushrooms. Wide-eyed, knees shaking, Connor held tight to his brother, Genann. Katbad led the reluctant bulls through the monolithic columns. The falling sparks scorched a white line across the backs of the black bulls. Genann pulled his tunic over his head. The wheels of the chariot scraped the sides of the pillars.

Three sizzling sparks scorched Connor's head, changing the color of his hair and his character forever. Katbad pulled, the boys beat the bulls with the reins, and the bulls strained. The chariot wheels turned in protest, scratching, scraping, sparking, and braking between the pillars of stone.

Connor's eyes ached. Fire and brimstone polluted the air. Foul smoke filled his lungs. Genann's strong arms held him erect so that Connor passed from this world into the next, his head afire from the sparks that scorched him. The chariot wheels spun clean. The bulls stood strong on the green grass of the glorious meadow. Connor sucked in the bracing air. His lungs cleared and a divine light flooded the top of his head.

Genann's brow glowed with light and life. Katbad remounted his chariot. The tails of the bulls swished with relief. All were affected with this breath of life from a meadow, untouched since its creation. At a signal from Katbad, the bulls started across the meadow to a hugh mushroom-covered mound at the base of the granite mountain.

Katbad looked down at Connor's lovely head. The front of Connor's hair gleamed blacker than a seal in shallow water. An angry streak of fiery red hair crowned the top of Connor's head. A helmet of golden hair caressed his neck, completing the transformation wrought by the scorching sparks. Feeling Katbad's gaze on him, Connor looked up at his father with eyes that had turned from blue to green.

The mark of the Druid comes in many shapes and shades. Connor the boy-king of Ulster crossed the meadow of mushrooms in a state of exalted transcendence. A divine light flooded his being, from the balls of his feet to the top of his tri-colored head. He had reached the essence of his Druid nature, living so completely in the moment that every second beamed an extension of eternity. Never so young and free; never so brave and bold; never so happy in his companions.

Beside him stood his clever brother and guide, Genann of the Brow of Light. Behind him, Katbad his father, King of the Druids of Ireland. Before him, the promise of immortality in the music of motion and the memory of his people. In an ornate chariot pulled by black bulls, this first family of the Druids of Ireland raced forth. They flew across a meadow into a place called Tír na nÓg, the land of eternal youth. In Tír na nÓg, a glory of warriors and worthies dwelt without disease or death, forever in their prime. Tír na nÓg is a state of eternal grace, the infinite gift of the

Celtic Druids. They took it with them when they departed. The bulls halted at the base of the mound. The boys stayed in the chariot. Katbad walked to the mound with the three-pronged javelin in hand.

Katbad the Druid studied the mushroom-covered mound, watched by his sons and the brave black bulls. He plucked two small mushrooms from high on the mound and threw them to the bulls. The bulls chewed slowly on the mushrooms, licking their tongues in appreciation, then the bulls danced a small jig to the day that was in it.

"Magic mushrooms," Genann whispered to Connor.

"There is magic in everything," said Katbad of the Druids in his ear. He plunged his three-pronged javelin into the mound and turned it slowly. The boys heard the sounds of iron bolts scraping. Fascinated, they watched a mushroom-shaped door open slowly in the mound.

"Follow, stay close." Katbad waited for his sons to scramble from the chariot and stand by his side. Together, the three Druids entered the mound. The door shut, closing off the outside world. Inside the light was unlike any seen on land or sea. Sunlight without warmth; moonlight without mercy; twilight without mystery. A lost world lit by lightning and peopled with the supernatural. Katbad smiled at his sons, proud of their presence, and with a wave of his javelin and a sprinkling of gold dust from his purse, Katbad wove three cloaks of invisibility over himself and his sons. Unseen by others, they were clearly visible to one another. Connor tried to touch Genann, feeling lightheaded and free.

Nothing corporeal remained to the boys. Laughing and dancing, they walked through each other. Shadows without substance. The gift of invisibility includes mild intoxication.

"Bright loves of my life, my beautiful boys," Katbad blessed his sons. They danced through and about him. He raised his javelin toward the ceiling. The eyes of the boys followed the arc of his arms. Genann saw it first.

"It's a monster mushroom. We're inside of a massive mushroom," he told Connor.

Then Connor saw it, too. The sloping veined ceiling, the drooping white walls, the seductive odor of morning mushrooms, the promise of nature's possibilities in a temple hidden from humans. As the boys followed Katbad, they heard a soft tapping sound that increased with each step forward. Tap, tap, tap. A murmur of soft, small voices rose above the tap, tap, tapping. Now they were in the center of the mushroom, under its soaring cathedral roof. In front of them lay a long rectangular table, and behind the table, on toad-shaped stools, sat six small full- bellied men wearing green tunics. Each man had a red leather sack covering an ample belly. Green caps with a black cock's feather covered the heads of the wee men, and with tiny hammers and trowel knives in each hand, they tapped diligently at the white mushroom, slicing slivers into silver cauldrons.

Sitting on tall toadstools beneath the wall in front of the six were two full-bellied tailors with crossed legs and large needles. One tailor had a spool of blood-red thread. The other tailor had a spool of black thread. At the head of the table sat a small, fierce, round-faced man. His right hand stroked his beard. His left hand caressed the contents of a crock. From his mouth, he chanted the history of the Firbolgs—the wee men with the large bellies. His name was Sreng the Strong. As he chanted the history, the tailors sewed swiftly from their spools, spearing their needles into the mushroom wall. The

red and black threads spread on the wall, emerging, entwin-
ing, enchanting, forming moving pictures of the words and
songs of Sreng the Strong. Thus began Sreng.

"Follow the thread; our dread it tells,
How we survived our living hells."

Sreng chanted the history of the Firbolgs, the wee men
with the bulging bellies. He told how his tribe was enslaved by
the Greeks and forced to carry rocks in leather bags to build
heathen temples. The tailors' threads etched cave paintings
on the wall to confirm the history conveyed in Sreng's chants.

"We grew sick and sad and sorry,
Hauling rocks from an endless quarry.
Our shanks, they shrank under constant weight,
Our bellies bulged, we lost our height."

The six wee men gave full attention to the chants of Sreng
and the cave paintings etched by the tailors' thread. Sreng
paused to pour himself a potion of golden liquor. Connor
the Invisible checked the contents of Sreng's crock. It was
half-full of mellow yellow gold that Connor's invisible hand
could not feel or steal. Sreng finished his drink and resumed
his chanting. He told how his tribe sewed their leather sacks
into leather boats to escape from the Greeks, and arrive on
an island green and splendid. Katbad waited until his invisible
sons lost interest and dozed off. History for the young lies in
the future. Katbad went into action.

Katbad the Druid drew back his arm. He threw his three-
pronged javelin at the threads of the wee tailors. The red and
black threads twisted and turned, curling about the prongs
of the javelin. Connor the boy-king of Ulster felt the exit of
invisibility from his form and vision. Red-eyed, he watched
the threads leap from the wall and entangle the tailors and

their fat, wee bodies. The restless threads snaked swiftly toward Sreng the Strong.

As the devil curled around an apple tree, so did the threads secure Sreng to his toadstool, his arms to his sides. On top of his head and under his chin, cutting short his chanting song, the threads trussed him as a goose for a feast. Then the threads trussed the guests at the feast, turning and tying the mushroom slicers on their toadstools.

Connor staggered, struck by a blow on his shoulder from his brother, Genann. No longer insubstantial, the boys had regained their human substance. Both looked toward their father, Katbad the Druid. When invisibility exits, the residue is a dryness of form and vision. Katbad pulled his javelin from the massive mushroom wall. He reached for the silver cauldron of sliced mushrooms in front of Sreng the Strong. Sreng's eyes narrowed in hate and horror, and a low moan of loss rose from his cohorts. Katbad smiled and poured the mushrooms into his leather satchel. Connor, conditioned to kingship, reached for the golden crock of Sreng. Now his hand could caress the gold inside Sreng's crock.

"Druids are healers, not stealers!" Katbad's javelin pinned Connor's hand to the table. Ashamed, Connor watched his father Katbad empty gold from his purse into the crock of Sreng. Genenn rubbed his brother's back, signifying his presence.

"What will happen to the wee men, Katbad?" Genann asked his father. Katbad smiled and rubbed his son's head, pleased at the question. He pointed at the crock of gold.

"In a couple of days, the wee men will lose weight and wriggle free. Sreng and I have clasped hands in the past and will do so again. On our way boys, we have a busy day ahead!"

Thus they left the inner chamber of the massive mushroom. Katbad had his sons lay on his grey cloak in the back of the chariot. The two boys fell fast asleep and did not awake until safely home in Katbad's courtyard.

Katbad the devious Druid smelled the mushroom he'd brought from Sreng the Strong. Mound mushrooms were the most powerful in cause and effect. Katbad needed all the help he could get to secure the throne for his son, Connor. On the day he'd regain his crown, Fergus could exile Katbad and Connor from the Red Branch. Katbad had done business before with Sreng, and would so again. Both were survivors, Sreng as the historian of his tribe, and Katbad as the King of the Druids.

Katbad the Druid studied Briar MacMalice. Briar was a tall man inclined to dark thoughts. His nickname was Briar of the Poisoned Tongue.

Briar had a wicked gift for satire and a tongue that could strip the skin off a sage. His vicious invectives raised blisters on the face and boils on the bums of his victims.

"Luck of the Irish to you, Briar," said Katbad the Druid.

"Luck is what I'm lacking at the moment," sighed Briar, afraid of Katbad's power.

"You are notorious for meanness and malice, Briar. Not once have you hosted a feast for King Fergus or the Red Branch Knights. Take note: those who give, receive."

"If I gave a feast and none came, I would be the scut of scullions. What do you need from me, Katbad?" asked Briar.

"If you help Connor hold onto the throne, I will help you throw a feast that will make you immortal in the memory of Gaels," said Katbad.

"Of course, I will help Connor. I love the boy," lied Briar of the Poisoned Tongue.

"Clasp hands, brother; you're a rogue and I'm another. Listen to me, MacMalice."

Katbad and Briar huddled together. The mushrooms bubbled away and the steam of dreams filled the kitchen.

From daylight on, the plains people of Ulster assembled on the pleasant field of many flowers, known as the hurley field of future heroes. Thus began the great Hurley Hooley, courtesy of Katbad the Druid. When the day was well aired, the plain people formed a hero's line enclosing the hurley pitch. Behind these goboys, the people cheered the young lads running onto the hurley field. Sons of Erin. Pure and perfect. Strong and stalwart. How a lad handled his hurley stick and balls indicated his potential to men and appeal to women. In this high state of excitement, Katbad had his son Connor drive his wondrous chariot around the hurley pitch. Bold, black bulls and brave young Connor waving his hurley stick ignited the applause of the people. On nearby trees, the birds perched, covering the leaves with feathers and the branches with excitement.

The hurley teams formed two straight lines in the center of the pitch. King Fergus and his Queen Nessa drove the royal chariot between the eager boys. What day like today? Even Old God dropped down from heaven on a white cloud to witness the great Hurley Hooley. King Fergus tossed the hurley ball between two boys. He drove fast for the sidelines before the clash of the ash. Hurley sticks smashed together and the match began. Surges of boys swept the ball up one wing of the pitch. Counter surges swept the ball down the opposite wing.

Great hurley heroes were born, battered, bruised, and broken that afternoon. Boys became men, warriors, leaders, followers. Few faltered. None failed. King Connor ruled the game. The ball seemed to seek out the broad base of his hurley stick.

Time and again, Connor's powerful pucks sent the ball spinning toward the upright posts with his team in hot pursuit.

"Play the ball, not the man," was the first and only commandment in the game of hurley in this era.

Connor tore loose from a forest of hurley sticks and began a brilliant solo dash up the right wing. Tapping the small ball on his stick, Connor ran for his life and the opposing posts. Connor dodged, ducked, and darted past the slashing hurley sticks of his opponents. None could stop this heroic hurler. Fifteen yards from the posts, he struck the ball, straight and true; faster than a speeding spear, the ball flashed between the posts.

Hundreds of birds swooped and whooped in a delirium of approval. Katbad the Druid shook his javelin. King Fergus embraced Queen Nessa. The black bulls waved their tails. A great bull roar from the crowd welcomed a new hero. A bull roar that shook the top of the Mountain of Mourne. A roar that awoke a savage brown bull from a dream of death. Death.

Above the Hurley Hooley, the one cloud in the sky kissed the sun, turning scarlet with delight.

King Fergus kissed Queen Nessa, and then drove his chariot onto the pitch to signal halftime. The boys still standing collapsed in place, storing energy for the second half of the hurley match. Fathers and mothers ran onto the field to minister to their sons. Injured boys were placed gently on shields and laid in rows before Katbad the Druid. With healing hands, Katbad moved among the boys, curing bruise and cut with salve and touch. When all were restored to normal, Katbad signaled the resumption of the hurley match.

At the same time in a different place, Jane Daw organized her female birds into small groups. Each group had a house to investigate while the occupants enjoyed the great Hurley Hooley. Houses with wealth and abundance were marked with an *X* on the roof. Houses lacking luxury were marked with an *O* on the roof. Thus, began the game of *X*s and *O*s, still played today.

Meanwhile, back at the Red Branch hurley field, King Fergus flung the coveted ball between the rows of boys. Once more, the clash of the ash quickened the spirits of the watching men. Once more, the budding manhood of the boys in their tight raiments warmed the blood of the women.

At the same time in a different place, Jack Daw began to steal everything of value from the houses with an *X* on the roof. This is how the bold Jack accomplished his task. First, he organized groups of his male birds to descend on the houses of wealth and abundance marked with *X*. The birds collected objects of worth into neat piles on the roof, according to the directions of the female Daws. As this pilfering proceeded, Jane Daw realized the magnitude of the task.

To transfer wealth from the houses marked *X* to the houses marked *O* might take until dark. The return of the tipsy owners could endanger the stealing birds if they were still looting. When in doubt, Jane Daw flew to the top branches of the highest tree. Here she could look down on her problems. Her sharp little eyes fastened on the castle of King Fergus at the Courts of the Red Branch. Something was blowing on the wind.

Twelve

IT WAS LONG the custom of the household of King Fergus to change and wash the sheet on his bed whenever he gave satisfaction to his bedmates. Last night it was Queen Nessa. As it was a feast day, there were seven—no, eight—sheets hung out to dry in his courtyard. These sheets were highly prized for their salutary effect on the blood. King Fergus left an impression wherever he lay. It was long the custom of King Fergus of the Red Branch to sell half of these sheets to the highest bidder and give the rest to those who needed them most.

Once again, Connor dominated the hurley game. His skill at solo runs left his opponents baffled and his supporters thirsty from cheering. None controlled the flight of the small ball as did Connor. None hit the ball so straight and true, so hard and fast. All eyes focused on the skillful Connor, king of the hurley hooley and king of Ulster, until the next day.

For tomorrow was a year to the day of Connor's time as King of Ulster. Tomorrow was the day for Fergus to take back his pledge and resume the throne of Ulster as the king of the Red Branch court. Dramatic days in the old odd country, courtesy of Old God on his cloud and Katbad on his chariot, not to mention Nessa and her schemes.

At the same time, in a different place, Jane Daw sent her female birds of a feather into the wood next to the courtyard of King Fergus. Now all Jane had to do was charm the birds off the trees into the courtyard, borrow three sheets of Fergus the Virile, and bring the sheets to three locations where Jack was working the second floors with his boys. Jane recalled a memory of Noah on his ark, where she and Jack had first met. Night, noon, and morning, Noah had to instruct many animals to do his bidding. This was the way of it for Noah. And if it worked for him, why not for Jane?

"For God's sake, borrow three sheets from Fergus the Virile and take them to Jack and his boys," Jane said. "You birds know what to do. Fly to it."

Jane watched as three sheets of King Fergus floated across the blue sky, held aloft by the strong beaks of the Daws. Above it all, Jane Daw directed her feathered offspring toward the brave Jack at his life's work.

Meanwhile, back at the Hurley Hooley, Connor was hurling away at a ferocious pace. On their flight to Jack Daw, the birds with the three sheets stopped for a cooling moment beneath Old God's cloud. The three sheets blocked Old God's view of the hurley game just as Connor pucked another ball between the posts. Elated, the crowd roared approval.

Annoyed, Old God blew the three sheets across the sky toward Jack and his Daws. Old God's breath blew tiny trickles of the essence of Fergus the Virile from his sheets onto the crowd below. The essence of Fergus warmed the thighs of the women who thought of Fergus the Virile before sleep. The women pushed closer to see Fergus. All this courtesy of

Old God's gift for mystery and mischief and the essence of King Fergus on a feast day.

Old God does not waste his breath. Meanwhile, back at the branches of trees surrounding the houses marked with *X*s and *O*s, the stealing proceeded, supervised by Jack Daw himself. The thieving blackbirds filled the three sheets of Fergus with goods from those who had them in the houses with *X* on the roof. These they deposited on the flat roof of a house with an *O* marked on its top.

Then the birds began their long day's journey into night transferring the goods of those who had into the homes of those who had not. Jack sent his wife onto the highest branch of the tallest tree, close to the hurley field. Jane Daw's function was to warn their thieving progeny when the Hurley Hooley ended, and thus save them from the anger of those who'd lost their store of life's blessings. In the meantime, it was 'take till your beak breaks' for those birds of prey.

The hurling game ended with the hero Connor carried high on the shoulders of his teammates. Musicians played his triumphant circling of the hurley field. Now began the vaunted feat of Katbad the Druid, to celebrate the last day of the Boy King Connor on the throne of Ulster.

Now Connor, alone in his chariot pulled by his black bulls, led a host of hostelers and wagons onto the hurley field. Thus began the feasting of the Hurley Hooley. The hostelers set long tables opposite the goal posts.

An Irish acre of butchers and bakers unloaded the wagons onto the groaning boards. Pails and bales of slimy snails. Dish after dish of venison and fish. Stewed lambs and chops of mutton, enough of both to stuff the gluttons. Quivering livers and shivering gizzards. Oxen roasted and oysters toasted.

Mullets with almond. Fillets of salmon. Cockles and mus-
sels; sprouts of Brussels; tubs and tubs of steaming spuds.

After these preparations came the libations for recreation.
Oceans of ale, ruddy and pale. Rivers of beer, from far and
near. Stout and porter; cider and lager. Pints and noggins, vats
and flagons. Whiskey stills and poitín kilns; casks and flasks.

And so the plain people of Ulster drank and ate more than
their share. Mound mushrooms flavored the food and mood
of the guests with a strong and subtle magic. All this sweet
confusion was courtesy of Katbad the Druid, to secure the
throne of Ulster for his son, Connor. Mood is as major to the
abdication of a king as any other factor.

Bards with harps, fiddles, and drums struck up a wild Irish
jig. Dancing girls by the dozens reeled onto the hurley pitch.
The dancers kicked high, clicked heels, swung left, swung right
to the beat of the bodhrán and the hand-clapping spectators.
The girls threw caution and costumes to Old God's wind, exciting the men and priming the women.

Following the dancers, Malachy the Minstrel played old,
sweet songs of love on his wild harp. Then Sceál Galore told
tales of Gaels and glory. Warriors of the Red Branch Knights
performed feats of arm. Druids provided interludes of magic
to confuse and amuse.

The day danced on until the sun set. And so the feast ended.
The celebrants reeled home with light in their heads. Husbands
embraced their wives, thinking of the swish and swirl of the
dancing girls. Wives thought of Queen Nessa and the seven,
no, eight satisfactions from King Fergus on a feast night.

In his house of marble halls, Katbad the Druid welcomed
his guests for the evening and saw to their sleeping chambers.
King Fergus and Queen Nessa occupied the ivory and silver

rooms. Connor and Genann fell asleep with no delay after their goodnights to kings, queens, Druids, minstrels, bards, blacksmiths, and the riff and raff of Katbad's house.

Seeing the feast end and the guests staggering home, Jane Daw flew to warn her husband. Flaven the Raven followed Jane at the request of Katbad the Druid. Along the way, Flaven swooped down to observe the erotic endeavors of the homeward bound.

The old played the games of their youth: rambles in the brambles, larks in the dark, rolls in the hay, bull in the bush, witch in the ditch, hog in the bog, bird in the hand.

They were a rural people. The young made it up as they went along, as if they discovered it for the first time.

Jane Daw fluttered her feathers as she perched alongside her husband Jack. Now all the houses marked *O* were filled with the goods from the houses marked *X*. All that remained for the Daws was the return of the three sheets borrowed from Fergus the Virile.

In his chamber of ivory and silver at Katbad's house, King Fergus pranced and practiced with his long sword. Queen Nessa watched Fergus refine his dance of life and death, wounding thrusts to deter and disable; skill with blows to kill all foes. This long sword of Fergus had won and maintained for him the throne of Ulster. Queen Nessa smiled at Fergus. She knew he'd use his sword tomorrow to regain his throne, if need be. But he would not kill Connor. Fergus the man loved Connor; Fergus the king loved his crown.

Connor moaned in his sleep. His brother Genann watched over him. Once a king was not a guarantee for life. Once a Druid, forever a Druid. In his empty kitchen, Katbad the Druid looked deep into the eyes of Briar MacMalice. Katbad poured a dram of golden whiskey with a mushroom bud float for the dour Briar.

"Luck of the Irish to you, Katbad." Briar sipped his whiskey, his mind on tomorrow.

For diversion, Old God assumed the face of a man in the moon to watch those below. By now, all the byplays in the byways were over for the people of Ulster. Still intoxicated by their feast of food, drink, love, and lust, they streeled home. The jackdaws flew over them with the three sheets of Fergus held in their tired beaks. The man in the moon blew a deep breath that tossed the sheets and Daws topsy-turvy.

The three sheets flapping in the wind subjected the equilibrium of the stragglers to severe distress, compounded by the mocking face of the man in the moon

So memorable was this event for those involved that the phrase "three sheets to the wind" signified the depths of intoxication from then on.

King Connor the Boy King of Ulster awoke with the sun. As always, Connor reached for his crown before he quit his bed. Crown in hand, he tiptoed past his sleeping brother. Standing before a silver shield, Connor saw himself as others did. Every inch a king, he placed the crown of Ulster firmly on his head. King Connor loved his crown.

King Fergus of the Red Branch Knights awoke with the sun. As always, Fergus reached for his long sword before he quit his bed. Queen Nessa stirred in the bed beside him. Today she'd remain queen to King Fergus or queen mother to her son, Connor.

Katbad the Druid awoke with the sun. As always, Katbad reached for his three-pronged javelin before he quit his bed. Alert and aware, the King of the Druids created an image of the crown of Ulster on the head of his son.

Cullen the Smith awoke to a growl of welcome from his wolfhound. As always, Cullen patted his hound's head before he quit his bed.

Malachy the Minstrel awoke to the loud snoring of Sceál Galore in the bed beside his, in Katbad's cellar. As always, Malachy touched his wild harp before he quit his bed. If snores told the story of the sleeper, then the music of his harp could only improve its climax.

Briar MacMalice awoke with a dry tongue and a sore head. As usual, Briar reached for his glass before he quit his bed. He gargled and drank the whiskey in his glass, then chewed the mushroom bud left there by Katbad the Druid. Then, as usual, he got out of the wrong side of the bed.

The plain people of Ulster awoke with the father and the mother of all hangovers, leavened only by the lingering lightness of the magic mushrooms. Those who awoke to newfound wealth in their homes blessed the reign of the Boy King Connor and the goodness of the Old God. Those who awoke to empty rooms cursed the times that they were in and the neglect of Old God in his heaven.

Those who'd lost formed a straggling gaggle of Gaels making their way to the hurling field for the ceremony of transferring the crown from Connor to Fergus.

Those who'd gained stepped out lively. They soon passed the vexed and wrecked who lost their wealth.

The peaceful passing of a crown from a boy to a king had no precedent in the history of Ulster royalty. Fergus the King left the arrangement of this ceremony to Katbad the Druid.

Massed bards and minstrels set the mood with waving banners and regal music on the hurley field. Behind a wall of shields held high by the knights of the Red Branch in full regalia, Connor prepared for his chariot ride around the hurley field. Dressed in his royal best for his last appearance as king, Connor circled his subjects in his ornate chariot; the black bulls, with the white stripes across their shoulders, rose to the occasion with waving tails and snorting nostrils.

On the advice of his Druid Katbad, King Fergus waited for Connor's last farewell to his subjects before he'd make his appearance and retrieve his crown.

Loose and lively, the newly fortunate were the first to arrive for the end of Connor's review. Bound by their good humor, they were welcomed by Briar MacMalice. He plied them with food and drink from his personal groaning board. Toasts to the grand year of Connor's kingship were fast and frequent, ignited by the sly tongue of Briar. They dared not discuss their new wealth for the fear it could disappear in the talk of it.

When they arrived, those newly bereft of fortune huddled to the left of Briar's groaning board. None mentioned their loss for fear of losing stature among their peers.

If misery loves company, malice embraces all. At least Briar MacMalice did, talking out of both sides of his mouth at the same time. Those on his left did not hear what he said to those on his right. Those on his right did not hear what he said to those on his left.

To those newly selected by fortune, he stated that Connor's year as a king had received Old God's blessing to multiply the wealth of those who deserved it.

To those newly deserted by fortune, he blamed their present state to the indifference of King Fergus on leaving the affairs of his kingdom to the care of a seven-year-old boy. Briar was afraid to fail Katbad in securing the throne for his son.

The Druid had promised help to throw a feast to make Briar immortal in the memory of Gaels.

By now, all the birds of Ulster had assembled high in the trees around the hurley field, whistling "Connor is king."

Katbad reviewed his strategy. The magic mushrooms from the mount. The endowed rings from Cullen the Smith. Both sides of Briar's mouth. Jack and Jane Daw. His son Genann. And, as always, the luck of the Irish.

Connor the Boy King stepped into his chariot. The wall of shields opened. He drove his black bulls around the hurley field, the crown on his head, the three-pronged javelin in his hand.

Briar led three mighty cheers for Connor as he passed his groaning board. Slowly, Connor circled the field to tumultuous applause until he returned to the wall of shields.

The wall of shields opened again. King Fergus and Queen Nessa stood tall on his chariot, driven by Ibor the Charioteer. Slowly, Ibor drove the royal couple down the hurley field. In a silence that bespoke worlds conjured by Briar and his poisoned tongue, Ibor stopped the king's chariot in the middle of the field, turned, and waited for Connor.

King Fergus drew his long sword and pointed it at Connor's chariot. Connor placed his crown on the middle prong of his javelin. The black bulls with the white stripe on their shoulders marched in step toward the chariot of King Fergus. When they were opposite each other, Fergus slipped his long sword under the crown on the javelin.

Thus, he transferred the crown of Ulster from Connor to himself. Placing the crown firmly on his head, Fergus had Ibor drive his chariot down the field. Instead of applause, Fergus and his Queen Nessa heard loud remarks from the people of Ulster, courtesy of Briar MacMalice.

"What Fergus sold for his queen's dowry, let it stay sold."

"What Connor bought for a year, let it stay bought."

"Fergus has known half the women of Ulster as king, now he'll know the other half: our wives and daughters."

"Connor has the look of a king and the luck of the Irish."

As a king, Fergus had never trailed in battle or lacked in courage. Was he to become a creature of ridicule at the insolence of a seven-year-old boy, in front of the people to whom he'd devoted himself? Shocked and awed, the furious Fergus had Ibor face the chariot of Connor. Waving his long sword and roaring his battle cry, Fergus startled his horses into a wild charge up the field.

Connor started his brave bulls in a stately walk toward the galloping white horses of Fergus. Queen Nessa grasped the sword arm of King Fergus. The surprised king looked swiftly into the eyes of his queen. Time and place vanished for both; all the women Fergus had ravished in his eventful life were mirrored in the lovely eyes of Nessa. He saw the end and beginning of love at a level he had never expected or wished for. Her ringed hand slipped down his arm and closed over his powerful hand. Both rings touched, crown to crown, connecting his heart to his head. Nessa and Connor had doubled the love in the life of Fergus. Connor was a boy Fergus had fostered as a king, and the lad he loved as a son, and Nessa reigned as the queen of his being.

Nessa smiled at Fergus and changed the course of Ulster's history. Fergus handed his long sword to Nessa.

"Swing close to King Connor, Ibor," he yelled. Ibor smiled and pulled his chariot close to Connor's. Fergus reached for the boy Connor as their chariots passed. With a king's flourish, he picked Connor from his chariot and placed the boy on his shoulder. With a warrior's grace, he transferred the crown of Ulster onto Connor's head.

Fergus pledged his loyalty to the Boy King Connor, with his long sword and his smiling face. Thus, Connor resumed the throne to become the most renowned king in the history of Ulster, to the thunderous applause of his people.

A modest summation:

Was it the birth of Connor, the rush to mushroom heaven, the great Hurley Hooley, the orgy and origin of sheets in the wind, Queen Nessa's eyes, or Old God's fancy that secured the throne for Connor MacNessa? These subjects still ensure intense scholarship among intense scholars.

I row my small boat through rough seas toward my island home. With the wind at my back, I scurry along the grass toward my stone house. On my shoulder I carry a leather sack.

Standing at my lectern, I empty my sack of writing materials for the long winter of short days. In an ancient flagon, I carefully place my new goose quills. Into marble inkwells, I pour my blackberry ink. On a rope of bullhide, I drape my sheets of vellum.

I run my hands over the calfskin containing my work in progress. With my fingers, I trace out the gold letters inscribed on the calfskin.

SETANTA THE WARPED ONE

I open the volume and study the blank page of parchment before me. Carefully, I dip my goose quill in the marble inkwell. The black strokes on the white parchment excite my very being.

I empty my mind of all distractions to continue the saga of Setanta the Warped One.

So be it.

Mael Moró

137

Chirteen

IT IS SOON told and long remembered how Setanta the Warped One fulfilled his vow to protect the property of Cullen the Blacksmith from predators.

Cullen the Blacksmith of Ulster did not find the grace in his heart to forgive the boy who killed his hound. He did not welcome Setanta into his house or provide for his food or shelter.

Exchanging the solicitude of a king for the solitude of a warrior taught Setanta to forage for himself wherever life led him. Alone, Setanta practiced and made perfect his skill with weapons on Cullen's demesne. He killed and skinned the game and geese he needed for survival. He could spear a leaping salmon in midair, swirl it around his head until the flesh separated from its bones, and remove its skin with a slice from his thumb.

To enlarge his lungs and strengthen his body, Setanta dived into lakes and fords. From schools of fish he learned to swim and breathe until he was as secure under water as on the land above. Cuddled and coddled by their concern, Setanta slept between his two horses. In time, Setanta became as one with the birds of the air, the fish of the streams, and the beasts of the earth.

A rough justice of necessity ensured the survival of those under the stewardship of Setanta, now called Cucullen, the Hound of Cullen.

Back at the Red Branch court, King Connor missed the excursions of his eccentric nephew. In preparation for an upcoming fair, the king sent a team of twenty-five boys to Cullen's house to improve their hurling skills under the auspices of Setanta.

Knowing the high regard for hospitality among the Ulster people, Cullen the Smith saw to the comfort of these young boys of consequence. Setanta stood aloof, a silent witness as Cullen's household prepared bed and board for the young hurlers. For three days, Setanta drilled the young boys in the ancient game of hurling.

Two days before the fair, Setanta assembled the team of young hurlers, skilled and sharpened under his guidance. On the plain outside Cullen's house, he put them through a rigorous series of exercises to strengthen the body and focus the mind. Who but a hero can inspire heroes?

Then came the sinister chanting on the morning wind. First to react were the two horses of Setanta. Ears and tails erect, they nudged Setanta toward the rough voices disturbing the day's equilibrium. Setanta listened closely. The boys huddled close, eyes on Setanta. Into view marched twenty-seven marauders from the Isle of Frongoch, sent to sack the House of Cullen. These are the words heard by Setanta and his team that morning:

> "We are torrents of torment,
> Flames from the Devil sent."

Closer came the invaders toward Setanta and his team of staunch hurlers. Dressed in black cloaks with ebony spears and dark shields, the thick-shouldered, bandy-legged band marched on.

They stopped close to the boys and Setanta, defiant and deadly. The boys looked to Setanta. He pointed his hurley stick toward the marauders. Clutching their hurley sticks, the boys ran to attack. Setanta whistled for his two horses and unloosed his leather pouch of marble slingshots.

A ruddy relic of a man swaggered forward from the vandals. He seized a boy in each brawny hand and flung them against their teammates. Two more boys he hurled at the hurlers. Dismayed by their possible nemesis, the boys ran from these fearsome foes. Left alone to defend Cullen's house was Setanta and his two horses.

Setanta slapped Ban, his white horse, with the flat of his hurley stick. Tail high and hooves kicking, the horse galloped after the running boys. Setanta leaped onto the back of his black horse, Dub. Watched closely by the felons of Frongoch, the black horse ambled toward them. Setanta stood tall on his horse's back, firm of balance and sure of purpose. In his right hand his hurley stick. In his left hand five sharp marble slingshots. He turned the left side of his black horse toward the swarthy men. The left side of an animal or chariot is an insult, an insinuation of cowardice. Setanta issued his challenge:

"Save body and bone,
Be good—or Begone."

A brawny braggart hefted his ebony spear, and stepped to the fray.

"Run away, wee boy
Or stay here and die!"

Setanta flipped his marble slingshots in the air. He struck them firmly with his hurley stick. Straight and true, the slingshots flew toward the scurvy rabble. The first removed the Adam's apple of the boastful braggart. Two more blinded the left eyes of his brothers beside him. The fourth shot landed into the open mouth and ripped out the back of the neck of the robber holding the cross-eyed bull with the crooked horn.

Deep in his bowels, Setanta felt the beginning of a warp seizure. To forestall an imminent slaughter, Setanta let loose his clarion call to conflict. None who heard it that day forgot it. His white horse galloped into the woebegone wastrels. Kicking with his rear hooves, biting with his sharp teeth, ramming with his broad rump, the white horse battered the bandits.

Setanta slipped from the broad back of his black horse. He slapped the horse and watched the animal leap high into those still standing. Clutching his hurley stick in both hands, Setanta waded into the messy mass of bleeding bandits. Slashing, smashing, bashing, he laid low the remnants of the swarthy scoundrels.

From then on, Setanta was the first served at meals and celebrations in the House of Cullen the Blacksmith. He kept his distance from others who approached too close to him. He was Setanta the Warped One. First among heroes; a warrior from the other side. Alone and aloof, he survived on courage, cunning, and immortality in the memory of his deeds.

From the age of seven to the age of fourteen, Setanta protected the home and estate of Cullen the Blacksmith. In the province of Ulster, his valor became legend, reflecting splendor on his uncle, King Connor MacNessa.

Cucullen, the Hound of Cullen, was a name bestowed on Setanta by the satirist Briar MacMalice. A name conceived in jest was born into immortality by the deeds of Setanta. Many came to challenge Setanta. None overcame the lad's assurance; none survived Setanta's assault when attacked in battle.

A sword as long as a boat's rudder struck the door of Cullen's fort.

"Open, Cullen, open," roared the voice of Fergus the Virile.

Setanta opened the door. Holding his sword, Fergus lurched into the courtyard. Bloody and bowed, wounded and woebegone, Fergus stared at Setanta.

"Fergus, where is King Connor?" asked Setanta.

"He's out there on the field of battle. Find him. Save him."

Setanta passed Fergus into the dark night, lit by a fitful moon. Setanta's eyes from the other side watched banshee bitches lift corpses in mocking embrace before transporting them to desolation and despair.

This night had a thousand eyes, gleaming in the dark. Two turned into a man with half a head on his shoulders. On his back, the man with half a head carried half a body.

"Have you seen King Connor?" asked Setanta.

"Help this poor man with half his head carry his brother's body. Relieve me of my burden, friend."

The half-headed man flung half of his brother's body at Setanta, knocking him to the ground. The dying howled their derision. The man with half a head sat on Setanta's chest. His open wounds dripped blood onto Setanta's face. The black and white horses circled Setanta and his assailant, seeking an opening to aid the youth. Setanta's right hand closed tight on the handle of his hurley stick. Hefting high his hurley stick, Setanta struck the half head from the shoulder of its owner. The bloody half of the bloody head skidded over a trail of severed limbs. The black horse kicked the headless body from

Setanta's chest with his rear hooves. The white horse kicked the half body of the brother of the headless man with his rear hooves. Setanta took his revenge in his own peculiar way. First, he slung the body of the headless man across the back of his black horse, tying hands to filthy feet.

Using the half head of the headless man as his sliotar ball, Setanta played the ancient game of hurling. Straight and true, he struck the half head ahead of him with his sturdy hurley stick. The blood red eyes of the severed head blazed with pain and fury, lighting the road ahead. When convinced he had the full attention of the half head, Setanta chanted to what was left of him:

> "If you find King Connor and he's not dead,
> I'll bury your body beneath your head.
> Fail, dear friend, in this endeavor,
> And you will rest in pieces forever."

Those who died without all parts attached or close by would be so marked for eternity, and not welcome to the world of the ever young. A king not whole in body and mind could lose his throne. The half head acknowledged Setanta's command by nodding the remains of his aching head. Setanta hurled ahead in his search for King Connor. Now began Setanta's chant to alert the king of his presence on the field of battle:

> "King Connor, King Connor,
> Please answer your nephew Setanta."

Doubtless and dauntless, Setanta followed the flaming eyes of the rolling head, searching for signs of King Connor. Both Connor and Setanta were from the other side, endowed with great gifts and epic cruelties, as necessary for eternity and memory.

The half head of the headless man vanished into the dark night. Setanta blinked. The horses stopped. Sound had replaced sight on this bloody ground. To the left lay the bog and coffin holes of the vanquished. To the right stretched the dark unknown. Ahead was the ground where the half head disappeared. About and behind, the dead and dying cursed their fate.

A crimson column of light flashed on and off ahead, as if arising from the earth itself. A voice roared near this light that shined in the darkness. The voice of King Connor of Ulster:

"You, red-eyed knave,
Depart my grave."

Setanta walked to the edge of a coffin-shaped bog hole where the voice and light emanated. A half head with flaring red eyes erupted from the bog hole and rolled toward him. The teeth from the mouth of the half head fastened on Setanta's toes to break its forward momentum. Seizing the moment, Setanta grasped the half head and pointed its crimson eyes into the bog hole below. Here King Connor lay prone on a cord of corpses, slowly sinking and sinking slowly into the endless depths of an Irish bog hole.

Setanta gauged the depth of the coffin hole. At least three tall warriors deep. Nothing to hold on to, slimy walls of putrefying muck, the stuff of nightmares and bog holes. Down was a slippery slope. Coming up with the body of a wounded king was another problem.

Setanta looked around. Behind him a black and a white horse. Dead warriors on the cold ground. Limbs without owners. Below him a king in a sinkhole. When in doubt, do. Setanta set to work. He hauled the corpses of the three tallest warriors he could find to the side of the bog hole. Below him Connor the king snored the rasping breath of a sick man in a bog hole on a dark night.

Setanta made a snake's ladder of the three dead warriors. He tied feet under armpits, one to the next, with sword belts, shield straps and armor girdles collected from the dead. When finished, Setanta pulled and pushed, lowering his column of corpses into the bog hole. Then he removed the body of the headless man from his black horse. Setanta secured the neck of the top corpse to the broad shoulders of his black horse with a rope of sword belts. Bloody work, indeed. He arranged the half head with the crimson eyes to light the coffin hole and began his descent to rescue the king.

It is not easy at the best of times to climb down a ladder of corpses into a bog hole of sucking foul matter. To do so on an evil night when the bog hole is host to cords of warrior corpses is another story.

Holding tight to the hair of the top warrior, Setanta lowered himself down his column of corpses by the light of the crimson eyes of the half head. At the top of the bog hole, he found grips for his hands and holds for his feet on the body parts of the dead he'd tied together. Setanta slipped past faces frozen and surprised by death. The eyes were the worst, tinted red and terrified by the corpse light within and the crimson light above.

The smell increased the deeper he descended into the coffin sump. Mud that sweated ancient blood and bile. The stink of the recent dead. Vomit. Snot. Fear. Bloody slices. Gaping wounds. Missing noses. Bowels. Bones of pulp, battered and bruised beyond redemption. Hacked necks. Slashed breasts. Flayed flesh. Crushed skulls.

Setanta's feet landed on the broad chest of Connor, expelling air from the king's lungs in a gurgling rush. The sound of the night diminished at the bottom of the bog hole where the dead ruled. Setanta stepped from his uncle's chest onto a corpse below him. The crimson light showed Setanta that King Connor lay on a pallet of four dead warriors, the width of the coffin hole. Two more pallets of warriors supported this top layer of corpses. Beneath all, the sucking sounds of the bog floor slowly swallowing another corpse into its maw. A sinking feeling. The balance shifted among the corpses, tilting left and then right as a body disappears into the sink-hole for eternity.

Setanta shook his right foot loose from its immersion in the belly wound of a bloated corpse. He stepped over the king's body to kneel at the breast of a brawny dead charioteer. He laid his head on the king's body, listening for a heartbeat. It was still strong and steady, but he detected a slight flutter. In this feted air, Setanta felt the fingers of death everywhere.

King Connor's eyes were closed. His mouth curled in a cruel sneer new to Setanta. Death features its own welcome. Setanta tried to lift Connor into a sitting position, but encoun-tered resistance to moving the king's body. He ran his fingers over Connor's body. The powerful hands of the corpses on which Connor lay clutched the arms of the king in a death grip. To each his own. Setanta tried to pry these dead fingers from their last embrace of the king. It was arduous work. Another body sucked below by the insatiable bog hole. The floor of corpses tilted again. A low groan from King Connor. The smell of death increased. King Connor spoke:

"Setanta, I have a vision. A dream of a crock of gold as big as a mountain." He fell silent again. Setanta sliced through the wrists of the dead grasping the king's arms with his gold-handled sword. The type of work he was born for. Best done in the dark.

When finished with his handiwork, Setanta propped the body of the king against the lowest warrior on his corpse pole and secured them together with sword belts and armor girdles.

A whistle from Setanta and his black horse surged forward. Slowly, the caravan of three corpses, a sleeping king, and a boy named Setanta were pulled from a coffin hole by a straining black horse. Finally, Setanta sprawled beside the half head with the crimson eyes. With this as light, Setanta unwound the fingers clutching the king and tossed them into the bog hole. Setanta untied the king of Ulster from the dead soldier he was tied to. The black horse knelt beside Setanta and he removed the corpse from the horse's back. He tied the king's body onto the horse's back.

When finished, Setanta stood beside the bog hole and spat into it. A voice spoke in the night, a voice from half a head with flaming eyes:

"Here's my head. Where's my heels? Where's the rest of me?"

Setanta smiled. He back-heeled the half head of the headless man into the bottomless pit of the bog hole.

They set forth into the dark night, seeking shelter for the ailing king. His horses seemed anxious and upset, bumping and stumbling into each other. This awoke King Connor. He chanted to Setanta:

> *"On this bloody night,*
> *Stay tight to the right;*
> *At the Crystal Spring,*
> *Make a left again,*
> *Where this king once rode*
> *To a snug abode.*
> *There you light a fire,*
> *Before I expire."*

Setanta followed Connor's instructions. Dub and Ban drank from the spring water as if from the elixir of life. A young whelp of a hound barked a welcome in the distance.

"Head for the hound; You're homeward bound," said King Connor, eyes still closed. The horses cantered left toward the dog that barked in the night. Soon they arrived at a small snug house. Setanta opened the door and entered the house of his father. The house he was conceived and born in.

Inside the house, Setanta found a well-appointed room with a fireplace stacked with seasoned oak logs. He carried King Connor into the house and settled him on an elegant couch of brown bullhide in front of the fire. Setanta kindled a blazing fire for the king. The king's body heated and his limbs regained their use. Setanta explored the small house that seemed to expand with his presence. He felt very much at home, as if back in the womb again. In the cellar, he found flagons of coal-dark beer and golden vats of mellow whiskey. He brought a tray of drinks to King Connor. Fire and whiskey—very frisky. Slowly he poured a tot of whiskey down the king's gullet. Setanta felt like a host in his own home, entertaining royalty. Outside, Dub the black horse chased Ban the white horse around the field they were born on.

King Connor opened his eyes, his face a royal flush. He looked into the fire and spoke to Setanta.

"I could sit up. I could eat a roast pig. I might live."

Setanta helped the king to sit up. "I'll go find you a roast pig."

Setanta went from the house to find a pig. As the luck of the Irish would have it, he smelled the aroma of roast pig down by the pure spring water of the crystal fountain.

Setanta whistled up his horses and set forth for the king's dinner. Straight and true, they soon arrived at their destination, lit by a blazing fire pit. A swarthy man of ferocious aspect was turning a roasting pig on a spit with one hand. In his other hand, he held his wicked sword, knob polished to a fire-thee-well. He wore a torn tunic, blood-splattered from filthy feet to unwashed hair. Eyes red with smoke and slaughter. Mouth drooling with a surfeit of appetite and ignorance, a deadly combination.

"Luck of the Irish to you, man of the roasting pig," said Setanta and stepped into the firelight with his two horses behind him. The ruffian of the roasting pig swung around and pointed his sword, knob and all, at the bowels of the youth.

"Can I help you, boy of the two horses?" His voice was rough winds over desolate spaces.

"I'm seeking a roast pig for a sick friend," said Setanta.

"There is only enough pig here for me and the brother," said the swarthy man, drool dripping down his chin.

"And where might the brother be?" asked Setanta.

"Begob; he's right behind you. He's got a bigger sword than I have for your back." The surly scoundrel looked closer at the two horses with Setanta.

"I'll swap you the roast pig for your two horses, boy, and I'll throw in your life to sweeten the deal."

"Whom might I be talking to?" asked Setanta.

"I'm Gob Mac Nob, and that's the brother, Begob Mac Nob covering your rear." Gob was far gone in villainy.

"Is the pig cooked yet?" asked Setanta.

"One more turn on the spit and its meat would revive the dead for a last supper," boasted Gob Mac Nob.

"All right. I'll say farewell to my horses and the bargain is struck." Setanta kissed each horse three times on the neck and whispered instructions in their ears. He smacked the black horse Dub on the rump. Dub did his horse trot over to Gob Mac Nob and stood behind him. Ban the white horse cantered behind Setanta in search of the brother Begob Mac Nob. Setanta walked toward Gob Mac Nob and the roasting pig.

"That's close enough, boy. Stay in the light where we can see what you got," ordered Gob, thrusting his sword toward Setanta.

"That's a fancy sword for a fancy boy. Take it out slowly and let's have a look at it," sneered Gob Mac Nob.

Setanta unsheathed his gold-handled sword and pointed it toward Gob's weapon.

"It's a gift from King Connor of Ulster."

"A king's gift is a beggar's blessing. Bring your sword here and help yourself to the pig," said Gob.

"The king might miss his sword," said Setanta.

"O, that king is in a bit of a hole at the moment, isn't that true, Begob?" asked Gob.

"Gob, if he's where we left him, he's below concern about swords and supper," Begob Mac Nob said from directly behind Setanta.

The white horse snickered, alert and alive.

"Come and take my sword, you mangy maggots," Setanta said, and spat in the eye of Gob Mac Nob.

Gob hefted his weapon with two filthy hands and advanced on Setanta. Gob started swinging his sword back for his killing stroke. Setanta whistled to his trusty steeds, dropped to the ground, and lay still. Dub the black horse high kicked Gob Mac Nob on his bum with his rear hooves. Gob ascended over the prone Setanta at an angle of forty-five degrees behind Setanta. Begob Mac Nob raised his particular sword for a slicing blow to split the youth's head in twain. Behind him again, Ban the white horse high kicked Begob Mac Nob on his bum with his rear hooves.

Begob Mac Nob ascended over the prone Setanta at an angle of forty-five degrees to the perpendicular. The two brothers met in midair over Setanta's giggling body. Gob Mac Nob's sword, knob and all, sliced the body of his brother, Begob Mac Nob, in twain. Begob Mac Nob's sword sliced Gob Mac Nob's head in two. Setanta rolled out of the way as half a head and half a body fell where he recently lay.

With his horses behind him and a roast pig on his back, spit and all, Setanta returned to the snug house of his father, Lugh of the Long Hand.

Setanta saw to the feeding and care of his uncle, King Connor of Ulster. Before a roaring fire, they ate well of a delicious roast pig.

"Let us go to the House of Cullen the Smith," said a restored King Connor. On the way back to Cullen's Fort, King Connor heard the moaning of a wounded warrior in a low ditch.

From the broad back of the white horse, Connor spoke to Setanta. "Yonder is the night chamber of my son, Cursa."

Sliding from the back of his black horse, Setanta found a severely wounded boy crying in a wayward ditch. He was Cursa, a favored son of King Connor of Ulster. Setanta bound up the boy's wounds with healing herbs from his pouch. Cursa was the same age as Setanta, a boy who'd gone to war with his father against the enemies of Ulster. Feeling close to Cursa in age and essence, Setanta carried the boy on his back. Behind him, a wounded king on a black horse followed along with a protective white horse. Dawn's curious rays informed Setanta of his whereabouts concerning his arrival at the House of Cullen the Smith. The king opened his eyes and spoke to his son:

"Cursa, I had a dream of a crock of gold as big as a mountain." Connor closed his eyes again. Setanta looked closely at King Connor. He was not the same king Setanta had known for the last seven years of his life. Lines of tension tightened Connor's face. His left shoulder thrust upward, as if always on guard. His mouth drooped in a tiny sneer, licked open and often by a moist red tongue, as if curiosity was now replaced by a cruel certainty.

FOURTEEN

WHAT SETANTA SENSED in King Connor's face did not bode well for those who knew only kindness in the king's character. A night on a cord of corpses in a bog hole does not bring out the best in king or commoner. Setanta was never the same after his descent into the coffin hole. He left his childhood behind in the bog hole. From then on, he had less time and more tension with the merely human. For a year after Setanta rescued him from the bog hole, King Connor stayed close to the Red Branch home. Something dark and disturbing surfaced as impatience with events that interfered with his pleasure. A night in an Irish bog hole is not conducive to good conduct. Connor's passions overcame his privileges to an extent that caused concern. Katbad the Druid arranged a meeting with Fergus the Virile on top of his tower housing the oracular throne. This was the one safe house in Ulster.

During the troubles of King Connor, they met on a clear and starry night. "The battle lost by King Connor and his heroes might restore equilibrium," said Katbad the Druid.

"We need Setanta by the king's side. He's the best we have in Ulster." Fergus loved Connor as a foster son and a king.

"Many dogs were given to Cullen over the years to release Setanta's pledge of protection. None reached maturity on Cullen's estate."

Katbad loved Connor as a son and a king. He touched the throne with his right hand. Fergus and Katbad were men of the world they lived in.

"If a Druid saw to a hound to replace Setanta..." Fergus looked at Katbad.

"If a warrior could return Ferdia to Ulster, King Connor would have a hero fore and aft. A new generation."

Then, as now, the consequences were seldom predictable. Katbad the Druid learned as much from dreams as mortals from life. In the enchantment of sleep, he saw the great hound of Lugh of the Long Hand. A hound greater than any other hound in courage and combat to the foes of Lugh. A magic hound that left mead or wine in its wake when immersed in water.

Leaving his son in charge, Katbad bid farewell to his pupils and stepped onto his chariot. His black bulls set off in high style to find Setanta, and then a hound to replace Setanta as the Hound of Cullen. A Druid's life takes many roads, not all run straight and true.

Katbad met Setanta near the abode of Cullen the Smith. Alone, Setanta sat on a boulder. After salutations, Katbad spoke to Setanta.

"A youth of consequence is a man of action. Setanta, King Connor needs a hero." Katbad gestured to Setanta to join him on his chariot. The bulls walked toward Cullen's fort, listening intently to Katbad.

"I had a dream of the hound of your father, Lugh of the Long Hand. If I find this hound for Cullen, will you leave him and serve King Connor?" asked Katbad.

"Connor is my king. Ulster is my destiny," said Setanta.

"How do I find the House of Lugh of the Long Hand?" asked Katbad of Setanta.

"My horses know the way. King Connor found the house by a hound barking in the night," said Setanta.

"That is the hound I'm looking for," said Katbad.

Katbad the Druid stood on Setanta's chariot. He watched Setanta kiss each horse three times on the neck. Setanta whispered in the ears of both horses, then spoke to Katbad.

"Tonight I'm dining with a wealthy landlord who will buy a ring from Cullen to help him find a wife. This is not the way of a warrior."

Katbad let the horses set the pace. Dub and Ban cantered along with tails high and ears erect. Nothing untoward happened to Katbad. Setanta had cleared the province of outlaws and churls. The horses stopped at a crystal fountain for a deep drink. Across the clear air, a young whelp barked a welcome.

The horses trotted toward the barking dog. They stopped at the front door of a narrow house. A black whelp ran three times around the chariot. Katbad bestowed a Druid's blessing on the House of Lugh of the Long Hand. The game began. The horses ran smoothly behind the black dog. He led them on a merry chase across fields and fords. Old God followed on a scudding cloud, wondering what he'd drop from the sky in the way of mischief and misfortune.

A salty rush of air and three soaring seagulls welcomed Katbad to the rough seas between Ireland and Alba. The black hound sniffed among the rocks along the shore. He scrambled atop a slab of rock above a walkway to the ocean and barked at the crashing waves. The horses stopped and waited for a signal from the Druid. Katbad listened intently to the whelp's barking. A yelp for help; a bark of arrival; a growl for approval; a rumble of readiness; a call to something on, beyond, or below the roaring sea.

Satisfied they were in the right place, Katbad turned the horses for Cullen's fort and Setanta. Whatever he'd set in motion would evolve in its own way. His loyalty ran to his son, King Connor, and the province of Ulster.

Because of the dramatic calendar of Connor's birth, Old God had kept his distance from the King of Ulster. Another king was born in a stable in Bethlehem at the time of Connor's birth. A desert wind from this new god-king cleansed the world of wily tricksters like Old God and his ilk. In Old God's day, the world turned on chance and mischief, survivors and spectators.

For three days and nights, the whelp crouched on the sea-wracked rock and barked at the waves. On the night of a new moon, his calls were answered. From beneath the sea surfaced a beautiful woman in a silver gown. She swam ashore toward the barking dog, seaweeds clinging to her crimson tresses. The elegant woman and the excited dog walked into the dawn. Her name was Macra, Maid of the Mist and Foggy Shower Clouds. Macra's father, an odd sea god named Sainrith, Son of Imbath, was a cousin far removed (the farther the better) from Old God himself.

The name Macra weaves in and out of the oral history of Old Ireland. Macra was the warrior wife of Nuada of the Silver Hand. Both were slain by mighty blows from Balor of the Evil Eye. These vivid characters we will meet in our old tales, if we survive the times that are in it now.

Macra and the whelp walked easily through the fallow land of Ulster, followed by Old God on a crimson cloud. Bypassing all small and medium holdings, she settled on the largest house she found. This was the land and home of Crunniac, a rich landlord whose wife had died from overwork in building up her husband's wealth. Crunniac lived with his sons and sorrows. A man with a tongue as loose as his wallet was tight, Crunniac's prosperity remained his priority.

Without a word, Macra and the whelp moved into Crunniac's house. She set the house in order, cleaning, cooking, and tending his domestic animals with a sure and knowing hand. Macra slept by the cooking fire, the whelp by her feet. A small red glow in the hound's eyes flashed death to those who approached Macra without respect. Macra kept well the House of Crunniac. There was no lack of food, clean linen, or the essentials for civilized existence for Crunniac and his two sons. All this with no inroads on his wealth. Macra's order begat order that caused Crunniac's tongue to prattle and his wealth to increase. His tales of Macra's prowess became the talk of the tenants and spread through the province. Briar MacMalice brought the news of the beauty of Macra to the ears of King Connor.

One fine morning, Macra entered the bedroom of Crunniac, the hound at her heels. Closing tight the door, Macra removed her clothes. Enchanted by her beauty, Crunniac's tongue failed him. He gazed in silence at the fall of the crimson hair on her lovely skin, and her cool and limpet green eyes. Slowly, with the assurance of immortality, Macra made a mystical sunrise right hand turn at the foot of his bed. This ritual from the other side doubled the good fortune for whoever used the bed for love that night. As swiftly as she disrobed, Macra and the dog vanished.

This left Crunniac in a high state of excitement. A heavy knock on his bedroom door cut into his fantasy.

"Who's there?" yelled Crunniac, covering himself.

"It's Briar MacMalice, an envoy from King Connor."

Crunniac rushed to open his door and Briar sauntered in. Had Briar seen Macra leave his room? wondered Crunniac.

Aloud, he said to Briar, "Welcome to the envoy of King Connor."

"A welcome is what the king would appreciate tonight. He would not intrude, but news of the wonders of your housekeeper has intrigued his interest. He is searching for a hound for his nephew Setanta," Briar said and left.

Nothing would have it for him but to cause as much mischief as he could. Above all, he knew that a man was judged by his hospitality and largeness of spirit, especially where a king was concerned.

Between Macra's turn in his bedroom and Briar's sardonic eyes, Crunniac's self-control unraveled. He issued conflicting orders to his household until all were confused in an uproar of apples and ales. Macra saved the day. She awoke Briar from his nap after his middle of the night trip. Briar rubbed his red eyes and stared at the beautiful woman with the crimson hair.

"We would appreciate the advice of the king's envoy in preparing for Connor's stay in the House of Crunniac," Macra said and smiled. Briar sensed she saw right through him. A woman as devious as she was desirable. Did she see the jealousy and passion in his eyes?

"We'll clean the house from top to bottom, prepare for the feast, and arrange a bedroom for King Connor," Briar said, and left his sleeping quarters.

They set to work together, trailed by the whelp. A babbling Crunniac followed until silenced by a sardonic look from Briar MacMalice. Crunniac slipped away to count his blessings and his kitchen silver. A landlord who feasted a king such as Connor in his house would command respect for the rest of his life.

If the king's feast was satirized by the likes of Briar MacMalice, the host would become a figure of perpetual ridicule. Macra had the house aired from top to bottom. She brought the outdoors indoors with fresh flowers, shrubs, and shamrocks. Briar advised Macra on Connor's taste in food and comfort. Outside the house, oak logs were cut and stacked alongside three roasting pits; three plump pigs were slaughtered and slathered with savory sauces. Fresh linen tunics were prepared for the household. Dark beer and ruddy ale prevailed in the kitchen. Beautiful maidens, local musicians, and wandering bards were collected by the eager chariots of Crunniac's sons.

Unspoken between Briar and Macra was the king's privilege of first choice of any woman where he slept, and of his interest in Macra because of Crunniac's loose tongue. They came to the choice of bedrooms for the king's pleasure. Briar left to bring back the king's wreath. A wreath of roses fixed to the door of the king's bedroom to ensure privacy for the royal privileges.

Macra rushed to pull Crunniac from the kitchen. She brought him to stand between his bedroom and that of his sons' next door.

"King Connor must not sleep in your room tonight," Macra said to Crunniac. The hound at her feet growled in approval.

"But if Briar picks this room for the king?" asked Crunniac.

"Listen to me, man. Do not turn the blessing I put on this room today into a curse tonight." Macra punched Crunniac on his shoulder.

Briar returned with the royal wreath, licking his lips. Had he heard what Macra said? She wondered.

"I'll leave the choice of the king's bedroom to you, Macra. Connor likes a canopy over his bed, and the softest women—I mean linen—under him. Whichever room you choose, hang this wreath on the door before the king retires." Briar handed the wreath to Macra.

"When I've finished preparing the king's bedroom, I must leave. I will not be here tonight," Macra said.

Briar moved closer to Macra, touching her hand, ignoring Crunniac. "The king comes for you tonight, Macra," he said.

"No man has a privilege on me. I come and go as I please." Macra held the royal wreath on the bedroom door of Crunniac's sons. "I need a dagger," she said.

Briar handed Macra his short, tongue-shaped dagger.

She stuck the dagger deep into the door and hung the royal wreath on its horn handle.

"Farewell, Macra. I will miss you tonight." Briar backed away from Macra. Ireland abounded in beautiful and dangerous women. Briar backed out of view but not out of hearing.

"Tonight, Crunniac; be in your room late tonight. Do not let your tongue reduce your future. Tonight I will fulfill your blessing and double your fortune." Macra opened the door with the dagger and set to work. She energized the two sons of Crunniac into changing their bedroom. Drapes of red velvet on the wall, green rugs on the floor, oak logs arranged by the fireplace, a canopy of red silk on a frame of blackthorn adorned the royal bed. The softest linen covered the bed.

Macra departed as she had come, swiftly and alone. None saw her go, not even the hound she left behind. As the sun set, King Connor arrived in a flurry of chariots and banners. Macra's hound barked a welcome to the king and jumped aboard his chariot. They were well met. A hound with unconditional love and a man with a king's appetite for the same. They bonded together, both from the other side.

In the feast hall, Crunniac bent in two before the king.

"Your honor, King Connor, welcome to my home," babbled Crunniac.

"And when do I meet Macra, the paragon?" asked King Connor.

"Macra comes and goes, King Connor," said Briar.

"You told me of Macra, Briar; I hope it's not a wild chase for a tame gander," said King Connor, looking at the women assembled for his welcome.

"The real feast awaits if you retire alone, King Connor," said Briar. This was a time in King Connor's life when privileges and perversion assumed the same proportion. There were none to say him nay, and lots to fulfill his yeas.

Briar and Crunniac saw to the king's program for the rest of the evening. Ale and board games. Music and tales of heroes. Dark beer and roast pig. Bones collected for the hound at the feet of the king. The life of a king when not at war. Briar slipped away when Crunniac fawned before a bored King Connor. Bored and tired enough to prefer soft linen to warm women.

Briar could not pull his tongue-shaped dagger from the bedroom door. Macra had a way with a dagger equal to any man. Briar stuck a silver knife he'd borrowed from Crunniac's table into Crunniac's bedroom door. With a smooth grasp of the royal wreath, he transferred it from one door to the next.

He dedicated his evening's work to his long-time collaborator, Old God himself, and returned to the feast. The evening wore on and wore out King Connor.

"Yes, King Connor."

"No, King Connor."

"No trouble at all, King Connor."

"My honor, King Connor."

"My Macra, King Connor."

"My wealth, King Connor."

"My house, King Connor."

"My, my, my, King Connor."

The prating of Crunniac sated the king. Briar escorted Connor to Crunniac's bedroom to escape the prattle of the host. The hound stayed close to the king's heels.

"Where is Macra?" asked Connor from his bed.

"She will return and double your blessings when all are retired tonight, King Connor," Briar replied. The hound lay at the foot of the bed.

Briar returned to the feast to assail a befuddled Crunniac with more ale. Never had Crunniac feasted a king. Never had Crunniac the option to talk to heroes. Never had he seen a naked goddess with crimson hair, public and private, from the other side. All this in one day. When he staggered to his bedroom the royal wreath of roses on the door welcomed him.

The low growling of Macra's hound from inside his bedroom stopped Crunniac. Behind him, Briar pushed Crunniac into his sons' bedroom. Briar directed him to the bed with the red canopy. Crunniac fell fast asleep. All of his dreams had occurred when awake. Beware days like this. Dreams have a place and price on them.

Outside the sons' bedroom, Briar transferred the wreath from Crunniac's room, and retired to gloat on his night's work. It warmed his bone and chilled his blood. In the dead of the night, the silent Macra returned. She presumed that the door with the wreath contained a bed with a king, and the bed behind the wreathless door contained her feckless lover, whose blessing she'd double on this night of the new moon. Her hound greeted Macra by crawling on his belly to lick her tender toes.

In the still of the night, Macra slipped off her cloak and tunic, and slid into the bed of the sleeping king. Mistaking him for Crunniac, Macra kissed him three times on the neck and whispered in his ear. She aroused him from his dream of a crock of gold as big as a mountain.

Under a new moon, a king and a goddess became a man and a woman. It is better for all when the reverse occurs.

In the morning, Macra awoke in singular isolation. The king had disappeared with her whelp hound. Crunniac was not available when most needed. The knock on her bedroom door was not familiar, but insistent enough for her response. It was Briar MacMalice himself, warts and all. "King Connor sends his gratitude for your hospitality and extends his invitation to a return engagement at his Red Branch home," Briar said.

"Oh, and this is in exchange for your gift of a hound." Briar handed Macra a ring from the personal forge of Cullen the Smith. She put it on the bedroom table without looking at it.

Setanta heard about the hound of Macra when he made a visit to the house of his uncle, King Connor MacNessa. The hound was now the foster hound of Katbad the Druid. A hound without fault or flaws, reared by a school of Druids. King Connor walked alone with Setanta.

"Setanta, I will tell Cullen I have a hound to replace you. We need to restore vitality to the Red Branch. I have sent a messenger to Ferdia to return for a great fair to celebrate your release from Cullen and your return to arms for all of Ulster."

Setanta knew then that his destiny as a hero was taking an exciting new direction. Ferdia was the only warrior mentioned in the same breath as Setanta. Ferdia, who'd gone to Alba, Europa, hell, and heaven to learn and practice his craft as a hero warrior. Ferdia—as good a man as any who walked the earth, but as good as Setanta, himself? If not, he could teach Ferdia a trick or two or three. If better than Setanta at this moment, he could learn a trick or two or three from Ferdia.

Either way, the world's borders opened for a Setanta ready for experience and adventure. First comes courage. On his way back to Cullen, Setanta went to see the hound at Katbad's house. He rode through the open gate of the courtyard. No sight nor sound of human inhabitants. Before he'd time to dismount, a furry black ball of fury slammed into him and sent him sprawling sideways. He lay on the ground, the snarling teeth of the black hound inches from his throat. His hand crept to his knife.

Setanta, killer of hounds, lay at the mercy of the dog trained to replace him. He did not move for fear of the glistening teeth of the canine brute.

"Down, hound, down." The commanding voice of Katbad the Druid brought the hound to kneel at his heels. Setanta released his grip on his knife and scrambled to his feet.

"I see you've met your match, Setanta. Do you think he can take your place for Cullen?" asked Katbad.

"He's more of a hound than any I've met, including the one I've killed. King Connor told me that I'll meet Ferdia at a fair." Setanta knelt and looked in the hound's eyes. Neither blinked or moved.

"Yes. Setanta and Ferdia—the meeting of the bright warriors. Let us hope for friendship for life."

The hound blinked, rolled over, and offered his genitals to Setanta. The young hero kissed the hound three times on the neck and whispered in his ear. Now they were bound for life, the hero and the hound.

Fifteen

FROM THEN ON, Setanta prepared for his adventures. After the fair, his release as the Hound of Cullen arrived. To protect the hound from any deprivations, Katbad kept his Druid's eyes close on the animal, and his door closed to strangers.

Nine months to the night King Connor coupled with Macra, the fair for Setanta began. Briar MacMalice arrived at Crunniac's house with an invitation to him and Macra from King Connor. Macra refused to meet with Briar, lying in the locked bedroom. Heavy with twins, she did not need his prying eyes or caustic tongue. After Briar's departure, she summoned Crunniac to her bed and birth chamber.

"Crunniac, look and listen to me. If you insist on going to the fair for Setanta, you must promise me that you will not mention my name there or the fact that I am pregnant. If you do, you will suffer consequences beyond your comprehension," Macra charged Crunniac.

"Of course, Macra. Whatever you say, Macra. Your command is my wish from now on, Macra." For Crunniac, words had no connections with deeds.

King Connor let it be known that the focus of the great fair for Setanta would center on the racing of horses and chariots. This sport of kings introduced into the Celtic World by Setanta's father, Lugh of the Long Hand, became the passion of the province of Ulster. People wagered on their favorite animals, the men on the horses, the women on the chariot drivers.

To prepare for the fair, Setanta trained his horses on the broad meadows near the house of King Connor. The black horse held the edge in speed. The white horse favored endurance over the distance. The racecourse used by King Connor was a natural oval bounded by oak trees. Here, Connor planted his royal tent beneath the shade of an ancient oak.

Setanta lined up his two horses under the largest branch of the old oak. King Connor's throwing a spear at the old oak began the race. Those who started before the spear struck the tree were eliminated. Setanta flung his spear at the old oak, then ran and leaped onto the back of his black horse before it hit the tree. Dub the black horse ran at a blistering pace that set the grass aflame. The white horse stayed behind, choking on the smoke from the smoldering grass. Filled with the thrill of the race to come, Setanta threw back his head and laughed. What he saw behind him stopped his laughter. A lithe young man of superb form and feature rode his white horse two lengths behind the black horse. By the time they were in the home stretch, they were neck to neck, nose to nose, a black and white blur of man and beast. Setanta transferred a wild burst of energy from his thighs to his black mount. They drew ahead. Demonic with delight, Setanta flashed his squinter's grin at the rider of the white horse.

He noted a gleam of light in his green eyes, a long spear in a muscular arm. The arm flung the spear toward Setanta. It nicked the ear of Setanta's black steed and embedded itself in the shaft end of the spear struck in the old oak tree. In pain and shock, the black horse pulled back its neck. Nose to nose, the two horses flashed by the quivering spears in the old oak tree.

Neither had won nor lost the race. They rode on. Setanta pointed ahead with his short spear, indicating another lap of the racecourse. The green-eyed rider in the short tunic of forest green nodded ascent.

Once more around the oval track, neither gave way. Flying down the home stretch, Setanta sensed a slight decrease in the speed of his black horse. The edge went to the white horse. He drew ahead, approaching the finish line of two joined spears protruding from the old oak tree. Setanta flung his short spear. It curved in front of the white horse and stuck into the shaft end of the co-joined spears. The three connected spears swung back and rebounded to whack the white horse on the forehead. Startled, the white horse broke stride. Once more, both horses passed the finish line in a dead heat. Both riders took a swift account of each other. Who could throw a spear with such assurance? Who could ride a horse with such skill? From Setanta's point of view, who was the green-eyed man who mocked him with a wink and a wave of his arm as he leaped from the back of the white horse and vanished into the forest?

The whole of Ulster gathered to celebrate the emancipation of Setanta from his years as the hound of Cullen the Smith. Setanta's courage and cunning had struck a kinship among the men. His good looks and his warping superpowers excited the women. All this and a fair of food, drink, and horse racing, too.

For Setanta, it provided a moment to implant an image of his prowess and appearance among the people of Ulster. To this end, he groomed both his horses. He trimmed their tails,

curled their forelocks, brushed their coats. For his showing at
the fair, he fastened his blue tunic about his muscular shoulders with a carved clasp of gold from the forge of Cullen the
Smith. Black as midnight were his straight eyebrows. The center of his grey-green eyes a challenge. His mouth, an invitation and a mockery. His brow a meditation on all he surveyed.
Wise in judgment, skilled as a warrior. First in feats of fortitude, a protection against predators. Setanta moved through
the fair to secure his position as an immortal at the Court of
the Red Branch.

The racing of horses came after the chariot events. In
between, before and after, came the feasting and drinking.
Crunniac arrived early, dressed in his best, under the watchful
eyes of Macra. She repeated her warning not to mention her
name at the fair. Another watchful eye noted Crunniac's arrival.
Briar MacMalice licked his tight lips. He passed through the
fair to clap Crunniac on his shoulders.

"Luck of the Irish to you, old friend. Welcome to you from
King Connor. He's sent you a welcome cup." Briar passed a
goblet of ruddy ale to the delighted Crunniac.

Those about him gazed at him with wonder and respect.
A welcome drink from King Connor himself. Surely, Crunniac
was a man of consequence. Maybe he'd tip them a winner at
the races if they listened close enough, and listen they did.

"And how is your fine mare at home?" asked Briar.

"O, Macra never fared better," boasted Crunniac.

"Is she as fast as ever?" Briar asked in a loud voice.

"Nothing on land or water could match her speed,"
Crunniac bragged.

While waiting for the start of the chariot races, Briar
brought Crunniac another foaming ale in an enormous

king-sized goblet. Soon, Crunniac turned foolish and flustered in the excitement of the ale and the chariots charging past. As expected, King Connor's chariots won the day. This sat well with the crowd, who loved their king, especially at a fair.

"Have you ever seen anything faster than the king's horses?" yelled Briar so more people could hear him.

"Yes, I have; Macra skimming across the waves could outrun King Connor's horses," boasted Crunniac in a loud tone.

When the people around Crunniac heard this, they became restive and murmured against him. Crunniac took this as a sound of approbation. Briar fanned the flames.

"You mean you know a mare that can outrun the king's horses?" Briar exclaimed.

"My Macra can outrun the wind—not even King Connor's horses could catch her," roared Crunniac, fueled by ale and befuddlement.

"Inform the king of this blasphemy," Briar said out of the side of his mouth, to those closest to Crunniac. Random crowds are as rowdy and raw as the weather. Six stalwart informers rushed to inform King Connor of the traitor at the fair.

King Connor heard a commotion at the edge of his compound. Three stalwart heroes stood to arms, there to protect the king. King Connor was talking to Setanta, who had just arrived with his two brave steeds.

"Welcome to your fair day, nephew. Today you'll be a hero of the Red Branch," said King Connor.

"Where is Ferdia, King Connor?" asked Setanta.

"He says he lacks a horse to race against you and will meet you another day, Setanta," said Connor.

"If that be the case, Ferdia can borrow my white horse for the race."

The black whelp at King Connor's heels started barking as the commotion outside the compound increased. A brawny hero approached the king with an angry informer in tow. King Connor bade them welcome. The whelp hound kept barking so Connor did not hear all he was told. Willful or happenstance, this is the way of kings.

"A man is at the fair who boasts of—"

Arf, arf, arf, barked the whelp. "—who can outrun the king's horses," said the hero. The informer nodded assent.

"Well, if it's a challenge, let it stand. Tell him to fetch his animal today and we'll have a fair race after the horse races," said King Connor.

Those who heard the king applauded. The three heroes escorted the informers back to Crunniac's side. Two heroes grabbed Crunniac by the shoulders. He stopped his prating and started praying. Briar smirked at his discomfort. Old God was watching out for his own.

"Go get your mare. The king's horses will meet you in a fair field open to all comers. I will escort you home and back again," said the tallest hero with the sharpest weapons.

"I can't ask Macra to race; she is about to give birth," cried Crunniac, suddenly aware of his stupidity.

"If Macra does not accept your challenge to race against all the king's horses, then all the king's men will dismember you both for blasphemy," said Briar, to the applause of those around him.

The three heroes escorted the craven Crunniac to his abode. Meanwhile, back at the racetrack, Setanta led the parade of horses and riders around the course. The hound of Cullen was the man of the day. Roars of applause from the men crowding the track. Screams of acclaim from the women sitting on the shoulders of the men to catch a glimpse of the legendary Setanta the Warped One, defender of the border, protector against predators, fearless in feats of arms, vigorous and impetuous, irresistible and exciting, honorable and extraordinary.

The steady beat of the bodhrán and the plaintive strains of harpers' strings set the pace for Setanta and the riders behind him. Such a bright summer day for a fair. The wind from the north. The smell of roasting ox and spitted pigs for the noonday feast. Lilies from the valley. Wild Irish roses. Wild blackberries. Wild Irish men, crushed close to wicked and wanton women. All aroused, flushed faces, erect nipples, pagan pleasures.

Setanta soaked up the adulation of the assembled multitudes. A low roar like the ocean before a storm turned his attention. Behind him onto the racecourse rode a solitary horseman on a white horse. The horse belonged to Setanta and was named Ban. The rider belonged to the people and was named Ferdia. A great cheer arose to welcome home Ferdia, the boy hero fostered at the Red Branch of King Connor MacNessa.

Ferdia rode and looked like a hero. He took his steed alongside Setanta at the head of the column of riders. Setanta squinted at Ferdia. The last time they met was on a wild race around this course. Then Ferdia wore a flimsy girdle of gold silk next to his skin, and over that, supple black bull's hide as his battle harness. On his fair head, Ferdia had a gold battle helmet, decorated with precious stones from the East, a gift from a female admirer.

Setanta surged with an energy emanating from the blush on Ferdia's cheeks and the sparkle in his clear green eyes. Heroes love their reflection in others. With these two, the rest could leave the fields of love or battle. Setanta and Ferdia, the equal of all before and after. Ferdia mocked Setanta the Squinter, winking at him with his left eye, tilting his head to the side. He did this so well that Setanta's initial anger turned to laughter. Setanta whistled. Ban the white horse reared high, feet flailing. A shocked Ferdia held tight to the curled mane of his steed, hunched forward, battle helmet askew. Setanta mocked Ferdia, hunching forward in the same awkward manner as Ferdia had. He did this so well that Ferdia laughed. Something male, elemental, and eternal passed between them, a gift of joy in the discovery that each was as capable of laughter as of slaughter.

After the parade of the riders, the feast of the fair began, followed by the race of heroes. In the wagering for the winner, the men favored Ferdia because of his age and height. The women favored Setanta because he was Setanta the Warped One. Excitement inflamed the people of Ulster. Spectators are as immortal as heroes. Both bear witness and transfer memories, the stuff of legends.

By this time of day, Macra arrived, covered in a red clock, with a chastened Crunniac and her escorts. The redheaded, very pregnant Macra sat apart and aloof. She had refused to come at first because of her condition, wishing to be home to give birth to her twins. Only when the escorts threatened to kill Crunniac in front of her had she consented to come. Immediately after the horse race, the king's chariot would race against all challengers. The only challenger to King Connor's matched grey horses moaned of her pangs as her time approached.

As Setanta and Ferdia broke bread together at the feast, they circled each other, probing for weakness. For all they had in common, they were aware that the uncommon had as much consequence in victory as skill and strength. The riders and horses lined up opposite King Connor. In front of the old oak tree, King Connor stood in his racing chariot. At full attention, he lifted high his long, black spear. Ferdia tipped the wink of Setanta's squint to him. The spear flew straight and true across the snorting nostrils of the racehorses and struck deep in the oak tree.

They're off! Old God flew low on his scudding white cloud to follow the horses. From the start, Setanta and Ferdia drew ahead of the pack in a two-horse race. Around the oval track they thundered, inches apart. Ban and Dub galloped together. Setanta and Ferdia crouched low on their steeds, pumping power into their mounts, a study in concentration. So fast and spectacular a race silenced the crowd. Into the home stretch fast they flew, presenting an outline of a black horse to those on one side of the course; a white horse to those on the other side.

So they flashed past the long spear. A dead heat at the finish, and still they kept on going, not slowing, no quarter given, none taken. A race to a finish known only to Old God above and the devil below. Ferdia rode into the woods. Setanta stayed alongside him. Quickly, they disappeared from view. The crowd grew restive. The race of the year. No sign of the heroes. They threw sticks and stones at the other horses and riders. Sensing the onset of a riot, King Connor had his charioteer drive his matched greys onto the racecourse. This stilled the restive crowd for a brief time.

"Who challenges the horses and chariot of King Connor in a race open to all comers?" yelled the wily Briar MacMalice. This focused attention on the chariot. Again, the rowdy and rambunctious crowd grew surly.

Briar flung a small clod of grass in an underarm throw toward the king's chariot. This initiated a burst of flying sods across the course from the gurriers in the crowd. The horses skittered under the assault. This had never happened to King Connor before. Briar pushed the shaking Crunniac onto the course in front of the king.

"This man boasted all day that his wife could outrun the king's horses. Let him answer to the king," yelled Briar.

"Bring forward the wife."

"Kill the husband."

"Let the bitch run for her life."

"Do not fool us twice."

"There's a winner in every race."

"Run the woman."

"Whip the man."

Thus roared the crowd, edgy and excited with pagan excess.

The red-headed woman in the red cloak came forward. Pushed by the king's men, Macra stood by Crunniac.

"Your husband has boasted of your speed. Now, either he or you will race my horses. If you lose, you die."

Macra looked at her husband. He fell to his knees and sobbed before all. Briar led the boos from the crowd. A sorry spectacle for a fair day crowd to see.

"Can you save me now, husband?" Macra asked. Crunniac hung his head in shame. Macra faced the crowd.

"Do not take advantage of my condition," she pleaded. Macra discarded her cloak and stood swollen with twins, about to give birth.

"Has not a woman borne each of you? Wait till I give birth. When I'm well, I will race whomever you want me to." Macra bent double with her birth pangs. The crowd had lost its sense of mercy. None spoke for Macra. Another victim of the mischief of Old God.

"Shame, shame, shame on you and your children's children to the ninth generation," shouted Macra.

King Connor could abide this no longer. He turned his back and retreated to his tent.

"You know my name and you know my unborn twins, Connor. My name is Macra. Remember it well in this hour of infamy," she called after the king.

Briar ran across the course and took the king's place. He pointed toward the woman and the chariot with his spear, as if asking an opinion on whether to start this terrible race. This released a desire for a dastardly deed among the spectators. Briar aimed his spear and flung it at the old oak tree.

Setanta and Ferdia raced through the thick forest. First one, then the other surged ahead. Ferdia set the pace, hell bent for the glory of his name as the first hero of the Red Branch. Setanta rode to prove his arrival as a warrior and for his release from the bounds of Cullen the Smith. The faster and wilder the ride, the closer they came as kin and companions. To know there is another in the world as oneself is rare among men and never among heroes, except when young and unwise in the ways of the world. These two raced on, mocking and laughing, and becoming men in a forest deep with the shadows of Old God's deeds. Out of the forest they raced, across broad meadows and sparkling streams. Across the all-embracing earth of Ulster.

Briar's spear struck the oak tree. The king's chariot charged forward and the pregnant Macra fumbled after it, her long red hair curling over her shoulders. The unruly mob laughed at Macra and her shaking stick of a husband. It was good enough for both of them, a braggart and his bitch. Most had wagered on the king's grey horses to win the race. A few were ashamed for Macra's condition. After all, she had brought it on herself. Why would a beautiful woman, a red-haired one, marry such a sparrow fart as her husband? Macra inhaled deeply and began her race after the king's chariot. The jeers of the mob ceased. Macra ran faster than any human they had seen, like an ocean wind across the cliffs on a storm-tossed day. The sky darkened as Old God's cloud followed her, blotting out the rays of the sun. Halfway around the track Macra drew level with the matched greys. Looking neither left nor right, she ran straight and true alongside the sweating steeds.

Setanta had the time of his young life, galloping wild and free alongside Ferdia. His mind clear, his body strong, his heart beating with a strange excitement. Along the banks of a swift stream toward a waterfall they charged. Who would prevail?

Ferdia rolled off his horse at the waterfall. Cooled by its radiant spray, he shook his left fist at Setanta.

The left fist is the challenge among the boys of consequence at the Red Branch to a wrestling match. Whether one by one or altogether, Setanta had never lost in wrestling to the boys of Ulster. He turned his horse toward the waterfall, standing tall on its back. Balanced and beautiful, horse and rider approached Ferdia, the challenger.

Setanta came level with Ferdia. He leaped from the back of his horse over the head of his challenger. Twisting in the air, he landed behind Ferdia. Swift, sure, fast, and furious, Setanta removed the supple black bullhide of battle harness from Ferdia and flung him to the ground. The gold battle helmet of Ferdia rolled toward the roaring waters of the waterfall. Another leap from Setanta over the prone Ferdia brought him to the banks of the stream. He scooped up the helmet and stuck it on his head at a rakish angle. Setanta raised both hands in a challenge to Ferdia. He sauntered toward Ferdia, covered with spray. A two-fisted gesture meant a challenge to an advanced form of wrestling known as strip and go naked, a favored sport among the boys of consequence. When they played the stripping game of wrestling, Setanta stripped all stark naked, without pulling as much as a broach from his cloak.

Heading toward the home stretch, Macra drew ahead of the king's chariot. Onwards she flew with no concern for king or company. A woman from the other side with powers beyond the human. Macra raced past the finish spear in the old oak tree. She had won the race and saved her husband's life. A grave silence greeted her. None could take their eyes off the pregnant Macra, clutching her swollen self in anguish.

Slipping behind Ferdia, Setanta clutched his opponent around the waist and neck. Quickly, he squeezed Ferdia's vital parts. Ferdia lost consciousness and hung in Setanta's strong arms. With a flourish, Setanta stripped the flimsy silk girdle covering Ferdia. The dizzy Ferdia spun toward the waterfall. Setanta caught Ferdia's wrist. He pulled the naked Ferdia to the safety of his arms, and held him erect.

Ferdia had proved no match for Setanta in the strip and go naked wrestling game. The best Ferdia did was to tear the broach from Setanta's blue cloak. Ferdia recovered his breath and wits, pretending to sag as if too weak to stand, clutching Setanta's cloak for support. Setanta lowered the limp Ferdia to the damp grass. When his back touched the ground, the wily Ferdia drew his knees up. He kicked Setanta's body from him. Setanta flew backwards, tripping over a rock.

Ferdia leaped to his feet, still clutching Setanta's blue tunic. Except for his calves and feet encased in straps of blood-red bullhide, Setanta lay as naked as Ferdia. Swirling the blue tunic above him, Ferdia approached the stunned Setanta. The spray from the waterfall revived Setanta. He whistled. His black horse charged forward, butting Ferdia in the back. Ferdia slammed into the rising Setanta. The blue tunic spun high and fell to cover both. Wrapped together, they struggled at the edge of the waterfall. A shriek of agony split the earth beneath their feet. They fell sideways under the thundering waterfall. Deep they plunged into the churning waters. The shriek grew louder.

The pregnant Macra let a screech of agony out of her that shook the earth and all in her vicinity. Collapsing to the ground, her pangs visible to all. Macra gave birth to twins, a boy and a girl. Again, she shrieked, so shrill that none dared lift a finger to help her. Finally, Macra stood, a bloody babe in each arm. The women sank to their knees. The men hung their heads in shame. Now all knew that Macra was no braggart's wife, but a goddess from the other side.

Macra spoke in a voice that rolled across the province of Ulster and stopped at its borders.

"Bad cess to you and your sons, men of Ulster. Listen close to me. My curse on each and every one of you for your arrogance toward a woman in childbirth. From this day forth and for the next nine generations, I call down this curse on you. Heed me well, Ulstermen."

None who heard Macra forgot her. The north wind still carries her words. The rain still sheds her tears. Neither forgives nor forgets the pangs of Ulster.

"In your time of greatest need, you will be afflicted as a woman in labor, alone, weak and wan, with none to help or heed. You will remain in this state for five days and four nights," so spoke Macra.

As it was said, so was it done. The men of Ulster lay weeping in place, weak as a babe against the curse of Macra, unable to move. Only the young boys of Ulster escaped Macra's curse. Only Setanta and Ferdia, deep in struggle under the waterfall where Macra's words could not be heard, were exempt from the curse of the pangs of Ulster. Macra gathered her babes to her breasts and departed.

Setanta and Ferdia rose together from the lake's deep waters. Wrapped together in Setanta's blue cloak. They breathed deep of Ulster's fresh air. They separated and swam for the shore. Setanta pulled his blue cloak behind him. All seemed as they had left it. Clothes strewn by the stream's bank. The two horses running forward to welcome them. The afternoon sun dried their tough young bodies.

And yet, both had a sense of something amiss. An anticipation of events beyond their experience. It was exciting, upsetting, and called for energies between Setanta and Ferdia. They were becoming brothers in arms, ready to die for each other. From then on, until death did them apart, when Setanta and Ferdia raised two hands to wrestle each other, the night belonged to them. Later, by moonlight, they ate magic mushrooms and bound with all around them. Coddled and cuddled between the two horses, Setanta and Ferdia spent their first night together.

Sixteen

FOR TWO DAYS and nights, they stayed together, like a young Cain and Abel, in a world empty of people. Then Setanta had a dream. A vision in his mind's eye. Katbad the Druid appeared to be standing over King Connor's bed, waving his staff. King Connor lay pale and petulant, racked with pain that came like waves from the ocean.

At sunrise, Setanta and Ferdia mounted the horses and rode back to the Red Branch. Side by side, they rode. Neither spoke. Both looked long and hard at each other. One was hail. The other rain. One was flame. The other fire. One was wind. The other thunder. Both were from the other side. Fearless forever. Ever at ease, but changed. From then on, until one killed the other, when Setanta and Ferdia raised their hands in a wrestling challenge, the night belonged to them.

There came a stillness when they neared the Red Branch home of King Connor of Ulster. Even Ban and Dub seemed subdued. The fields of play were empty of boys wielding hurleys or spears. No smoke arose from the great kitchens. No odor of roasting pigs or ox for the evening meal. No women picking flowers or vegetables in the fields of farmers. No wild harps tuned for the night's feast. Close to the Red Branch, small groups of women huddled together. Some were dressed as warriors with shields and spears and male accoutrements. These swaggered in place, clung to by women loose in dress and gesture. These Amazon women seemed attracted to Ferdia, as if seeing him for the first time.

There came a sound from inside the Red Branch House of King Connor of Ulster. The sound of the men of Ulster being assailed by the birth pangs from the curse of Macra.

They dismounted at King Connor's house. Setanta pushed open the massive red door. The house held one hundred and fifty rooms paneled with red yew wood. The male occupants in the rooms our heroes passed through were horizontal, stretched prone on their cloaks, disarmed and disheveled. They tossed and turned with the piercing pangs of childbirth, moaning and groaning under Macra's curse for five days and four nights. Setanta and Ferdia recognized many of the Red Branch warriors at their feet. Fergus of the Long Sword. Ibor the Charioteer. Conall Carney. Cullen the Smith. Briar MacMalice the Satirist, drooling out of one side of his face and slobbering out of the other.

King Connor's room lay at the center of the house. Overhead were screens of copper between bars of gold. On the floor lay King Connor, grasping his stomach in agony. Standing over him was Katbad the Druid, staff in hand and concern on his face. Katbad knelt over the king, feeding him herbs and potions. Setanta looked at Ferdia, listening to the low moaning of the afflicted men. Katbad arose and gestured for the two heroes to follow him. He led them to the great kitchen in the back of the house. Here his son Genann of the

Brow of Light supervised bored women stirring pots of pale gruel. The sounds of the suffering men diminished as they stepped outside through a kitchen door.

Finally, Katbad spoke to them. "I believe we four are the only men in Ulster not afflicted with Macra's curse. Since the men collapsed, the women here have lost the run of themselves. Show them there are still warriors on their feet."

Katbad looked at Ferdia.

"Ferdia, you have trained with Amazon women in Alba. Tonight, you stay with the budding Amazons here in the courtyard."

Ferdia nodded his assent.

"Setanta, tonight you stay in the House of the Twinkling Horde. Guard the weapons there, and try not to kill anyone."

When Setanta heard this, he knew that women were stealing weapons from the collection at the Twinkling Hoard.

"And what happens tomorrow?" asked Ferdia.

"Tomorrow, we will divide Ulster into two. Setanta will protect the east and Ferdia will protect the west. Tonight, show authority and strength."

* * * * * *

Setanta and Ferdia knew that their brief flourish of freedom was at an end. Outside King Connor's Red Branch House, they hugged farewell. Ferdia made for the courtyard, as far away from the moaning Ulstermen as he could get. Here he made his sleeping site for the night. The two horses lay down, offering him comfort and warmth between them. As was his custom, Ferdia stripped naked. Holding his spear in his left hand and his sword in his right, he lay flat on his back. Soon he attracted the strongest and boldest of the budding Amazon women in warrior garb. Softly the women beat on their shields and sighed his name into the night. Ferdia. Ferdia. Ferdia.

Ferdia cancelled an image of Setanta from his core. He flexed his muscles for the singing women. If he did not perform well, he faced death and disembowelment. Neither appealed to Ferdia, especially after his sojourn with Setanta.

* * * * * *

Setanta walked with authority and strength toward the House of the Twinkling Hoard. Some of the women he knew left the Amazons in battle garb to follow him. He paid them scant heed until he pushed open the door of the Twinkling Hoard, and then turned to face them. Many of the women had handed the naked seven-year-old Setanta from one to the other the day they immersed him in vats of cold water to reduce his ardor. These women smiled at Setanta. When one touches a god from the Other Side, the moment is forever. Setanta had images of one hundred and fifty naked women in his mind's eye, women who had watched Setanta grow into the most beautiful man in Ireland. In all his warrior's glory, smiling at the women, Setanta closed the door.

The acclaimed weapons of the Red Branch heroes were kept inside this house. Setanta walked through the rooms, touching the javelins, shields, swords, and spears. The "Twinkling Hoard" referred to the gold glittering on the sword hilts and shield rims, the silver outline on favored javelins and tall spears. Setanta had a vivid memory of begging King Connor for weapons and a chariot in this very room. Then he was a boy of seven, ready for his first adventure and warping into the immortal hero of Katbad's prophecy.

Setanta selected the most fearsome and ferocious of the weapons on display. The famous hacking sword of Fergus, the wounder sword of Laere the Charioteer, the triumphant sword of King Connor's son, Cursa. Nuada's immortal sword of light, the Claive Solus. The sword of deceit and dread of Dubtach. He carried these, and sundry shields, javelins, and spears, to the hallway facing the front door. Here he assembled his borrowed weapons into a half circle of power and protection against the wall. When finished, he leaned against the front door, listening for predators.

Setanta heard a softer sound than the whinging of the men. Plaintive. Seductive. A chorus of love and longing. A women's chorus.

Setanta. Setanta. Setanta.

The song from outside lit a fire that fueled Setanta's manhood. All thoughts of Ferdia left him. He unlocked the door. From his half circle of weapons, he removed the sword of light. This he placed by his bed. There was now room for one—or two—slim women to slip through the space left by the sword of light and join Setanta on his makeshift bed. Here he lay on his back, naked. In his left hand, he held the sword of light. In his right hand, he held his tall spear. The front door opened slowly. Two women entered and relocked the door. They stood silent and stared at Setanta. He lay naked and ready, a god from toe to tip, lit by the glitter of gold and the glimmer of silver, framed by a glow from the sword of light. Tonight he'd learn about women. Tonight, they'd learn about Setanta. "Warriors fight stronger when naked—they enlarge" was a precept Setanta had learned from Ferdia. Love and combat were ever the same to those from the Other Side.

* * * * * *

The morning after his night in the Twinkling Hoard, Setanta found it painful to mount his black horse. The morning after his night in the courtyard with the budding Amazon women, Ferdia found it painful to mount the white horse of Setanta. Katbad the King of the Druids blessed their day ahead with a Druid's prayer and sharp looks. To the low moaning of the stricken Ulstermen, they rode through the courtyard and then separated. Setanta rode east toward the coast, his area to protect from predators. Ferdia rode west to patrol the rest of the province.

As soon as he was out of sight and sound of Ferdia, Setanta dismounted and walked. Ferdia did the same. Both needed a good stretch of their legs to recover from the hectic night before. On and on walked Setanta, thinking of his heroic defense of the king's weapons against the desperate women of Ulster. His body drained of passion, his mind at peace, Setanta lost the last of his growing pains. Wherever he walked, he saw no men. The women called his name, reminding him of his night of love in the House of the Twinkling Hoard. So he walked onwards with authority and strength, avoiding any entanglements. A hazy vision of a wife and child formed in his mind's eye. A boy warrior, a hero of the Red Branch. Only out of himself would the likes of him come again. The black horse Dub nudged him from behind. Setanta turned around. A baker's dozen of young women were following him, singing softly. *Setanta, Setanta, Setanta.*

Swiftly, Setanta remounted and galloped away. From then on, Setanta became the most desired man in Ireland, at a level never seen before or since. As his warping for slaughter terrified his enemies, so did his aura for procreation activate female admirers. Setanta accepted this as his due for the short life promised by Katbad, the King of the Druids. As the day wore on, the worn-out Setanta fell asleep on the broad back of his black horse.

Ferdia had the knowledge of more Amazon women than any man alive in his time on earth did. This was his blessing and his curse. The Amazons had taught him more skills and tricks in close combat than any warrior he had ever met. Except, perhaps, one—Setanta the Warped One. One more year with Scatach the Shadowy One in Alba would equip him to kill any hero in Europe. Scatach the Amazon Queen. In his core, he'd prefer to fight side by side with Setanta against the enemies of Ulster. They were now brothers in arms, signed and sealed that day in the stream. Ferdia knew he'd lay down his life for Setanta. Ferdia would never cease learning the craft of the warrior until he could kill Setanta in single combat. This was the way of it in the time of King Connor of Ulster at the Red Branch. Ferdia had as strong a need for immortality as Setanta.

Tired of walking and thinking, he remounted the white horse. Soon he fell asleep on the broad back of his noble steed.

And so the two horses ambled through Ulster with no direction from their sleeping riders. As always, the two horses returned to each other. Both were bound to Setanta for life, being born at the same time as he. Finally, as the sun set, they met by a pure crystal fountain. Dub and Ban drank deep of the cool water, nuzzling each other. Our heroes slept on.

* * * * * *

King Connor MacNessa, High King of Ulster, awoke from the curse of Macra with an aching head, an agitated interior, and the face of Katbad the Druid inches from his own.

"Is is over, Druid?" King Connor asked.

"It seems you are the first to recover," answered Katbad.

"I could eat a roast pig. I had a dream of a crock of gold as big as a mountain," said Connor to Katbad. Connor appeared as kingly as ever as he looked first to his own concerns, above all others.

"I can arrange your feast. As soon as the cooks awake from the curse," offered Katbad.

"Were we attacked?" asked the king.

"No. I went to see Macra about removing the curse on the first day of it," said the Druid.

"And she agreed?"

"To extend the curse on anyone who killed an Ulsterman suffering from the pangs. One bad cess deserves another. Macra drives a hard bargain; the weight of her twins in gold and herself in silver." The Druid helped the king to his feet.

"What's that noise?" asked the king.

"The cries of Ulstermen in pain from the pangs."

King Connor reached up for his rod of silver with its three golden apples. He shook it three times. This was the king's way of ensuring silence in his kingdom. The wailing and whinging stopped and life resumed its ordained pace in the province of Ulster.

"Anything else of consequence?" asked the king.

"The women have lost the run of themselves."

"That may be an improvement," said the king.

"I speak as a father, Connor. Pay heed to Deirdre. Send her away to Alba for safekeeping. Anything that leads to the fall of the Red Branch may be blamed on her." Katbad looked deep into the king's eyes. Both knew devious sequences could have disastrous consequences.

Note Bene   1011, Anno Domini

Here I repeat that these are old tales of our ancients before the Divine Grace of Christ arrived on this Isle of the Blest. The worship of the bull, the valor of heroes, and the glamour of kings and queens were the concerns and conceits of our ancestors, as relayed in song, verse, and tales since their arrival.

The Geasa is a curse of restriction with dire consequences, even death, if ignored or flaunted.

The word "cess" means a painful curse on a person or their possessions.

It is my privilege to preserve this old history for people of the present, the curious of the future, and the glory of our past.

So be it.

Mael Moró

193

Seventeen

AFTER HIS ORDEAL in the bog hole and recovery from Macra's curse, King Connor rode alone into the night on his speckled grey stallion. Connor had a need for perfection in one form or another. Now was the depth of winter, a white cloak of fresh snow on the land. Tied across the front of Connor's saddle was a weaned calf, fresh meat for Deirdre and her guardian, Biddy Bentbook. The king's saddlebags held flagons of strong drink to sweeten the tongue of old Biddy, and earth vegetables to survive the winter.

King Connor dismounted before his snug, snow-covered house in a hollow at the base of an odd-shaped mountain. The waterfall that fed the stream by the house had frozen into a sheet of translucent ice. Connor lifted the calf from his horse and carried it to the sturdy oak door of his house. Three times the king kicked the door. Old Biddy opened the shutter on a side window. Deirdre, hidden from inquisitive eyes, stood close to the side of the window, peering through a peephole.

They saw the powerful King Connor holding high a bleating calf, stamping his feet in the snow. Deirdre joined Biddy

Bentbook at the window. Deirdre warmed the chill of the king. Deirdre. Deirdre. Deirdre. Divine of form and grace, and on the brink. A king's gift to himself. The most beautiful woman in the world. Entranced and exalted, King Connor put down the calf and slit its throat. Scarlet blood (the color of Deirdre's lips) splashed on the snow. A black raven (the color of Deirdre's eyelashes) swooped to drink the blood. The snow was virgin white (the color of Deirdre's skin). King Connor flayed the calf. Deirdre flayed his heart. Biddy Bentbook prayed for Deirdre. Biddy stayed close to Deirdre, never leaving her alone with King Connor. He called her away from Deirdre's side.

"Is it not time for bed? I want to speak to my foster child," the king said.

Biddy saw more need than nurture in Connor's eyes.

"You are the only man Deirdre has seen. Let her mature for seven more years."

Biddy looked him in the eye. Connor poured a tot for himself and Biddy. Deirdre sat aloof and alone. Deirdre. Deirdre. Deirdre.

"Deirdre is now fourteen. Return in seven years, King Connor. I will prepare Deirdre for the love of her life." Old Biddy Bentbook stared down Connor. Both knew the king would never wait seven years to see Deirdre again. Biddy and Deirdre watched King Connor ride away.

Inside the house of the king, under the watchful eyes of old Biddy Bentbook, Deirdre grew up. True to her promise to King Connor, Biddy kept Deirdre from the company of men. Biddy devoted her life to Deirdre. When she was seven, Deirdre saw her first man, a king of Ulster. An imposing presence for any but Deirdre. When she was seven, King Connor sat Deirdre on his knee and marveled at her potential. Perfection is an announcement not to be ignored. Connor knew he'd accrue command of Deirdre when his time was due. Deirdre paid small attention to King Connor. This aroused an alarm in Biddy. If the king lost interest in Deirdre and removed his protection, what then for the most beautiful child in the four provinces of Ireland? Katbad's prophecy was legend. Deirdre's love will last forever. Deirdre's love will kill thousands. Deirdre's love will destroy the court of the Red Branch.

Biddy Bentbook was an old satirist whose words could flay the calves of those she addressed. She grew old in comfort due to the high regard King Connor held for bard and poets. But she loved Deirdre more than herself. Hidden in her kitchen, Biddy kept a poisonous mushroom for herself and Deirdre. She knew when Connor rode off into the snow that she had until his return to decide the destiny of Deirdre.

After the departure of the king, the bond between Deirdre and Biddy Bentbook changed. No longer child and guardian, but two women under one roof. One old. One young. Deirdre had not a drop of feeling for King Connor, but she did have a curiosity to the ways of a man with a maid. In the evenings, Deirdre poured tots of whiskey for Biddy. They sat together before a crackling oak fire. Biddy's face grew redder and her love for Deirdre stronger. Silently, they'd stare into each other's eyes. Deirdre absorbed the gift of second sight from old Biddy's eyes. Knowledge beyond words about times yet to come. The reflection of the flames in Biddy's eyes cast visions for Deirdre. A young, godlike man in Biddy's right eye. Deirdre's form in Biddy's left eye. Then impressions strange and startling assailed Deirdre from Biddy's fierce old eyes.

Love. Love. Love.

Eternal love. Loyalty. Exotic Adventures. Friendships. Honor betrayed. Bloody days. Black nights. Epic slaughter. The fall of a kingdom.

Death. Death. Death.

* * * * * *

On a bright spring morning, Deirdre milked her cow in a meadow behind the house. Deirdre heard a voice. A song that came to her across the hills and down the mountainside. A song to haunt all who heard it. Deirdre closed her eyes and saw the singer of the song in her second sight. A young man, hair as black as a raven, skin as white as the snow. Lips as red as blood. A voice from above that raised all below.

Deirdre carried the cow's milk into the house. Red Biddy Bentbook relished a flagon of fresh milk upon waking. This morning, the milk had three times the usual cream. The songs of the birds were three times sweeter. Deirdre hummed softly the song that changed her life as it ended.

"Did you dream well, Deirdre?" asked the sly Biddy.

"Yes. My clearest dream ever. It came with a song from a man I'd marry upon sight," said Deirdre.

"Did he resemble a king?" asked Biddy.

"No. More like a god. Hair black as a raven, skin white as snow. Lips red as blood. Do you know such a man?" Deirdre looked deep into Biddy's eyes.

"Tell me the name of my true love," Deirdre said.

"Naóise, the son of Usnach. The sweetest songbird in Ulster," Biddy blurted out.

"Where will I meet my true love?" demanded Deirdre.

"At the mists of the waterfall. Naóise brings his father's sheep for food and water. When he sings, the sheep fatten in contentment."

"When will I meet my true love, Naóise?"

"Never. Never. Never! You are bound to King Connor."
Biddy twisted free from Deirdre's grasp.

Later that day, Deirdre took herself to the waterfall in
search of her true love. For three times seven days, Deirdre
made her pilgrimage to the waterfall. Rain or shine, in sunshine or in shadow, Deirdre arrived early and left late. At
noon each day, she'd strip naked behind an oak tree close to
the waterfall. Then Deirdre would walk under the misty spray
to cool her ardor and focus her mind on the vague figure of
Naóise the Singer. In the midst of the misty waters, she'd
sense Naóise behind her, touching her. Loving her always.
They were as Adam and Eve. Made from and for each other,
in legend and lore.

Deirdre awoke one morning to the song of Naóise in her
ears and heart. The milk for Biddy gushed and frothed from her
warm hands on the cow's teats. When Biddy saw the excited
girl and heard Naóise's song on the wind, she knew today
would change their lives forever.

* * * * * *

King Connor MacNessa awoke the same day from a dream
of a crock of gold as big as a mountain. He had a burning desire
to see the beautiful Deirdre again. Alone, he rode his speckled grey stallion toward the house of Biddy Bentbook and the
most beautiful woman in the world.

Deirdre. Deirdre. Deirdre.

Giving in to her ward, Biddy combed the long, golden
hair of Deirdre until it hung like a silk sheath on her body.
She helped Deirdre into a tunic of the whitest flax. On top of
this, a filigree of linen as delicate as a spider's web caressed

the breasts of the divine Deirdre. Even Deirdre's cow mooed in admiration as the maid set out to meet the love of her life.

Naóise, the son of Usnach, stood as handsome a man as any in Ireland. Tall, well boned, and virile, he enjoyed the gift of song to bring contentment wherever he went. A magnificent warrior, he had fostered with his brothers Aidan and Arden as heroes in the Red Branch of his uncle, King Connor MacNessa. When Naóise and his brothers formed a triangle of spears and shields, they could hold at bay the entire province of Ulster. When they sang together, women warmed amorous, men grew ardent, and animals peaceful. In this land of bards and poets, they were unique in valor, strength, and grace.

Deirdre felt the shamrock growing beneath her feet as she walked toward the waterfall. As usual, she stopped by the oak tree, where she'd disrobe each day. Here she saw a warrior's sword, shield, and spear standing guard over a neat heap of rich garments. Magnified by the rushing waters, the song of Naóise captured Deirdre's heart. Aroused and enchanted, Deirdre walked on shamrocks toward the singer.

Naked in the spray of the waterfall, Naóise sang for her heart's content. Deirdre's eyes devoured the first naked man she'd seen. Raven black hair. Snow-white skin. Blood-red lips. A god's body from the Other Side, strong and sure. Then and forever, there was never another for Deirdre, in thought, word, or deed.

Naóise closed his eyes to finish his song on a high note. When he opened his eyes again, he saw the most beautiful woman in the world walking toward him. She slowed as she passed him, burning his being with her grey-green eyes.

"Fine and fair is the heifer passing this way," was the best that Naóise could think to say.

"Heifers are inclined to elegance when there's a lack of bulls." Deirdre stopped to look at Naóise.

"The king of Ulster is the bull of this province," said Naóise. He knew who Deirdre was.

"I will choose between the two of you. And I will pick a young bull such as yourself." Deirdre closed in on the excited Naóise.

"Hold on, woman. What of Katbad's prophecy?" said Naóise.

"Do you reject me, then?" asked Deirdre, her eyes unblinking on the naked Naóise.

"Indeed, I do, for the best outcome of Ulster," said Naóise.

Hearing this, Deirdre stepped close to him and took him by his ears.

"These are two ears of shame and mockery, unless you take me with you." Deirdre pulled Naóise to her and kissed him all over his face. Surprised, the warrior tripped backwards. Both Naóise and Deirdre fell into the stream. Deirdre embraced Naóise. He held her in his strong young arms. Deirdre's golden hair floated behind her on the bubbling waters.

And O—Deirdre's love blush and the golden glory of her hair delighted the hot rays of the midday sun that set fire to her surroundings. The sun reflected the love from Deirdre to Naóise onto the streams, falling from the spire of the mountain.

And so sheets of molten matter formed a crown of gold atop and down the mountain. A crock of gold as big as the mountain celebrated the embrace of Deirdre and Naóise in the waters below.

* * * * * *

King Connor MacNessa rode hard until he reached a fertile valley near the neat house of Red Biddy Bentbook. Here he dismounted and rested his horse. While the horse nibbled the grass, the king climbed a small hill to survey his house at the foot of a mountain.

There, in front of him, appeared the crock of gold as big as a mountain.

The mountain he'd loved had utterly changed. The noon sun burned the mountaintop into a massive crock of gold, glinting on its melting snow. To King Connor, the cascading waters down the mountainside turned into veins of molten gold. An apparition from his dark night of corruption and death in the bog hole was in front of him. Wealth beyond reason. And Deirdre, the most beautiful woman in the world, lay waiting for him in his trim house at the base of his crock of gold as big as a mountain. A king's share of the world. Full of awe and swagger, Connor remounted his horse and rode toward his heart's desire.

* * * * * *

On matched black stallions, the two brothers of Naóise herded their father's sheep toward the meadows at the base of the golden mountain. Aidan the Dark had jet-black hair, dark eyes, and a hero's form. Arden the Red had red hair, blue eyes, and the strongest arms in Ulster. Four black and white sheep-dogs helped them herd the fat sheet of their father in pursuit of their brother, Naóise.

Aidan and Arden were curious for a glimpse of the fabled Deirdre. They presumed that Naóise preceded them on the same pilgrimage. The deep braying of Bran, their wolfhound, alerted Aidan on the flank of the sheep herd. Waiving to Arden, he rode toward the barking wolfhound. Aidan dismounted and hushed the excited Bran, who was the favored hound of his brother, Naóise. The love song of Naóise replaced the barking of the hound. Now Aidan knew that Naóise was singing of the beauty of Deirdre. His heart swelled with love for his brothers and the adventures they had shared together.

* * * * * *

King Connor awoke old Biddy Bentbook with three loud thumps from his sword on her front door. Deirdre. Deirdre. Deirdre.

Biddy opened the door slowly and looked up at the king on his horse. Strong and triumphant. It was how he wanted to appear to Deirdre, his ward and reward.

"Where is Deirdre?" Connor demanded.

"She is gone. Gathering mushrooms," lied old Biddy.

"Then I'll have no trouble finding her. The magic mushrooms grow best by the waterfall. We'll have them for a snack before we leave for the Red Branch," said King Connor.

A wolfhound barked in the distance. When it stopped, the song of Naóise enhanced the day.

"Who is that singing?" asked King Connor.

"Some stray shepherd who's lost his way," said Biddy.

"And found Deirdre! Bring me my spear, old woman." No singing shepherd would ruin this day for the king. Biddy stepped back into the house. Swiftly, she slammed and locked the door. Three times the angry king slammed on the door with his sword. Deirdre. Deirdre. Deirdre.

Inside, old Biddy leaned against the door. Opposite her hung the king's spear and shield. Awaiting his pleasure or anger, she closed her old eyes, thinking of Deirdre. Perhaps it was time for the poisoned mushrooms. For herself for betraying her king and protector. For Deirdre, to save the kingdom and stop the death of thousands. Sighing, she opened her eyes. King Connor stood in front of her, reaching for his spear and shield. A king's coming and going has more doors than conceived by his subjects. It's the first lesson of royalty.

Aidan was the first to see King Connor riding toward the waterfall. He recognized the king on his speckled grey stallion. Delighted, he prepared to sing out a song to welcome Connor. The king's horse reared high as he pulled it to a savage stop. Then Aidan's young eyes focused on what the king saw under the waterfall. In a golden stream, his brother Naóise embraced the beautiful Deirdre. Both were naked. The two had become one.

Aidan whistled a warning to his brother Arden. He drew his sword and pointed it toward Naóise and Deirdre. Together they whistled a warning for Naóise. He returned from the golden glow of Deirdre's embrace to see his brothers stampede their herd of sheep toward the waterfall. Riding full tilt, they charged into the herd in an effort to slow King Connor's wild gallop toward the lovers.

Naóise released Deirdre and swam for the bank of the stream. He scrambled ashore and ran toward his spear and shield. Even in the midst of danger, Deirdre's eyes could not get enough of the naked warrior running for his weapons through bleating sheep and barking dogs.

With his spear in hand and hate in his heart, King Connor booted his speckled horse through the crazed runaway sheep. His target: the naked Naóise, leaping and running toward him. Connor only had eyes for the man who had ravished Deirdre and made a mockery of his notion of kingship. He did not see

Naóise's wolfhound Bran snapping and biting his way through the sheep toward his master. Nor did he see Aidan and Arden ride to the protection of their brother from the top of the meadow.

Naóise reached his weapons at the trunk of an oak tree at the same time the king did. As Naóise's hand grabbed his spear, Connor's horse smashed into him. Naóise crashed sideways into the tumult of darting, farting sheep.

King Connor grasped his spear like a javelin. The surging sea of sheep rammed his horse's legs and defied his aim to kill Naóise. Connor dismounted and found his place. From here, he could pierce the heart of Naóise. He could pierce the bowels of Naóise.

Bran the wolfhound launched his defense of Naóise by leaping over six stray sheep and landing on King Connor's chest. The king's head slammed into the oak tree. Stunned, Connor fell to the ground. His eyes closed. He still held his spear.

Deirdre watched her naked hero pull King Connor from damage by the slashing feet of the terrified sheep. His brothers rode up on their black matched stallions. Young and godlike, like Naóise. The three brothers huddled together. Deirdre's second sight told her they were talking about her. Naóise left his brothers and ran back to Deirdre. He was still naked.

When King Connor recovered his senses, he was resting safely under an old oak tree. The sheep were clustered by the bank of the stream, eating and excreting their fears. The stream was empty and no longer golden. Nor was the cloak of gold on top of the mountain. He still had his spear in his hand. Connor pulled himself to his feet.

Deirdre stood inside a triangle of men, shields, and spears. When the three brothers stood thus, they could hold at bay the entire province of Ulster. Deirdre saw King Connor look at her in a way she never forgot. The king hefted his spear and boldly approached the brothers.

King Connor walked around Naóise, Aidan, and Arden, looking for an opening. He found none. He stood and spoke.

"I am King Connor of Ulster. I am your uncle by birth. I am your foster father as warriors to the Red Branch."

He pointed his spear toward Deirdre.

"Heed well the prophecy of Katbad the Druid. Deirdre will cause the fall of the house of Connor in Ulster. My kingdom. Deirdre will cause the death of heroes. Deirdre will cause the death of thousands. Deirdre is death to us all." The king stood opposite each brother, in turn.

"Deirdre is death," he said to Naóise.

"Deirdre is death," he said to Aidan.

"Deirdre is death," he said to Arden.

Connor stood still. He had their full attention.

"Release Deirdre to me. I will send her away from Ireland. If you keep Deirdre, you will all die. One-by-one, or all together. Everyone in my kingdom will try to kill Deirdre, to save the lives of thousands."

The king awaited an answer. Deirdre looked at Connor while the three brothers discussed her fate.

eighteen

I N OLD GOD'S day, a kingdom's worth was judged by the strength of its bulls, the valor of its heroes, and the wisdom of its king. Mac Bristle, the master herdsman of Ulster, kept the great bulls of the province on the fertile field of a wealthy landowner named Daire Mac Fiacna. The land on which they grazed and grew lay on the high ráth on the Cooley preserve.

The bane and thorn in the side and soul of Mac Bristle was the herdsman of Queen Maeve of Connacht. Mac Gristle was his name and malice his nature. In the length and breadth of Ireland, Mac Gristle remained the only herdsman to come close to Mac Bristle. In their abiding rivalry, they resembled the affairs of state between King Connor and Queen Maeve of Connacht.

The two herdsmen met for long periods and louder altercations as to who knew the most about the breeding of bulls. Rivalry begat hatred until their heated words scorched the heather, causing fish to swim back to the sea. There seemed no outlet for such intense debate because of the Geasa on herdsmen. No herdsman could slay another herdsman and not suffer eternal condemnation in the words of bards and satirists, and exile from the Other Side. The more Mac Bristle met with Mac Gristle, the louder the quarrel.

After a long night with new moonshine, Old God awoke with a headache that demanded the healing powers of sleep. This he could not do because of the roaring of Mac Bristle and Mac Gristle. On a whim, Old God turned the two herdsmen into two birds and went back to sleep.

The bird named Claw came from Connacht. The bird named Clamor came from Ulster. For half a year, they clawed and clamored each other in Connacht. For the other half, they clamored and clawed each other in Ulster.

The cantankerous cawing of the birds turned the air blue. This so upset the primal bulls of Ulster and Connacht that they neglected the needs of their mooning cows. Men rushed home to their scalding, scolding wives to escape feathers flying from Claw and Clamor and the dangerous disharmony between them.

For want of something better to do, Old God turned the birds into phantoms with the power to change shapes.

The phantom from Ulster had the name of Shade. The phantom from Connacht had the name of Shadow. Phantoms never attack each other, but Shadow turned on Shade. In the daytime, both phantoms became fire-breathing dragons, burning each other to the bone and beyond. At night, Shade attacked Shadow. Both became warlocks riding lightning bolts and farting thunder at each other. So pissed off were Shadow and Shade that they soaked Ulster and Connacht with a steady downpour that dampened any attempt at levity or lovemaking. Finally, Old God grew bored and changed the warlocks into warriors.

The warrior from Ulster had the name of Gash.

The warrior from Connacht had the name of Gore.

Gash and Gore sliced and slashed each other across Ulster and Connacht. By day and by night, the clanging of sword on shield kept infants crying and parents sleepless. They gored and gashed, sliced and slashed, until a small finger of flesh was all that remained to each warrior. Hurling insults and curses, Gore and Gash turned the air blue and crops wan.

Not having much left to work with, Old God turned the remnants of the warriors into two maggots, one dirty white and the other dirty brown.

The dirty brown maggot from Ulster had the name of Criss.

The dirty white maggot from Connacht had the name of Cross.

Enraged and alarmed, Cross bit into the maggot arse of Criss. Twisting and turning, sliding and slipping, snapping and snarling, the two maggots fell into a stream and were swept away from Connacht and Ulster. The stream gurgled into a riverlet, splashing into a lake that flowed into a river of black water. Here the story takes another twist.

There came to the black water to drink the most maternal cow in Ireland. Among all udders, this cow named Oxter had the best. Lapping the black water with a loud sound by the shore, Oxter drank her fill and swallowed the maggot named Cross, from Ulster, and the maggot named Criss, from Connacht. In Old God's day, maggots, for their size and weight, had divine powers of procreation.

Nine months later, the cow called Oxter carried enormous twin bulls in her womb. Oxter belonged to a wealthy landowner named Fergall MacManach. Fergall the Cunning foresaw great wealth and prestige in the birth of the bulls. He sensed the beasts were from the Other Side. Already, they were fully formed, from horn to rump, attacking each other inside the suffering cow named Oxter.

Fergall the Cunning knew the value of a great bull from the Other Side to the herds of King Connor of Ulster and Queen Maeve of Connacht. Because of the rivalry between these monarchs, Fergall decided to introduce the two rare bulls to the world at a great cattle fair near his home. Aware of the cupidity of kings, he extended an invitation to King Connor and Queen Maeve to be the first to view the bulls, on the eve of the fair.

* * * * * *

Setanta and Ferdia were called to the Red Branch House of King Connor of Ulster early one morning. King Connor and his cohorts addressed serious business pertaining to the security of Ulster before any other problems. At first light, Genann, the son of Katbad escorted the two heroes through the Red Branch House and its wondrous rooms until they reached an inner sanctum. The Chamber of Consultation was a circular room with a bullhide bench surrounding a circle of marble at its center. On the circular wall, carvings of great bulls abounded. The bulls had horns of inlaid gold and bright eyes of precious pearls. A dome of clear copper atop the circular chamber had nine skylights like enormous stars open to the elements of air and sunshine. In the center of the marble floor stood King Connor of Ulster, on his head a crown, and in his hand a wand of rolled silver with three gold balls attached. Seated on the bullhide bench surrounding King Connor were his trusted advisers and sages, men who raised the wellbeing of Ulster above other concerns.

Setanta and Ferdia sat silent and resolute on the bench, aware of the singular honor awarded them.

King Connor shook his silver wand three times. Genann of the Brow of Light entered the Chamber of Consultation once more. With his right hand on his father's elbow, Genann escorted the Druid to stand by the side of King Connor. Katbad's eyes were closed in a deep trance, his mind far from his body. King Connor touched the center of Katbad's forehead with the tip of his wand. Genann sat by Setanta.

"What sees the King of the Druids?" asked Connor

"I see blood. I smell death. Death in the afternoon. A great clash of men. Death. Two bulls. Death. Blood on the Red Branch. Thousands dead. Hacked. Separate the bulls! Save Ulster."

Exhausted and depleted, Katbad's head rolled to his chest. King Connor nodded to Katbad's son. Genann returned to his father's side and walked Katbad from the room. King Connor looked at the circle of men facing him.

"Last night, I had a message from Fergall MacManach telling me of two rare bulls due to be birthed soon. The bulls are fully formed inside the womb of the cow, Oxter. The bulls are reserved for royalty. What say you, Fergus?"

King Connor pointed his wand at Fergus of the Long Sword. Fergus stood and spoke.

"Fergall the cattle-jobber is not called Fergall the Cunning for nothing. If Queen Maeve of Connacht wants to improve her herd, she will pay any price. We know this. Two bulls from the Other Side would bode ill for Ulster if the bulls will follow a woman." Fergus sat down.

King Connor spoke. All listened.

"I had the messenger followed. When he crossed the border to Connacht, he was killed."

The king pointed his wand at Conall Carney and said, "We could send Fergus of the Long Sword to bargain with Queen Maeve of the Friendly Thighs. What say you, Conall Carney?"

Conall stood and spoke.

"Beware of queens baring all. If Fergus buys the bulls, he must bring them back to Ulster alive. Fergall will send another messenger to Queen Maeve. If the bulls are sold separately, Fergall could double his profit." Conall sat down.

King Connor thought before he spoke, looking around.

"We have a story about two bulls from the Other Side who may destroy us. Who here has the skill to tell another story about how we protect Ulster from the bulls?"

None moved until King Connor pointed his wand at Sceál Galore, the renowned storyteller.

"What say you, Sceál Galore?"

Sceál Galore stood by the king's side. All loved the tales of Sceál. This could be his most important story. They listened as if their lives depended on every word. Looking long and hard at Setanta and Ferdia, Sceál began his tale.

"With a black bull of ferocious aspect between them, Setanta and Ferdia rode forth from the Cooley Preserve..."

* * * * * *

With a black bull of ferocious aspect between them, Setanta and Ferdia rode forth from the Cooley Preserve. They were dressed as young herdsmen, up for the day at a cattle fair. Setanta wore a brown tunic tied at the waist with a bull belt, long brown britches tied at the ankles, with a blackthorn prod stick in his hand. Ferdia wore a tartan tunic, shades of Alba on his long hew trousers tied with leather laces, leather slippers on his feet, and a blackthorn prod in his hand. They sought out unknown and little traveled byways to avoid any problems the black bull might cause by its powerful appearance. Such a bull was not an everyday sight in Ulster or Leinster or any other province in Ireland.

After a long day with the black bull, Ferdia asked Setanta a question. He and Setanta had left with the black bull on instructions from King Connor before they heard the end of Sceál's story in the Red Branch.

"What do we do with this black bull?" asked Ferdia.

"We could sell the bull?" suggested Setanta.

"We could exchange the black bull for the two bulls from the Other Side?" asked Ferdia.

"We could find a cow from the Other Side for the black bull?" asked Setanta.

"We could bring all the bulls back?" asked Ferdia.

"It's Sceál's story. We need to hear what happens to the black bull from Sceál's own mouth," said Setanta.

"And where do we find Sceál when we need him?" asked Ferdia.

Finally, they arrived near the large holdings of Fergall MacManach at Lusk in Leinster. Early one fine morning, they secured the black bull and horses in a dense wood near an open field on which were working three times nine men and women. This field would be set for the showing and selling of cattle and the feasting of Fergall the Cunning's guests. Between the field and the fine house of Fergall stood the cowshed, an enormous barn for the protection of man and beast from the elements.

From the cowshed came enormous bellows of agony. The famed cow Oxter, still suffering birth pangs, had not yet delivered her twin bulls to the world. Setanta and Ferdia discussed their next move to secure the bulls of Oxter for King Connor of Ulster. Setanta went to walk the land.

Outside the cowshed stood a man armed with a cudgel for churls and a spear for serious work. Setanta noted the guard, the bellow from Oxter, and the lay of the land as he walked around the cowshed. None that he passed paid him any attention. He thought of what he had heard about Fergall MacManach. A medium-looking man in height, weight, and appearance, Fergall knew how to court fortune and woo wealth. Setanta stopped as close as he could to where the bellows of Oxter emanated. The door guarded by the henchman on the other side seemed the only entrance to the cowshed. Setanta heard voices between the horrendous din of the suffering cow. He sat down and leaned back against the outside of the shed. Surprised, he thought he heard his name mentioned. Closing his eyes, he concentrated on listening. A man's voice, medium in sound and effect.

"Setanta! What of Setanta? I've heard him talked about by the women," said the voice.

"Oh, Setanta. The Warped One. I started to tell a story about Setanta, Ferdia, and a black bull of ferocious aspect. I came here to find an ending to my story that would satisfy anyone, even myself."

To Setanta, it sounded like the voice of Sceál Galore.

"As regards your black bull, maybe I could take it off your mind—for a price," said the other voice.

"Never start a tale with a lot of bull unless you have an ending," said Sceál.

Setanta thought about this. He and Ferdia had left with the black bull before they heard the rest of Sceál's story. So, if Sceál did not know the finish of his story, it was up to Setanta and Ferdia to effect a suitable ending. Setanta listened closely. Sceál spoke between the bellows of the pregnant cow.

"Setanta is as much admired by women as he is feared by men, Emer," said Sceál.

"Is he as handsome as they say, the same Setanta?" Said the voice of a woman who could turn a boy into a man and return a corpse from his grave. Who was this Emer of the Cowshed? Setanta had to find out.

"Setanta is short in years and but long in deeds," Sceál said, sounding bored.

"Keep him away from my daughters, Ulsterman. He sounds like an idiot, not long for this world," said a male voice.

This voice must belong to Fergall the Cunning, thought Setanta, and Emer of the fine voice must be his daughter.

The cow Oxter let a shriek out of her that caused the demise of seven old women and twenty-one old men. Then silence. Setanta heard the sound of a medium man running through the cowshed toward the door. Swiftly, he ran in tandem on the outside of the cowshed. The door opened. A medium man in a high state of alarm yelled at the brawny brute with the cudgel.

"Quick, fetch Fiál and her brothers. Tell my children that Oxter's offspring are on the way. Run, man, run!"

The medium man disappeared back into the cowshed. As the doorkeeper ran toward the house, Setanta dove through the door before it closed. He crawled toward the darkest part of the barn, keeping his eyes closed to adjust to the interior light. When he opened them, he saw an enormous dun-colored cow lying on her side near the far wall. What he saw next changed the way Setanta looked at the world. It also changed the way the world looked at Setanta.

Inside the swollen belly of Oxter, two lumps of moving matter rolled together, separated, and bumped again. Two perfect pale hands, pink tipped, stroked Oxter's swollen paps in a labor of love. Sceál Galore and Fergall MacManach obscured the owner of the hands from Setanta's view. The hands were fascination enough for Setanta. He felt them caress his heart. A rich and rare pleasure flashed through his body, curling his toes, connecting his breast to his brain. A crackling flash in his good eye reshaped its pupil. A gold star with a silver outline imprinted itself on the center of his eye. The Warped One felt a golden burst of love leap from his heart toward the pale hands on Oxter's paps, leaving him dizzy with emotional intensity.

Setanta focused the power in his starlit eye on Sceál and Fergall. They moved to the rump of the heaving animal and revealed Emer to the enchanted eye of Setanta. Emer the Supreme of Form and Warmth. Emer of the Golden Hair. Emer of the Blue Eyes That Matched Her Tunic, revealing wonders of breasts and shoulders.

As Eve to Adam, so Emer to Setanta. Emer his first and ever love. The love star in Setanta's eye spun and sparkled with joy. It split into six tiny comets, orbiting the star in his iris. A single red dimple of delight opened on his cheek. Setanta felt his hands and feet crack and enlarge. Now he had seven fingers on each hand, and seven toes on each foot. All the more to love you with, my Emer, my angel, thought Setanta.

Oxter took control of the cowshed with a convulsive shudder and horrendous holler. A sharp white horn tore through the belly of Oxter near her rump. A sharp dark horn tore through her belly near her front. Emer screamed in shock. Two wicked sharp horns ripped bloody, erratic wounds on the heaving side of Oxter, moving toward each other. Entangled in bloody glop and each other, the two bulls pulsed forth from Oxter's opened wounds.

They hit the ground running. Twenty-one fingers tall, no give nor take between them. Pure hatred and reckless rage. Hate to live and die by. Rage to consume each other and thousands more. The bloody bulls ran in circles around each other, adding agility to villainy. Bellowing their arrival, the bulls charged at each other, heads down, horns straight.

Fergall the Cunning ran to save his bulls. Sceál Galore pulled tight the opened wounds of Oxter's belly, to help Emer sew them closed with her knitting needles. Setanta could not take his love-struck eyes off Emer. Fergall grabbed the bull with the curly white horn and yelled at Sceál Galore.

"Tie up that brown bull. I'm taking this one home before they kill each other."

Fergall ran toward the door with one bull under his arm. The brown bull kicked the ground in rage, and then charged after Fergall. Sceál and Emer paid heed to the saving of Oxter. Fergall slipped through the cowshed door, and then kicked it closed. The brown bull slammed into the door and staggered sideways into the open arms of Setanta, the love-struck Warped One. The blow to the brown bull's head from the door had knocked him witless. The blow to Setanta's heart from Emer was of a different dimension, and a much longer duration.

Setanta held the brown bull in his arms. He turned to walk across the cowshed toward Emer. Sceál walked swiftly toward him, blocking his view of Emer. She had her back to Setanta, still stitching the wounds of Oxter.

"Setanta! You're here! You have the bull. Save the day! Take him to Ulster before Fergall returns," said Sceál Galore.

"I'm here for the girl. You and Ferdia take the bull back. What's the bull's name?" asked Setanta.

Sceál thought for a while and then smiled.

"The brown one here is called Tawn Bo. The white-horned one is named Bawn Bo."

Setanta nodded. Leave it to Sceál for good names.

"Sceál, I must see Emer and talk to her."

"Not now, while she's stitching up Oxter. She will never forgive you if anything happened to Oxter because of you. I need a breeze and sunshine. I'm queasy. Come help me," said Sceál.

They walked outside and Sceál vomited. Storytellers are better at talking about blood and guts than being involved in the muck of it.

When Sceál recovered, he spoke strongly to Setanta, as follows:

"Setanta, you and Ferdia are to take Tawn Bo back to King Connor. This is direct from the king's mouth. Bring the black bull here, and then back to Ulster and triumph. Go, Setanta, I order you in the name of King Connor and the Red Branch. Go! Don't walk. Run! Before the return of Fergall." And then Sceál slipped back into the cowshed. Setanta heard the bolts slide into the holes, locking the doors. He slung Tawn Bo over his shoulder and ran back to Ferdia.

* * * * * *

Setanta dropped the witless bull at the feet of Ferdia, and took a deep breath.

"Ferdia, this is Tawn Bo. Sceál Galore is in the cowshed. He wants you to take Tawn Bo back to the Red Branch. Ride like the wind on the black horse. I'll take the black bull back to Sceál. You'll be a hero, Ferdia."

Setanta's squint affected him when he lied. Ferdia had learned this by now. He wished the luck of the Irish to Setanta and watched him ride back to Sceál with the black bull behind him. Ferdia slung Tawn Bo across the black horse and followed Setanta toward the cowshed, keeping out of sight. If Sceál Galore was starting a new tale, then it seemed to Ferdia he should hear that story from the mouth of the teller, not from a lying, squinting cad with his good eye on immortality. And whence the red dimple on Setanta's cheek and the stars in his eye?

Setanta rapped smartly on the door of the cowshed with his blackthorn prod. He heard the quick steps of Sceál Galore approaching.

"Who knocks on the cowshed?" asked Sceál.

Setanta provoked a loud roar from the black bull with his blackthorn stick. Sceál opened the door and Setanta rode inside the cowshed with the black bull behind him.

"Where's Ferdia?" asked Sceál.

"He decided to save time by taking Tawn Bo to Ulster. I'll follow him later. Where's the fair Emer?" Setanta dismounted.

"Emer? She went home to change her bloody clothes. Leave the black bull here."

Setanta loosened the halter from the black bull. Outside the cowshed, Ferdia covered Tawn Bo with his cloak and sat on his horse. He looked like a young herdsman with a calf on his way to a cattle fair. None who passed paid heed to him.

Inside the cowshed, Setanta had to deal with Sceál Galore.

"I'll make a short visit to Emer before I leave for Ulster," he told Sceál.

"Setanta, Emer's father has a bad cess for Ulster already. You should wait. When he's sold his bulls, he'll be more approachable," said Sceál.

"Approachable or not, here he is," observed Setanta.

Into the cowshed strode Fergall the Cunning. In his hand, a heavy stick. On the back of his head, a bull cap. Sceál greeted him.

"Fergall, it's about time you returned. Here is a gift from King Connor—the best black bull in Ulster." At last, Sceál had found a use for his black bull, something he'd thought of on the spot.

Setanta smiled when he heard this, and began grooming the black bull. Fergall looked at Setanta and the black bull with suspicious eyes, and said, "I'm here for the best brown bull in Leinster."

"When you took so long in returning, and I was still tending your cow Oxter, I thought to do you a good deed. I sent the small brown bull Tawn Bo back to King Connor of Ulster, toward the beginning of a beautiful friendship," said Sceál.

"Where's my brown bull?" Fergall thumped the ground with his heavy stick. Setanta stopped the grooming.

"King Connor said to tell you he needs one of Oxter's bulls to even the field against Maeve. Also, there are fierce warriors in Ulster," said Sceál.

Fergall pointed his stick at Sceál's heart.

"Queen Maeve has let me know there are fierce warriors in Connacht. Maeve won't argue about the price, as long as she goes home with two twin bulls." Fergall opened the door of the cowshed and whistled.

Ferdia heard a whistle from the door of the cowshed. The man in the bull cap waved his stick and seven brawny herders rounded the corner. They marched into the cowshed, ready to keep or break the peace as the occasion demanded. Ferdia moved closer to the cowshed door, waiting for a sound or signal to signify his next move.

Inside the cowshed, the seven herder-henchmen lined up in front of Fergall and Sceál. Setanta watched from behind the black bull.

"Sceál, heed me now. We are here to find the brother of the white-horned bull, the brown bull I left with you," said Fergall.

"I named him Tawn Bo, and his brother Bawn Bo," offered Sceál.

"We are here for Tawn Bo. Today. Now." Fergall rammed the knob of his stick into the stomach of Sceál. Breathless, speechless, Sceál collapsed to the ground.

"Grab that squinting brat. Don't kill him until we find Tawn Bo," ordered Fergall, pointing at Setanta and swinging high his heavy stick. It slammed down between Sceál's thighs, close enough to shrivel his vital part. Four husky herders marched toward Setanta. The Warped One whispered in the black bull's ear and kissed him three times on the neck. The herders moved closer to the black bull, blackthorn sticks in their hands.

Outside the cowshed, Ferdia wondered what had happened to Setanta and the black bull. He was soon to find out. A riot of motion and sound erupted from inside the cowshed. With pounding hooves and steaming nostrils, the black bull of ferocious aspect thundered from the cowshed. Impaled on each horn of the beast kicked a screaming, bleeding herder.

On the black bull's back sat Setanta, arms stretched high, holding aloft the two twitching herdsmen. The black bull lowered his head and flung high two contorting torsos with a wicked twist of his neck.

Setanta lowered his arms and then flung higher the two choking henchmen of Fergall the Cunning. The skulls of the flying goboys cracked together. Both dropped down dead, side by side. The twisting torsos flung by the black bull crashed down together, soaking the grass with blood, guts, and tears. Setanta skipped from the back of the black bull and cracked his knuckles.

Ferdia's mouth opened. Setanta had seven fingers on each hand, all the better to kill with. The Warped One put his arms around the black bull, whispered in his ear, and kissed him three times on the neck. Ferdia knew then that Setanta had a ferocity beyond any he'd encountered in his young life. Setanta clasped the bull by the horns, swung his legs around the belly of the beast, and thus they trotted back into the cowshed.

Ferdia rode his black horse after Setanta through the door of the cowshed. Tawn Bo stretched and blinked his eyes awake, slipping from Ferdia's grasp. Tawn Bo tumbled onto the grass of the cowshed, rolled over, and regained his standing. The black bull trotted toward a surly herder with an upraised club. Beside the doorposts, two burly herders sprang forward to clobber whoever was on the bull's back. Their blackthorn sticks smashed together, shattering in pieces. Setanta dropped from the bull's belly, rolled free of its flashing hooves, and stood before the startled herders. With swift swings of his blackthorn, he dealt three stunning blows to the heads of Fergall's herdsmen. They fell in place, witless and helpless.

Setanta strode toward Sceál Galore and Fergall the Cunning. Not once did he acknowledge the presence of Ferdia on his black horse. The black bull followed Setanta, stopping when he did.

Setanta the Warped One focused his starry eye on Fergall. His seven fingers tight on his blackthorn stick, Setanta raised it high above Fergall's head.

"Stop, Setanta! Let me talk to Fergall," pleaded Sceál.

"Talk. Be quick. My blood is rising," said Setanta.

"Fergall—listen or die. You need to sell two bulls to Queen Maeve. There are two bulls here and the one you took home," said Sceál.

Fergall the Cunning looked from Setanta to Sceál Galore. Hard boys from Ulster. Birds of a feather. Cocks of the north.

"If I don't sell Maeve two twin bulls, I'm a dead man," Fergall said.

"Sell this black bull and Bawn Bo, the white-horned one, to Maeve," said Setanta.

"Maeve will be expecting twins," repeated Fergall.

Sceál Galore looked around and about to put a better ending to the story of the bulls. Oxter the cow exhaled a deep sigh of relief. Tawn Bo knelt beside her, sucking at her upper udder, relaxed and healthy. Sceál watched Oxter and Tawn Bo. He closed his eyes and spoke.

"Fergall, tell Maeve that you took one bull home to stop him from killing his brother. The black bull left behind sucked Oxter dry. By the time you came back to the cowshed, the black bull had grown to a full size."

"Why would Maeve believe that?" asked Fergall.

"Because the bulls are from the Other Side," said Setanta.

"Tell Maeve you will sell her the big black bull for the same price as his smaller brother, Bawn Bo. This way, she gets the best of the bargain," said Sceál.

"If Maeve buys the bull story, you live. If we don't take Tawn Bo to King Connor, you will die," said Setanta. "Today."

Fergall the Cunning looked from Tawn Bo, asleep at Oxter's enormous udder, to the massive black bull.

nineteen

FERDIA RODE HIS black mount out of the cowshed. Behind him came Setanta with Tawn Bo across the shoulders of his white horse. Sceál Galore stood in the doorway with Fergall the Cunning. The black bull cast a fierce eye at Oxter, and then changed his mind. Ferdia sensed that Setanta had ignored him in the cowshed to teach him a lesson. There is no equality among heroes. First comes courage. Then what may.

The afternoon sun caused deep shadows along the side of the cowshed. Returning to see how Oxter survived her needlework, Emer the Fair of Face and Figure walked in the warmth of the sun. Emer felt loose and lovely. Meeting creatures from the Other Side elevates the essence of life. Was she not after saving a valuable cow named Oxter from certain death? Was Emer not among the most desirable women in all of Ulster? Was Emer not excellent in voice and speech? Was Emer not noted for her embroidery, wisdom, and chastity? And why was she thinking of chastity? A flash of light caught her eye. There. From the shadow of the cowshed, a voice called her name. The light beamed her way, a hue of love from a star-filled eye. Shielding her eyes from the sun with a pink-tipped perfect hand, Emer stared into the shadow.

A young man on a black horse. A hero strong and fit, bold and resolute. Behind him, in deeper shadow, the brother of the white-horned bull slung across the shoulder of a white horse. The rider of the white horse appeared as a fading vision at the tail end of a dream. The face of a man with stars in his eye. A face that would never grow old on the body of a god from the Other Side.

"Emer. Emer." His voice baptized her name as his own. Emer underwent a transformation. It bound her blood to her brain, her heart to her head, her soul to the search for this outline of a fancy. And it all vanished around the corner of the cowshed. The creatures from the Other Side. A black and white horse, a tawny brown bull, and a man-god with stars in his eye and her name on his lips.

* * * * * *

Setanta and Ferdia received no public praise for bringing Tawn Bo to graze, grow, and revive the herds of Ulster on the Cooley Preserve. The affairs of state between King Connor and Queen Maeve hinged on a traditional rivalry between Ulster and Connacht. The character and condition of these two strong and eccentric monarchs were such that an invasion by one or the other seemed an imminent threat at all times.

King Connor acclaimed this adventure of his two heroes and raised them high among his inner circle of warriors. This brought Setanta into his own among the women of Ulster. Those who witnessed him grew to worship his agility in athletics, bravery in heroics, and dexterity in all things physical.

The love-stars in his eye invaded the day and night dreams of a generation of wives and daughters.

Setanta, a name assured of immortality in the sound of it.

Setanta, a name of resounding elegance, soft, sad, and significant.

Setanta, a name for fame on a form for fornication.

Wherever Setanta went, his female admirers followed. They climbed on the backs of husbands and betrotheds to throw wild roses at the Warped One. Three husbands and two youths were strangled by the wild spasms of the legs of excited women on their backs as Setanta rode by.

The men of Ulster discussed the passion of their women for Setanta. He'd have less effect upon their wives and daughters if a wife was found for him. They said it was only out of himself that the likes of Setanta would come again. This increasing concern for Setanta's domestic arrangement reached the ear of King Connor.

Having first access to the women of Ulster for years made King Connor sympathetic to this plight of his subjects, especially concerning their daughters. The king sent out messengers looking for a wife for Setanta in the provinces of Ireland.

For nine months, the messengers searched in every town and fort for a king's, warrior's, or landowner's daughter to suit and sooth the Warped One. To no avail. There was no woman to match the verve and versatility of Setanta.

Setanta had a memory burned on his eye of Emer the Fair. To escape the attention of his admirers, Setanta began his courtship of Emer. He took concern in his approach and appearance. A new, wonderful chariot driven by his black and his white horses. A new and ambitious charioteer named

Laeg Mac Rian drove Setanta straight to his destination, the fields and fort of Fergall the Cunning and the home of his daughter, Emer.

Along with her sister, Fiál, Emer supervised a class in knitting and embroidery for her foster sisters who lived around her father's fort. Emer heard the sounds of a chariot approaching. The hooves of horses, the clang of weapons, the rumble of steel wheels. Fiál stood on a large boulder.

"I see a chariot with two horses large and shapely, swift and comely. A black horse elegant in outline, power, and performance. A white horse, striking and slender, splendid in speed, strength, and endurance," said Fiál.

"What of the chariot?" asked Emer, an image of a white horse forming in her mind's eye.

"A golden arc yoked to a yellow bridle. A high lovely wicker body, the chariot shafts curved, made of steel," said Fiál.

"Who occupies this rare chariot?" asked Emer.

"In this chariot is the most beautiful man I have ever seen. A crimson dimple on one cheek. A hue of love flashes from one eye. Seven fingers on his fierce hand hold a blood-red spear."

"How is he dressed?" asked Emer.

"His clothes proclaim a man going courting for a wife. A hooded smock of the finest linen clings to his strong body. A purple cloak of great value threaded with golden stitches on his shoulders. A gold-hilted sword in his sheath. Black as night eyebrows."

"Who drives the chariot?" asked Emer.

"A slender charioteer. Tall, with curly red hair held in place by a gold and silver headband. Strong, competent, adventurous; he drives his horses as if connected by invisible reins," Fiál finished. She sighed with desire. This made an impression on the love-struck girls around her. Emer stepped apart from the others, arranging herself inside and out.

When the chariot drew nigh, Setanta vaulted from it and landed in front of Emer the Fair. A warm wind whirled around them. Birds whistled at the sight of Setanta and Emer together. Emer raised her eyes to look at Setanta. He blinked at her beauty. A gold star with a silver outline imprinted itself on the center of his squinting eye. The love-star sparkled with joy, splitting into six tiny comets in orbit around his iris. Both of Setanta's eyes relished the perfection of Emer's breasts straining against her blue smock. Setanta smiled at Emer. She was the first to speak.

"You should know that I have a sister, Fiál, who is older than me, and should be first approached. Fiál also excels in needlework," said Emer.

Setanta stood tall and started his courtship of Emer.

"I have fallen in love with the sister of Fiál, who stands in glory before my love-struck eyes. I will rest my weapon in your sweet valley," swore Setanta, staring at Emer's perfect breasts.

"No man rests in this country, unless he performs the feat of the salmon leap, carrying twice his weight in gold," said Emer.

"I will carry twice my weight in gold for Emer. Forever. I will rest my weapon in your sweet valley," swore Setanta.

"No man will rest in this country until he kills three groups of nine men with three single strokes of his sword, leaving the middle man of each nine alive and strong," said Emer.

"As you wish it, so shall I do it. I will rest my weapon in your sweet valley," swore Setanta.

Finished with words, they let their eyes do the talking. Like a rainbow at noon, Setanta's love filled Emer's grey-green eyes with the hue from the comets circling his iris.

Fiál and her foster sisters, the daughters of landowners living around Fergall's fort, circled Setanta's chariot as if around a sacred place. From his curly red hair to his winged cloak and bull-hide boots laced high on his curving calves, Laeg the Charioteer enjoyed his time as an object of amorous interest. Being a charioteer to the Warped One had its benefits.

* * * * * *

That evening, neither Emer nor her sister Fiál spoke of the wonderful chariot and its handsome occupants before their father. Fergall the Cunning kept a sharp eye on his daughters. He also kept a sharp ear open for news or gossip, essential to survival in an uncertain world. It was not long before he learned of the doings of Setanta and his charioteer that afternoon.

The daughters of the landowners who lived near Fergall told their fathers of the two beautiful horses and men they had met in the meadow while knitting. Setanta and his starry eye were the center of the tales told at dinner by the girls. Soon enough, the landowners retold the story to Fergall the Cunning.

"Setanta the Squinter has fallen in love with Emer! The madman who would have killed me in my cowshed is now courting my daughter. I will prevent this, to my death," swore Fergall.

He went to a secure room in the bowels of his fort and locked himself inside. He thought long and hard about what he knew of King Connor of Ulster, and how he ruled his kingdom. Finally, a glimmer of a scheme, simple and audacious, evolved in his mind's eye. He gave thought to gifts to effect the disposition of a king toward him. His own gift was of changing his shape and personality, as needed, to further his ambitions. Being a perfect medium in weight and height, he did not attract attention, except by his clothes and accoutrements. Taking his sharpest dagger from his weapon trove, he shaved off his beard and mustache.

* * * * * *

Sceál galore returned from his adventure with Setanta and the bulls of Oxter to resume as the doorkeeper to the Red Branch of King Connor of Ulster. His duty was to greet and approve those who sought an audience with King Connor. He knew well the affinity of the king for music and story telling, for visitors from other countries, and for warriors, heroes, and beautiful women. Wine and strong drink were always welcome, as were exotic weapons.

At a festival, the young heroes of Ulster displayed their prowess in arms to the king of the Red Branch. Sceál worked the door to provide an audience for that night's events. As was the custom, many sent presents to King Connor to ensure entrance, with something on the side for the doorkeeper. Sceál arranged the gifts for King Connor in an ascending order of interest, to raise the entrance fee for those who wished to attend.

And never before had King Connor received such wonderful gifts as from a clean-shaven, amply girded foreigner. The suave stranger spoke with a Gaulish accent. Adorned in rich garments, he presented his impressive gifts to Sceál Galore, blinding the doorkeeper to reality. The first gift, a perfectly formed crock of silver filled with gold coins from Gaul, stopped all who saw it.

"Tell King Connor I represent a prince from Gaul who has heard great things about the Red Branch and would appreciate an alliance for mutual benefits," said the man from Gaul.

He clapped his hands and his two retainers appeared with more gifts. One brought a clear bottle containing a green-tinged liquor. This he placed beside the crock of gold. Again, the foreigner clapped his hands. The second retainer brought an elaborate drinking vessel in the shape of a raised cock's tail. The stranger bowed low and presented Sceál with a long-handled silver spoon.

"This is a stirring spoon for mixing the green liquor with your Water of Life whiskey. If done in proper proportions in the cock's tail vessel, the result will be an enchantment of taste and intoxication beyond your wildest dreams," said the stranger.

Sceál thanked the Gaul and went to see King Connor. He told him of the gifts.

"The gift giver is here to report on the progress of the Red Branch heroes to his prince of Gaul," said Sceál, gold coins dancing in his mind's eye.

"Your opinion on the gift giver?" asked King Connor.

"So average he's invisible. Neither inspired or aspiring. Sincere and—"

"Bring him and his gifts here before the cock crows," sighed the king. Sometimes Sceál had a problem getting to the heel of a tale.

The king was so taken with the gifts that he invited the Gaul to be his guest at the chariot feats the following afternoon.

* * * * * *

For the first time, more women than men attended the chariot feats of the young heroes of Ulster. They came to see Setanta. His fame and renown spread like a fever among the females. In appearance, audacity, and execution of skill, Setanta set the pace for others to follow. His charioteer Laeg Mac Rian had bonded with the Warped One in reckless daring. Both young, fearless, and immortal, they dominated the chariot races. None had a warrior's stance and glance like these two darlings of the daughters of Ulster—and also of their mothers. Setanta and Laeg, the awe-inspiring chariot, and the beautiful black and fabulous white horses, seemed an extension from the immediate to the immortal. Setanta's name a sigh on every woman's lips, his form an image in their mind's eye, the very air warmed and swirling around his chariot as he thundered past the king's pavilion. Nine chariot lengths behind came Ferdia, and then Conall Carney, and then the rest of Ulster's young warriors. It was Setanta's afternoon.

King Connor presented Setanta with a silver-hilted dagger from the Twinkling Hoard, for his prowess in the chariot feats. Setanta noted the rotund foreigner by the king's side. Like flakes of snow from above fell wild roses on Setanta, flung high by the women as he bowed before the king. The charioteer Laeg drove his high-stepping horses at a stately gait in front of the excited spectators. Setanta raised high his precious dagger. A pack of screaming women surged forward, arms outstretched, eyes blind with desire. They rushed to embrace Setanta. The horses' gallop in eluding the amorous women matched their speed in winning the chariot race.

Later, the frazzled Sceál had his worse night ever as the doorkeeper of the Red Branch House. Maintaining order of the screeching women beseeching entrance to see Setanta inside exceeded his skill. Sceál had difficulty in telling the boys from the girls, because many women dressed as men to ensure admission. He rejected promises of carnal intimacy for the privilege of entry. He ignored threats of a slow death if denied access to the Warped One. Salacious glances from insatiable mothers and daughters assaulted his sensibility. Glimpses of thighs, buttocks, exposed breasts, obscene gestures, rude remarks, upset his dignity as a doorkeeper to the king of Ulster.

Inside the Red Branch, the young heroes waited to display their feats of arms. Three remained for the indoor feats. Setanta, Ferdia, and Conall Carney ate together at a small table near the kitchen, each preparing for his next adventure in his own way.

Never had the Red Branch hosted so many at a feast. Never had so many women packed into the great hall, sitting at the long table and wandering about seeking glimpses of Setanta the Warped One. The kitchen had an immense demand for immediate food. The servers rushed to provide roast suckling pigs, haunches of venison, flitches of bacon, beef from tongue to tail, pigeon pies, fresh and smoked salmon, nuts, acorns, ale, dark beer, and whiskey, the Water of Life. These dominated the attention of the king and his guests.

When most of the plates were cleared, King Connor had a chance to survey his domestic domain inside the Red Branch. Connor's attention was absorbed by the Gaul beside him, his constant companion throughout the day.

The foreigner placed the cock's tail drinking vessel in front of the king of Ulster. He poured a dram of whiskey into the cock's tail vessel, and said, "I believe you call whiskey the Water of Life, King Connor."

The king nodded, feeling that tonight had a special significance beyond his ken. The stranger uncorked the flagon of green liquor he'd brought as a gift to the king, speaking in a soft, persuasive tone.

"I float a measure of our green liquor on top of the whiskey in your cock's tail vessel. I mix both together with the stirring spoon, and so—the Gael and the Gaul—fire for the body, smoke for the mind."

Wisps of smoke curled around King Connor from the cock's tail vessel. The stranger filled two drinking bowls with the smoking mixture.

"Luck of the Irish to you, King Connor."

The stranger drank his smoking bowl to show the king the purity of its contents. King Connor watched and waited. A sly smile of pleasure softened the face of the foreigner. Satisfied, the king sipped his own smoking bowl, absorbed in its taste and texture.

"Luck of the Irish to you, Gaul," said King Connor. Slowly, with a subtle effect that intensified the colors, sounds, and pleasures around him to an exalted degree, the smoking bowl worked its magic on the king. The next drink tasted better to Connor, extending the moment to the momentous.

"You will listen to me, and only to me. And I will tell you of wondrous things," said the stranger by his side, stroking the back of the king's hand.

"Look around the Red Branch tonight. See what is to be seen, King of Ulster."

King Connor did as the stranger suggested. As he surveyed his guests, his felt his world shift. It seemed that tonight the women in the Red Branch were lewd, lecherous, far-gone in villainy and drinking. The husbands were prim, proper, and austere, a reversal of the usual at these feasts. The focus of all was not on the king, but the youngest hero in the Red Branch, Setanta the Warped One.

"King Connor, when does the feat of the apples take place?" asked the stranger, pouring another smoking drink for King Connor.

"When the table is cleared of all dishes, or it's done on the ground. Tonight, let the apples fall where they will." King Connor clapped his hands three times. The chatter and clatter in the great hall ceased. Three servers brought three bowls of red apples to the end of the table. The wild harps of the king's minstrels escorted the three heroes to King Connor at the center of the long table. Setanta faced the king, flanked by Ferdia and Conall Carney.

"There are two feats left. Setanta has the lead after winning the chariot races," King Connor said.

Setanta bowed in acknowledgement. The women crowded behind the king, staring at Setanta in his garb of valor, with his star-filled eye and the scarlet dimple on his cheek. Slowly, the great hall filled with his name. Setanta. Setanta. Setanta. A trinity of taps from the tongue on the top, lower and top teeth, an open cry and then a sigh. Setanta.

"Walk the table, nine apples aloft. Touch or drop nothing. Setanta, you begin," said King Connor.

Setanta walked toward the three bowls of red apples. There were nine apples in each bowl. The women watched him.

"Touch or drop nothing," the king had said. This meant he'd have to be as dexterous with his feet as with his hands. Setanta stood on the table. Seven toes on each naked foot. Seven fingers on each hand. He scooped the nine apples from the bowl and set them flying in a circle above him. Such grace and agility elevated the spectators. Carefully, he stepped along the table filled with drinking and eating vessels. The stranger from Gaul mixed another whisky and green liquor in the cock's tail vessel with the long silver spoon, whispering in the king's ear. The smoke from the vessel drifted toward Setanta, blown by the foreigner as he stared at the soaring apples. Setanta sensed it first in his head—a loosening, a lack of control, a removal from the immediate. He focused again on his juggling feat, blowing his way through the smoke. The stranger poured another smoking bowl for King Connor and himself. He tilted the cock's tail flagon toward Setanta and waited for the Warped One to walk into the smoke. Setanta's eyes tilted upward, focusing on the nine spinning apples. The drifting smoke curled into a ring around his shoulders. Slowly, the stars in his eye began to spin in the same direction as the apples. The women pushed closer. None could take their eyes off Setanta. He disappeared in the smoke rising between the king and the foreigner, the Gael and the Gaul. The apples flew in all directions, chased by the covetous women.

When the smoke cleared, King Connor's head was tilted back, adrift in the land of smoky dreams. Beside him, the stranger tossed a red apple from hand to hand. He smiled at Setanta, and then bit into the apple. Setanta shrugged and stepped off the table. King Connor shrugged and smiled at Setanta. The women watched the Warped One walk away. Setanta had never dropped an apple before, nor would he ever again.

The king clapped again. Ferdia and Conall Carney marched together to stand before King Connor. The women at the table began to move in the direction of Setanta. The stranger whispered in the king's ear. King Connor stood to talk, his eyes red and his mouth moist.

"Ferdia, Conall—walk from the table's end to opposite my royal seat. On the ground, nine apples aloft. Drop or touch nothing. The first to arrive here is the victor," said King Connor, and he sat back in his chair.

Setanta watched Ferdia and Conall walk to the bowls of apples at the table's end. The king clapped again. Ferdia and

Conall scooped nine apples each from two bowls, and juggled them high in the air. Side by side, they stood, arms extended, bodies straight, apples circling overhead. King Connor clapped his hands. Ferdia and Conall stepped off swiftly, alert and confident. Alongside the long table they strode, hands juggling, apples flying. A sight for all to behold, except for the women watching Setanta restore his equilibrium. Setanta. His name was as a drumbeat in the voices of the women enamored of his presence and appearance.

Conall Carney kept pace with Ferdia, step by faster step as they approached the king's royal seat. Faster flew the apples, swifter moved their hands. Then Conall made his bold move. He sprang forward, twisting in a half circle past the surprised king. He landed on his knees, arms outstretched to catch and keep his apples in the air. Ferdia leapt forward, but too far to catch all his apples. One rolled along the table and hit the cock's tail vessel in front of King Connor.

The pressure was now on Ferdia. If he lost the next feat of heroes, he'd be eliminated, and the contest would be between Setanta and Conall Carney. Ferdia was the oldest of the three. He was the most renowned and revered of the young warriors. Until the arrival of Setanta. Setanta the Squinter. The Warped One. Just as Ferdia adjusted to the ferocity of Setanta, along came Conall Carney to best him, by trickery, at the apple feat. There and then, Ferdia decided to return to Alba to restore his skills at the hand of Scatach the Shadowy One—*after* his win tonight, at the feat of the rope.

Twenty

C ULLEN THE SMITH stood Setanta, Conall, and Ferdia at equal distance in front of the long table. He draped his long rope over the shoulder of each so that it reached from wall the wall. Bending his massive torso for perspective, Cullen the Smith secured one end of his rope into an iron hook he'd hammered into the wall. Shoulder height of the three young warriors, Cullen walked to the far wall, pulling the rope until it touched the shoulders of Ferdia and Conall, both of whom were taller than the Warped One. Satisfied, Cullen secured the long rope to the wall with another iron hook.

Once more, the three heroes were escorted to the king at the center of the table by minstrels playing wild harps. After a brief consultation with the stranger by his side, the king spoke.

"Ferdia, you will walk the rope from the left side of the hall. Conall, you will walk the rope from the right side of the hall. You will receive your weapons opposite my presence. Who stays on the rope, wins. Setanta, you will watch and wait."

Setanta resumed his seat and his surveillance of the feat of the rope. Opposite him, near the kitchen, Conall Carney sprang from the floor to land on the taut rope. He smiled at Setanta, his foster brother in arms. Both lived for, with, and in the moment. Both would die the same way.

Ferdia grasped the rope with both hands. He vaulted upward and straddled the rope. Ferdia slid backwards as he watched Conall blow him a mocking kiss. When his feet touched the wall behind him, he waved at Conall. When Conall waved back, Ferdia pushed sideways against the wall with his bare feet. A strong ripple raced through the rope, almost dislodging Conall Carney. He stepped backward until he found his balance by touching the wall behind him. Setanta smiled as applause filled the hall. The king lifted his smoking glass in tribute to his young heroes. They both walked the rope toward him until he signaled them to stop.

King Connor reached over the table and grasped the rope in both hands. With all his strength, he pulled the rope toward him and released it. The rope twanged from side to side. Ferdia and Conall swayed and listed, but remained standing. Now came Cullen with the weapons, standing in front of the men on the rope.

"You know the rules of combat?" asked King Connor

"Yes. Weapons: three blunt javelins, one wood shield," answered Ferdia.

"Yes. Conduct: always forward until a falter or fall," answered Conall.

"Step back three paces," ordered the king.

Ferdia took three short javelins in one hand from Cullen the Smith. He slid his other arm through the grip on the back of the shield of wood. Cullen then passed the weapons to Conall. When both were armed, King Connor clapped his hands. Ferdia and Conall leapt at each other, all feet off the

rope. Ferdia stabbed with two blunt javelins at the blue eyes of
Conall Carney. Conall slammed down with his wood shield,
aimed at the nose of Ferdia.

And so it began. A slamming of weapons between Ferdia
and Conall. No killing edges on shields or javelins. No let
up in fury of assault and attack. Conall's initial surge forced
Ferdia back. Slow, relentless, Conall pressed on, breaking
two of Ferdia's javelins. All were silent, listening to the crash
of the shields, the whacks of the javelins, and the roars of
the warriors.

Ferdia bent beneath the ferocity and frenzy of Conall's
onslaught with his wooden shield. Balanced on one knee,
Ferdia held aloft his own shield, absorbing the power of Conall's
savage blows. He slid his remaining javelin under the right foot
of Conall and braced himself. Conall raised high his shield for
his stunning final strike. Ferdia slammed his shield into Conall's
kneecaps. Conall's knees buckled sideways. Ferdia dropped his
shield and grabbed the javelin under Conall's foot with both
hands. He heaved Conall across the table onto the lap of the
stranger beside King Connor. Ferdia lurched forward, falling
face down onto the rope. Wrapping his hands and feet around
the rope, he saved himself from falling. When he recovered
his breath, he soon righted himself.

Ferdia! Ferdia! Ferdia!

His name became a masculine chant as the men in the
feast hall saluted his feat, thumping their feet on the ground
and elbows on the table.

Setanta! Setanta! Setanta!

The women sang in counterpart to the men.

Conall rubbed his kneecaps. Next time, he'd use them to
slam into the face of Ferdia when raising his shield. Next time.

* * * * * *

The three warriors were seated on stools facing King Connor, awaiting his review of their feats at the festival. Each had won. All were equal. Unless they partook in another combat round to determine the winner. King Connor stood to show the table two silver-hilted daggers from the Twinkling Hoard. These he presented to Conall and Ferdia amid applause and music from the minstrels. Though each of the young warriors believed himself the best, the three agreed that the kingdom of Ulster had never had such a triumph of heroes together at the same time and place. King Connor raised his hand for silence.

"My friend from Gaul will give his review and recommendations to Ulster's own. Pay heed, my heroes," said King Connor.

The stranger sipped from his smoke-filled bowl and began to talk.

"Ferdia, as the oldest, you kept your best to the last. My only suggestion is to practice feats of arms with those of similar or higher skills. Hostility and energy, Ferdia, will make you invincible."

Ferdia thought of his mentor in Scotland, Scatach the Shadowy One.

The stranger continued. "Conall Carney, a victorious warrior never admits defeat. Great is the glory before you, if you survive the wiles of your opponents. First comes courage, and first in courage is Conall Carney."

Conall Carney thanked the stranger for his advice and interest. And now the stranger turned his attention to Setanta.

"Setanta, precision and decision in your chariot won you the day. As you are the youngest hero, my advice to you is to travel to Alba to learn the ways of the warrior. Alone. Seek out Donall Mildemale. You will flourish under his tutelage. Ask Donall about Scatach the Shadowy One. If she accepts you as her pupil, you will be the first and finest warrior in Europe. If this is your destiny, Alba is your destination."

Setanta did not thank the stranger for his advice. He said nothing but thought the more. And of all his thoughts, those of Emer were ever the sweetest.

* * * * * *

Before his departure for Alba, Setanta rode his black horse to say farewell to Emer. Back to the fields and fort of Fergall the Cunning, the father of Emer he traveled. He dismounted from his horse, whispered in its ear, and kissed it three times on the neck. Then he lay down to rest after his long journey. Soon enough, the black horse reached the rock on which had stood Emer's sister when Setanta's chariot first arrived. As was their custom, Emer and Fiál were instructing a class of girls in fine embroidery. The horse seemed to appear to Emer as a vision from a dream. She walked over to touch its neck, her inner eye on a man with stars in his eye. The great horse nuzzled her cheek.

Emer climbed onto the rock and mounted the horse. Soon enough, they arrived where Setanta lay in the shade of an old apple tree. Emer slid off the back of the horse and lay beside the sleeping Setanta. Gently, she caressed his hair, his eyebrows, his eyelids, his eyelashes. Setanta smiled, pleased at his dreams of Emer. Her soft touch and warm breath. When he awoke, he thought he had passed to the Other Side. The land of the ever young. A state of grace, called love by some. Desired by all. Enjoyed by few.

* * * * * *

Later, Setanta told Emer about his adventures at the chariot races and the Red Branch. When he mentioned the foreigner from Gaul and his smoking cock's tail vessel, Emer caught his arm.

"That stranger is my father, Fergall the Cunning," said Emer. "He has sworn to kill you to keep us apart."

"He told me that if I go to Alba, I will return as the first warrior in Europe," Setanta said.

"Many study with Scatach the Shadowy One. Few survive her intact and whole," warned Emer.

"I will go to Alba. I will return to Emer," swore Setanta. He embraced Emer and showed his love. In return, Emer gifted Setanta with a body shirt embroidered with her skill and love. A shirt that told the tale of the Tree of Life, a favored love story of the Celtic Gaels.

Two lovers separated by death were buried on opposite banks of a swift-flowing stream. From each grave sprang a tall oak tree. The strongest branch from each oak reached out to embrace over the stream. This became an inspiration for all and a courting stop for young lovers. A full moon cast a shadow from the embracing branches onto the stream below. The contrast of a rushing stream with the steadfast shadows of love's arms begot the name the Tree of Life. Against the will of the people, these romantic branches were cut down to make harps and wands for bards and Druids. In the middle of the night, when all but dreams slept, the winds plucked the strings of the harps. This music of lovers yearning to embrace inspired a swift re-growth of the branches, stronger than ever. The wands from the braches were famous for subtle strength and magic powers.

Emer helped Setanta don her gift of a body shirt. The two branches of one Tree of Life reached embroidered arms across Setanta's strong shoulders in a clever embrace. She had the sister of this shirt covering her breasts, the sweet valley in which Setanta swore to rest his weapon. Both also swore to remain pure until they were reunited, unless one died. Then they parted, Emer for home, Setanta for Alba.

* * * * * *

By the time Setanta returned to the Red Branch court, Ferdia, his foster brother, had departed for Alba. Some say Ferdia left to become the foremost warrior in Europe under the tutelage of Scatach the Shadowy One in Alba. Other say he left for the love of Scatach's daughter.

Fergall the Cunning left the Red Branch to return to his daughters. He left behind him a favored spy, a left-handed man named Suloscal. They were as one in their attitude toward the world and the people in it. Suloscal passed as a traveling herdsman wherever Fergall needed information, assassination, or both.

Within a day of his return, Setanta told Conall Carney of his plan to study the warrior's art under Scatach the Shadowy One and Donall Mildemale in Alba. Immediately, Conall volunteered to go with his foster brother to Alba. The two heroes told Katbad the Druid of their planned adventure.

The next morning, King Connor called Setanta and Conall to his court. He walked with them to the House of the Twinkling Hoard, the repository of the weapons of the immortal warriors of Ulster.

"I hear you pair are off to Alba soon," said King Connor. Both looked at him.

"You may take your choice of weapons from the Twinkling Hoard—on one condition." King Connor opened the door and ushered them inside the house of weapons.

"I need a sea voyage to restore my vigor. In exchange for the weapons, I offer the company of a king. It has been many years since I danced with Scatach the Shadowy One."

Setanta knew it was a high honor to travel as a companion bodyguard to the king of Ulster. Both he and Conall were ready for any and all adventures. Awed and excited, they pledged allegiance to King Connor and each other with weapons from the Twinkling Hoard. King Connor appointed Fergus of the Long Sword as King of Ulster in his stead. Katbad the Druid was selected as adviser and enforcer to Fergus, for the good of Ulster.

The three set sail on a full tide and a strong wind. King Connor traveled in the guise of an envoy to the court of the Red Branch, escorting two young heroes to Alba to further their warrior skills. Setanta sensed there was more to King Connor's return to Alba than a dance with Scatach.

Meanwhile, back at the Red Branch, Suloscal set off for the fort of Fergall the Cunning. Left on Fergall's doorstep as a boy of thirteen by a wandering mercenary, Suloscal slid through life, a witness and a hearing post to the times that were in it. He told Fergall of the departure of Setanta for Alba after a visit to Emer. Also of Setanta's companions, King Connor and Conall Carney.

"Emer and Setanta must never come together. Be ready to sail on the next boat to Alba," Fergall said, and made ready to leave.

He and Suloscal traveled to Alba as a cattle-jobber and his drover. Both had done business with Donall and his daughter

Dornall before, buying and selling bulls and cows. To compliment the growing wealth of Donall, Fergall was always welcome to the home of the Hero-Maker.

This time, Fergall sent Suloscal to call on Donall's daughter, Dornall. This is another story, soon told. Suloscal brought a vivid red hairband for the unruly red hair of Dornall. He arranged a secret meeting between her and Fergall.

"Who is the guardian of Setanta and Conall?" asked Dornall.

"He is a king. King Connor of Ulster. He has more than one reason to return to Alba," said Suloscal. He noted the soft way she named Setanta, knowing this would be of interest to Fergall the Cunning.

Donall Mildemale had cold blue eyes, red hair on his head and brawny chest, and perfect balance in all his movements. He made the three Ulstermen welcome to his home, and kept his daughter Dornall apart from his visitors. This because of Dornall's proclivity for young warriors and her wicked nature if rejected.

The first lesson under Donall's instructions was walking barefoot on the pierced flagstones. These had a hole over a fire kept hot by a blowing bellows. Setanta and Conall walked barefoot over hot, smoking flagstones until their soles were black and leathered. Both showed fortitude and persistence in this trial by fire. Donall praised his pupils' courage to King Connor.

Setanta and Conall went down to a swift stream close to Dornall's small house. Unseen at an upper window, Dornall studied Setanta and Conall as they soaked their burnt feet in the stream. Dornall fell in love with the strong, perfect body of the man with stars in his eye. Setanta, body and burnt soles, invaded the heart and mind of Dornall. That night he became the center of her dreams and schemes as none had before.

King Connor's dreams were of Deirdre and revenge. He knew that Deirdre and Naóise had fled Ireland to Alba. His spies and pursuers kept the king informed as well as they could of Deirdre's wanderings. Naóise and his brothers, Aidan and Arden, survived as traveling mercenaries and bards. Deirdre survived on her love for the handsome Naóise and his love for her. King Connor thought to enlist the aid of Scatach the Shadowy One in the destruction of Naóise and his brothers and the recapture of Deirdre the Beautiful.

Fergall's dreams, like Setanta's, were of his daughter Emer. The difference was that of duration. Setanta saw his love for Emer binding them both together for life. Fergall dreamt that he would separate Setanta from Emer. This way she would marry into wealth and prominence and increase the family fortune. He had raised her with one purpose in mind, to wed a king or a rich man. Tomorrow he would meet with Donall's daughter Dornall and plot how to separate Setanta from his king and companion. To this end, he had taken Emer's shirt of the Tree of Life from her embroidery bag. Fergall the Cunning was well named.

Conall Carney dreamt of his friendship with his foster brother, Setanta. Together invincible, they would leave a legacy of the Red Branch of Ulster to endure as long as Gaels told tales. Brave all, until Conall and Setanta. Ulster was his world. All he needed. All he wanted. Conall was an eagle of protection over the province.

The second day of Donall's training began with an examination of the feet of Setanta and Conall Carney. Satisfied with their leather-hard skin, he took them to a field of spears, walking barefoot all the way. King Connor followed behind the Hero-Maker and his two pupils. Already the king was

homesick for Ulster, his Red Branch bed, and the company of
heroes at feast and play. Alba was for the young and reckless,
the thistle sharper than the shamrock.

He watched the balanced Donall open a gate into a small
field enclosed by wooden fences. Setanta and Conall entered
the field with Donall, who closed the gate. The three were barefoot, black of sole, and full of vigor. Donall led the two boys to
a small haystack in the center of the field. Setanta and Conall
obeyed Donall's directions, observed closely by King Connor
of Ulster. Setanta and Conall pulled the front of the haystack
aside, opening a shed-like wooded structure covered with hay.
They pushed on both sides of the haystack shed. It rumbled
backwards on hidden wheels, revealing a wooden contraption
covered with solid gear levers. Donall walked the field, fleet of
foot and sure of balance. The boys followed in his steps, paying heed to his every move.

Fergall followed close on Suloscal's heels through the front
door of Dornall's house. In his left hand, he held a present for
Dornall, something to complement her supreme gift. Dornall
had the sweetest voice in all of Alba. The glory of her song
induced visions of splendor among those who heard her, especially when Dornall was in love. Much depended on the quality
of the young warriors in her father's house. She had not slept well
since her first glimpse of Setanta washing his feet after a hot day
on the fierce flagstones. The three sat at a round table. Fergall
gave his gift to Dornall, wrapped in linen as red as her hair.

Donall stood on a raised platform behind the wooden contraption in the field of spears. By turning the wooden gear
levers, rows of spearheads sprang up like tall blades of grass
in an empty meadow. Setanta and Conall had to step lively
to prevent the spears from piercing their feet. Swiftly they

learned it was as much about balance as having calloused soles on their feet. For an hour, they walked the spear-tops, and then rested. Each had tiny specks of blood on his soles, but no major incisions.

And so the first half of the day went. Donall gauged their progress, raising the tips of the spears until they reached as high as those carried by a troop in a battle march. Neither Setanta nor Conall failed or faltered as Donall manipulated his gears and spears. He bent some sideways, some forward, some backward, some higher, some lower. Do or die time for the Ulster heroes. Do they did, as if born for this. Halfway through the day, they lay in the shade and slept for an hour. Donall had never had pupils as apt and able as Setanta and Conall. He knew his fame and fortune could rise with the knowledge he had tutored two such remarkable warriors, both mentored by a king as fabled as King Connor MacNessa.

Donall's daughter, Dornall, removed Fergall's gift from its red linen bag and clapped her hands with delight. A small, perfect harp from the original branch of the Tree of Life. She tuned it softly and hummed a love song that brought the birds who'd heard it to perch on her rooftop. All sang until Dornall. All harpists until Dornall. Fergall had done business with Dornall and her father before. He was a well-traveled man in his business of selling bulls and cattle. As Donall's wealth and fame increased, he invested in land and cattle. Who better at the cattle business than Fergall the Cunning? Dornall did not question his motive, but accepted his presence. And presents.

"I have a problem with Setanta. Do you know him?" asked Fergall.

At the name of Setanta, Dornall's fingers coaxed a trilling love note from the harp.

"I have not met him. I stay away from my father's house and his pupils," Dornall lied.

"I need to separate him from his companions as soon as possible. He is sworn to protect King Connor and will stay with him until death," Fergall said.

Dornall thought how much easier it could be to seduce Setanta if he were alone. She paid close attention to the plot outlined by Fergall the Cunning to affect the swift return of King Connor and Conall Carney to Ulster. She nodded agreement to all Fergall's suggestions for that evening. Then Dornall asked Fergall one question.

"Does Setanta like the color red?"

"Setanta is a Celt. He always wears red when traveling. He likes to redden his hands in the blood of his enemies," answered Fergall.

The harp emitted delighted trills. When Setanta and Conall awoke, they noticed a new arrangement of the tall spears at Donall's hands. The first row of spears was straight. Succeeding rows were bent in all directions at different angles. They watched Donall as he performed his feats of climbing a straight spear, balancing on its top, and leaping to another spear-top, at random. This Donall did with ease and grace. Then he repeated his journey across the spear-tops with his sword and javelin in hands, and shield on his forearm.

Setanta cracked the knuckles of his seven-fingered hand. He spread wide the seven toes on each foot. He knew these extra digits gave him an advantage over Conall Carney. A warrior accrued every advantage available because there are few second chances in the ranks of death.

Setanta embraced Conall Carney and then shimmied up a straight spear. He balanced on one heel, swinging his sword as if in the heat of battle. Conall saluted his friend Setanta, foster brothers until death. Donall had never seen a pupil like Setanta the Warped One. Setanta concentrated his energy with a low battle cry that carried him back and forth across the spear-tops as if a seagull skimming the high tides. Then Setanta did his salmon leaps from one spear-top to the next, from one side of the field to its opposite. Backward, forward, sideways, Setanta transversed any and all arrangements of the spears by the startled Donall. Setanta's last leap carried him high into a low-flying cloud, out of sight to Donall and Conall. Had the Warped One vanished to the Other Side? Setanta landed on the wooded contraption in front of Donall and leapt to the ground beside him. A brace of geese were pierced by Setanta's sword and two plump blackbirds quivered on the top of his javelin. Donall realized he had nothing more to teach Setanta, that this pupil exceeded his teacher by a wide margin.

Setanta and Donall concentrated on training Conall Carney for the rest of the afternoon. One on each side of Conall, they instructed him in the art of balance, and the feat of warrior battle on a spear-point. The fearless Conall learned fast with two such mentors. His love and admiration for Setanta now knew no bounds, nor did his confidence in himself as a warrior of the Red Branch.

Twenty-One

WHILE HER FATHER'S house was empty, Dornall entered. She found Setanta's room by the quality of weapons stacked in a corner and an embroidered body shirt with two branches reaching across a stream. The legend of the Tree of Life. Swiftly she arranged the shirt on the top of javelins so that the branches pointed toward her own small house. Then she arranged the sister shirt of Emer, given to her by Fergall the Cunning, in a similar manner.

Outside her father's house, with the aid of Suloscal, Dornall set a cunning trail of parallel branches on the grass in a circuitous route to her house. Here she bade farewell to Suloscal and sent him on his way. Inside, as in her father's house, she prepared the immortal food of the Gaels, as instructed by Fergall. This included a sprinkling of Fergall's potion over the berries, acorns, and seasoned chestnuts. Alongside these plates of nuts and berries, she left a large goblet of Alba's best whiskey. Then Dornall lay down for her beauty sleep before the arrival of Setanta.

* * * * * *

After a day of spear hopping with Conall and Donnal, Setanta returned to his room, exhilarated and exhausted, thinking of Emer. Setanta looked to his love gift. He blinked his left eye. Had his squint upset his vision? Was he seeing double? He walked to the javelins against the wall. The sister shirt of Emer touched his own Tree of Life shirt. Both embroidered branches now pointed toward the small house of Donall's daughter, Dornall her name, unseen and unheard since his arrival. His good eye noted a trail of parallel branches to Dornall's house. Ever ready for love and adventure, Setanta slipped unseen from Donall's house. A vision of Emer drew Setanta toward the small house. How or why she had sent him a lover's trail aroused his romantic nature. He pushed open the front door and advanced to the small table. Laying aside his javelin, Setanta chewed on the nuts and blackberries. Another dream of Emer formed in his mind, shaped by a love melody from a heavenly harp. He sat at the table. This food and music tasted new to Setanta. So did love. It flavored his world, endowing him with increasing pleasure in his person. He drank from the goblet. Alba's water of life. God's kiss wet his lips and warmed his heart. The love harp circled the crown of his head, slid down the byways of his brain, and enlarged the scope of his imagination. A delicious relaxation of his body followed. Then the dream of Emer pushed the world away. Setanta embraced the music from Dornall's harp, leaned back in his chair, and slept.

King Connor and Conall Carney sat at a round table in Donall's house. They ate of the nuts, sloes, and blackberries in front of them. Connor poured two drinks from the flagon on the table. He toasted Conall.

"Luck of the Irish," said Connor the King.

"To the Red Branch of Ulster," replied Conall.

They drank. It seemed then that a heavenly harp played an exile's lament of exquisite longing outside the window. Dornall's harp wove an aislinn for Connor and Conall. They fell asleep. A beautiful woman appeared in their dreams, and transported them to the court of the Red Branch. Never had they missed Ulster so much. Never were they so glad to return. Yet there remained a stillness around the Red Branch that chilled the heart. Dornall's soft voice spoke over the harp.

"Men killed—women raped—cattle abducted. Queen Maeve will ravage Ulster until she captures and returns the bull Tawn Bo to Fergall, its rightful owner. The men of Ulster, in their hour of need, will lay stricken with Macra's curse of the birth pangs. The Red Branch will diminish and die unless King Connor and Conall Carney return to save the province of Ulster."

Outside the door of Donall's house, his daughter Dornall finished her harp playing. Swiftly, she returned to her home and Setanta. Shortly afterwards, King Connor awoke from his aislinn, a vision of the red court in his mind and these words in his ears—men killed, women raped, cattle abducted. Connor shook Conall awake.

"We must return to Ulster immediately. Get the horses ready. I'll tell Setanta and thank our host," said King Connor.

He could not locate Setanta or Donall in the house by the time the horses were at the front door. Thinking only of Ulster, he mounted up and rode for his life. Conall rode beside him. They did not notice Donall talking to Fergall the Cunning in the field of spears. They did not notice Dornall dancing with her harp outside the front of her house. They rode for Ireland and Ulster, heart and home.

Setanta awoke from his dream of Emer the Fair to the reality of Dornall, the daughter of Donall. Dornall of the Lumpy Bumps. Dornall of the Beetling Brow, framed by the roughest red hair in creation. None rougher. Ever. Except for the spiky black bushy hair between her knees. Setanta blinked. A bad day for his squint? He closed and reopened his eyes. No. Emer was in Ireland. He was in Alba. And Dornall before him. Knees like boulders, feet behind, heels in front, one lame, the other halt. Hands like hamhocks. Teeth like a wolf's. Gums like a badger's. Eyes black, one crooked, one crossed. Setanta reached for and emptied the flagon of Alba's whiskey on the table. There are limits to the warping, he thought for the first time. Setanta moved to keep the table between them.

"Your friends have gone back to Ulster, Setanta," said Dornall in her musical voice. She placed a small harp on the table.

"The music of love awaits, Setanta. It will play forever between us. Say but the word."

Setanta's heart was charmed by the voice and words of Dornall. It was the frame from which they came that upset his equilibrium. Where was Emer in his time of need?

"I am betrothed to my first and only love," said Setanta.

The righteous are bold when it suits them. Dornall pressed forward.

"Her name is Emer. Her father will kill you—or her—to prevent a wedding. No sweeter music than mine shall play for you, Setanta, now or forever," swore Dornall in a voice to topple any man's virtue.

She blew a love-breath that stripped the clothes from his body and outlined his lineage from the Other Side. Had the Warped One met his match? Dornall pressed forward, a song of love's surrender and chastisement on her lips. A siren call to excess. Each note of Dornall's song weakened his resolve to stay pure until he returned to Emer. All that separated the naked Setanta and the advancing Dornall was his round-knobbed javelin on the tabletop between them.

As her song ended, Setanta and Dornall both reached for his javelin. Their hands met. Setanta's javelin sliced a long gash in Dornall's palm. She screamed. A gush of blood spurted from her, splashing onto Setanta's hand. He lost his grip on his javelin. It rolled off the table. Red blood on his hand restored Setanta's vim and vigor, and his vow to Emer. Gathering his clothes and slippery javelin, he ducked under the table. Dornall's legs stood apart, blood dripped from her open wounds; Setanta squeezed between Dornall's thighs. Her legs wrapped around his body. The spiky hair between her knees lacerated his back, splashing blood from shoulder to hip; wriggling and pushing, using his blood as a lubricant, Setanta emerged from the rear of Dornall. Eyes wide open, he ran through Dornall's open door.

* * * * * *

After his escape from the clutches of Dornall, Setanta sought to find the fort of Scatach the Shadowy One. He missed the high company of king and companion. Weary and wary, he avoided all because of fear of Fergall's cunning and Dornall's sorcery. Who could he trust in a strange country of unknown perils? He persevered for three long days and dark nights, avoiding the high and low roads of Alba. Gradually, his ebullience returned. Ferdia, friend and foster brother, was honing his skills with Scatach the Shadowy One. Fergall himself had told him he would be the first warrior in Europe if he studied with Scatach the Amazon. All Setanta had to do was find the fort of Scatach, near an isle called Skye.

On his third morning alone, Setanta slept under an oak tree, dreaming of Emer. He awoke to drops of warm liquid on his breast. Stirred and shaken, Setanta awoke to see a glorious white horse standing over him. Framed by the rising sun, the sea-green eye of the horse dropped another salty tear on Setanta. This tear fell on his forehead, over his eye from the Other Side. The all-seeing eye of his warping.

Fully alert, Setanta's eye from the Other Side warned him not to trust the emotions stirring in his breast. Sometimes the head knows more than the heart. The great white horse moved to the left of Setanta, and he saw the outline of a green-cloaked woman astride the beast. Obscuring her face was a wave-white cape falling on her shoulders from her head.

"Whither your direction, traveler?" The woman's voice was an echo of love seeking its source.

"I seek the Isle of Skye, the fort of Scatach the Shadowy One," Setanta said.

"All know of Scatach, sister to Queen Aoife, the wildest warrior on the earth. What would you offer if I took you to a bridge between Alba and the Isle of Skye?" mocked the woman in green.

"Kind lady, I offer my sword, my short javelin, and myself," said Setanta.

"The weapon I want is attached. Setanta, mount behind and ride the waves to the Bridge of Last Endeavors," she patted the rump of her wonderful white horse. Setanta wondered how she knew his name as he sat behind her. Sliding his arm under her green cloak, he let her naked flesh warm his own.

They rode out of the forest onto a wild, curving coastline. The white horse plunged into the sea and charged along the crest of the waves as if on the racetrack near the Red Branch of King Connor. Thus they traveled until the sun set. Setanta behind a lady in a cloak as green as the sea, on the back of a white horse. A teardrop on his heart from the green eyes of the white horse had created realms of pleasure between Setanta and the lady. And the white horse. The vision of Emer vanished from his mind. Setanta's young arm absorbed the surges of the lady in green from the smoothness of the steed's strides.

Mane flying, tail erect, the great horse left the ocean to gallop up an inclined hill. He stopped outside a wooden house on top of a grassy cliff. Setanta helped the lady in green down from the horse. He followed her into the house. The white horse snickered as if laughing at him. He turned around. The white horse galloped across the ocean toward the setting sun, circled by a rainbow mist.

Setanta walked into an empty house. No sign of the vanished lady in green. A blazing oak fire crackled in a bedroom. Setanta placed his sword and javelin on the king-sized bed. Stripping naked, he lay on the bed. The flickering flames cast colors on his thoughts. The last time he had lain naked with his weapons was in the Twinkling Hoard at the Red Court. Then an onslaught of Amazons. Tonight one lady in a green cloak. Come one, come all. First comes courage. So Setanta dozed off, his hand on his javelin, his mind in the clouds.

He awoke to find himself straddled by a lady whose green cloak covered both of them. Her face still hidden by her white cape. Her hands in front of him, clutching his javelin. Higher rose the javelin, aimed at his middle eye. A blood-red hairpiece fell across his neck. Carefully, he moved his hands to grasp the ends of the hair braids. The woman in green rode him as she had the horse. Surges of pleasure in the joust of love. Setanta's fingertips touched the hair braids of the lady. He bided his time. She'd drive the javelin into his forehead when she'd had her fill of him. She shook in a thrill of agony and ecstasy.

Setanta pulled her off balance, wrapping her hair around the bedposts. As she jerked forward, the javelin missed his head and rammed into the bed frame. He wrapped his legs right around her, holding her in place as he slid his left hand around her throat. The seven digits, strong and relentless. He squeezed until she went limp. He pulled his javelin free of the bedpost. Still holding her neck, he pushed the green cloak and white cape from the lady between his legs. Dornall, the daughter of Donall the Hero-Maker. Dornall, feet behind, heels in front, one eye crooked, the other crossed. Both closed at the moment. Before mounting the white horse, she must have removed the spiky hair between her knees. He waited until her eyes opened. She stared at him. No one had ever treated her like this before.

"When will the white horse return?" he asked.

"Tomorrow at sunrise," Dornall's voice rasped.

"Will he take me to Scatach the Shadowy One?"

"He comes for a lady in a sea-green cloak," she said.

"Where does he come from, Dornall?" he asked, caressing her throat.

"He is the lord of the deeps, the seas, and the oceans. Are you going to kill me, Setanta?"

"I do not kill women. As yet," he said.

They did not speak again until the sun rose, laying as they were throughout the night. A knocking, like a horse kicking, shook the house. The door slowly opened. Dornall stood in her green cloak and white cape. Outside stood a tall, handsome man of animal grace and magnetism. He wore a wavewhite shirt, a sea-green kilt, and a flowing white cape. His eyes green, his hair white, this lord of the morning bowed deeply before the lady in the green cloak.

"Where is the squinter?" he asked.

Dornall pointed toward the ground, prompted by the point of Setanta's javelin in her back.

"Whither the journey, Dornall?" He had deep rolling tones in his voice.

Dornall pointed north. "To Scatach the Shadowy One."

He bowed deeply, until both palms touched the ground. His wave-white hair grew long and luxurious, covering his body from head to feet. Dornall stepped back into the house at the request of Setanta's javelin.

A figure in green sat on the lord of the morn, as he transformed himself from the human to the mystical. Finally, the great white horse with the flowing mane strutted in a circle, a lady in a green cloak and white cape on his back. Inside the house, the naked Dornall plucked a sad melody from her new harp. All in all, she considered herself lucky not to be the first woman slain by Setanta, by love or force or both. She savored the cold hate building in her veins.

Dornall had not told Setanta the legend of the white horse with the green eyes and riptide mane, called the Kelpie. All who saw him loved his grace and beauty. A tear from the Kelpie's green eyes, whether as man or beast, would render its recipient a slave to love of the creature forever. The Kelpie appeared always at sunrise. At sunset, the Kelpie rode the wave back to his palace in the wild whirlpools of the ocean.

There he reigned as King of the Mermaids, who tended to his every need as he sat on his coral throne.

Dressed in Dornall's green cloak and white cape, Setanta sat easy on the Kelpie's back. They cantered down an inclined trail to the ocean from whence they came. Once more, they were riding the crests of the waves toward the Isle of Skye, home of Scatach the Shadowy One. So smooth were the great strides of the Kelpie that not a drop of salt water touched any of the fourteen toes of Setanta. An ease and intimacy bound man and horse, kindled by the green tear dropped by the Kelpie on the heart of Setanta.

In the late afternoon, the Kelpie flicked Setanta with his tail. They returned to the seashore, charging along the curving coastline. Setanta caressed the Kelpie's upright ears with his seven-digit hands. He pressed his powerful legs around the creature's back. They would know each other if they ever met again.

The Kelpie snorted three times and galloped straight at a sheer black cliff. Setanta prepared to leap for his life. The Kelpie lunged sideways into the mouth of a narrow cave. The Kelpie charged forward, lighting the way through the cave by beams of green from his emerald eye.

Setanta held tight, crouching low to escape the startled bats disturbed from their sleep. None dared touch the Kelpie or his rider. Along the bottom edges of the cave scurried enormous water rats, chased by Manx cats from the Isle of Man. Resting in a pool at the side of the cave lay a large three-headed monster from a loch called Ness. As far as he could see, Alba was as odd as Ulster, thought Setanta.

Finally, he saw daylight ahead. His spirits soared as they left the cave and dashed into a dark, dense forest. They skimmed past trees with sinister branches. On the forest floor, a cutting grass with sword-sharp blades slashed at Setanta's seven-toed feet. His tough-as-leather soles blunted the grass, but it damaged the hem of his green cloak. Wild-eyed forest creatures fled from the long strides of the Kelpie. The deeper they rode into the forest, the colder it became. No rays from the sun had warmed this part of the black forest. Each breath exhaled hung on the air. Setanta's extremities were losing contact with the rest of him, his ears and nose icicles ready to crack. The Kelpie's magic powers propelled them forward, never straying from his way through the Forest of Frost. Setanta's only source of heat lay between his legs, the broad warm back of the Kelpie. He knew if he did not move his limbs soon, he'd die from the frostbite of the bitter cold. Yet if he dismounted, and his legs were weak, he'd freeze in place, and never see Ulster again.

Cwency-Cwo

BACK IN HER father's house, Dornall collected twenty of his special spears. Each spear-tip had a shape and its curse to enter and kill a vital body part if thrown in anger at its target. Dornall—vengeance her name and vicious her nature when thwarted by desire. None had riven her as deeply as Setanta. None would pay as dearly. Standing on a wood bench, Dornall removed the power shield of her father from its hallowed place on the wall. She carried it outside and placed the spears on top. When all lay to her liking, she stripped naked and knelt on the shield of her father. Raising high her twisted arms, she sang a heavenly invocation for aid. Her beautiful voice attracted the scald crows in Alba. A black cloud of birds raised high the shield of Donall with his daughter and spears aboard. They covered the naked girl with black feathers to keep her warm and make her one of their own. Like a small cloud in a thunderstorm, they scudded across the afternoon sky in pursuit of Setanta and the Kelpie. The lovely voice of Dornall removed all obstacles from their flight of vengeance.

Setanta clasped his arms around the neck of the Kelpie for warmth. He lay his cheek against the silky skin of the beast, and rubbed his legs and feet along its haunches. The cold air scalded his lungs and froze the stars in his eye. Only an image of Emer kept his heart warm and the blood pumping in his veins.

With a swoop and a swish and shower of black feathers, the shield of Donall flew into the black forest. The Kelpie was the first to hear the twitter of the scald crows behind him. He twisted his neck and flicked Setanta with his tail. The shield of scald crows drew level with the Kelpie and his rider. The bird woman standing on the middle of the shield had a long spear in each hand. A bitter song of revenge raised a raucous commotion from the scald crows. They flew closer to the Kelpie until there was a spear's length between them.

Setanta's cold lungs could not muster up his battle cry to commence his warping. Dornall drew back the spear with the two eyeballs carved on its tip. She pushed it forward until its point was inches from Setanta's starry eye. Satisfied that they knew each other, she drew back the spear for its fatal throw. The Kelpie snorted. With his elegant tail, he flogged the frozen Setanta from shoulder to wrists, from thighs to toes. Dornall sang in ecstasy at the punishment of Setanta. Straight and true, the scald crows flew the shield alongside the magical Kelpie. Restored to vigor, his blood warm and wicked, Setanta stood on the back of the Kelpie. The green cloak trailed behind him, revealing his strong, heroic body.

Lust for Setanta delayed the launching of the spear in Dornall's right hand. Her crossed eyes caressed every nook and cranny of his being. Her feathered form recalled every touch of Setanta, every scrape and shape of him. The Kelpie saved the day for both of them.

He flicked his long tail around the ankles of Dornall, whipping her off balance. She fell flat on her back, the air knocked from her lungs, both spears erect. Seizing the moment, Setanta leapt from the back of the Kelpie to the tips of the spears, as he had learned from Dornall's father. He slid down the shafts of the spears, landing astride Dornall. The shield wobbled under Setanta's weight, shaking loose a scatter of scald crows. Setanta hoisted Dornall to her feet. He lifted her high and dropped her on the back of the Kelpie, facing the tail of the beast. The Kelpie sniggered and snorted. Setanta leapt onto his warm back, facing Dornall. The cold drew them together in a tight embrace, enhanced by the smooth strides of the white horse. Behind them flew scald crows, bearing the shield, the spears of Dornall's father snug on its length.

And so the three bonded again, the Kelpie and Dornall, ridden smoothly by Setanta, until they left the frozen forest. Now they were crossing the Plain of Missteps, full of wild and wondrous animals. Beneath the flying feet of the Kelpie lay bottomless quagmires and smoking bog fires of toxic intensity. Setanta and Dornall were lost in each other, paying small heed to their dangerous surroundings. The Kelpie knew the way to make the crooked smooth and destinations available to those lost in the wood.

Sunset began as the Kelpie and his courting couple reached the end of this world and the beginning of Scatach's. The Isle of Skye, where the Shadowy One lived in a secured fort, began in shade and shadow, fog and fear. The Bridge of Last Endeavors connected Alba to the vague outlines of the rocky Isle of Skye. A bridge built before Old God was young, it ended at the wooden gate to Scatach's fortress. It spanned a deep gorge of tempestuous waters filled with ravenous creatures of the ocean deep.

Setanta dismounted, kissed the Kelpie three times on his neck, and whispered in his ear. Replete and completed, Dornall watched Setanta walk toward the Bridge of Last Endeavors. If he returned to say good-bye to her, she'd let him leave. If not—well, she'd always have the ride on the Kelpie. Setanta stepped onto the bridge and walked slowly forward. The middle of the bridge rose high and flung Setanta from its end. He landed at the feet of Dornall, who was standing by the Kelpie. She put her foot with the heel in front on his chest and had an attack of the giggles. The Kelpie threw back his head and had an attack of the sniggers. Setanta waited for them to finish. He rose to his feet and began a swift run at the bridge. Reaching it, he launched himself into a long jump that brought him close to the center of the bridge. Once more, it bucked high, flinging him forth. Only by using his balance and grabbing onto the side of the bucking bridge did Setanta escape being thrown in the roaring waters below. He pulled himself together, scrambled back on the bridge, and returned to Dornall and the Kelpie. Setanta sat and stared at the bridge. It was not in his character to be discouraged. He'd collect his energy, restore his spirit, and try again.

On the Isle of Skye, high in the looking tower of her fortress, Scatach the Shadowy One watched the antics of Setanta. Beside her stood Hamish Mac Scatach, her son of limited opinions and endless ability as a warrior.

"Another lad from Ireland, from the cut of him," sneered Hamish, jealous for affection.

"More than a lad, to reach here with the Kelpie and Dornall," said Scatach, closely watching Setanta. Hamish looked at his mother. Shapely legs in laced leather leggings, a very short kilt of iron rectangles, a black steel-studded leather bodice.

A sliver helmet shaped like a ship's prow on jet-black hair. A face to die by and for. Famous for ease with sword and spear, Scatach reigned as the foremost teacher of young warriors. None had her level of cunning and conquest sought by those who sought the same for their young warriors. Hamish had heard of only two Amazons her equal at arms. Her wild twin Aoife and a queen in Ireland named Maeve. Hamish knew his mother Scatach had a soft spot for youths from Ulster. She favored Ferdia, the foster brother of Setanta, Naóise and his brothers, Aidan and Arden, and any she felt in the mood for. Because of her hectic pace, she could not put a name on the father of Hamish. The custom of fostering boys did not prevail in Alba as it did in Ireland. Scatach directed the attention of Hamish toward the Kelpie and his companions.

Setanta prepared for his third attempt to cross the Bridge of Last Endeavors. Scatach watched in admiration as he flexed his sword and javelin. Hamish watched in mortification as the Kelpie nudged Setanta in the back to get his attention. Hamish only had his mother's attention when he killed someone. The Kelpie knelt before Setanta. Without bidding farewell to Dornall, Setanta mounted the Kelpie. They rode in the circle of the sun, golden gods from a golden past.

Straight and true, the Kelpie galloped for the bridge, watched by the angry eyes of Dornall, the jealous eyes of Hamish, and the star-struck eyes of Scatach the Shadowy One. The Kelpie's hooves blazed to the bridge, and he leapt high over the roaring waters below. Setanta flashed with energy as he entered a grand adventure. The Kelpie landed in the middle of the bridge. It revolted, rising high and flinging both toward the foggy outline of Scatach's forest. Hamish rushed down from the tower. He'd greet this brash intruder with a spear in his back at the front door. Maybe then Scatach would appreciate her son's need for attention.

The tail of the Kelpie slapped a farewell to Setanta's back, and dropped down into the roaring waters beneath the bridge. Setanta flew forward, breaking his fall with a javelin jammed into the door. Scatach ran from the tower, slamming the door of her daughter Utach's room in passing. In the courtyard, Hamish stood by the door with his spear raised.

His balance restored, Setanta turned to ascertain the fate of the Kelpie in the wild waters below. A long spear ripped the shirt from his body, smashed through the door, and pierced Hamish in his heart. Scatach watched her son in his death throes, impaled against the door in a deathly embrace. She turned and walked slowly back to her daughter Utach's room. As in life, so in death Hamish lacked the attention of his mother.

The cawking of scald crows drowned the death rattle of Hamish. Dornall directed the hundreds of birds flying her father's shield to close in on her target, Setanta. She'd thrown her first spear at the Warped One from Alba. Now she was three spear lengths away from her second throw. Setanta flashed his eyes at Dornall. She held back, excited by his youth and glamour. He turned his back on her and grasped the haft of the embedded spear in the bridge door. Wild-eyed, she stood on the shield.

All this was watched by Scatach and her daughter, Utach, in the room facing the bridge. Neither blinked in their fascination with Setanta and his moves. Both thrilled with passion at his presence. Scatach pushed Utach away from the window.

"Go below; find the name and nature of the man who killed your brother," she ordered her daughter.

The lovely Utach was soon across the courtyard. At the bridge door, she stood beside the body of her brother, Hamish. On the other side, Setanta braced his seven-toed foot against the doorframe. He pulled free the spear from the heart of Hamish. A slab of the door cracked off as the spear emerged. Emer's Tree of Life shirt fell to the ground, its embroidery ripped and stained with the heart-blood of Hamish. Utach stepped back as her brother's body fell in front of her.

Sensing Dornall's need to see the stars in his eye, Setanta spun low and flung the spear sideways at her. She stepped left and threw her second spear at Setanta. Straight and true, Setanta's spear struck the shield and sent it spinning back to Alba. Screeching dizzy scald crows knocked Dornall flat on the curve of her father's shield. Dornall's spear skimmed past Setanta's head and tore another crack from the door. Now the lovely Utach could see Setanta through the spear-cracks in the door. He stopped and arose with Emer's tattered shirt. His seven-digit hand shook and tears flushed the stars in his eye. Setanta pressed the remains of the shirt to his heart and tied it around his neck. Utach glimpsed the long red wound torn by Dornall's first spear on Setanta's side. A bright red ray of the setting sun lit the Bridge of Last Endeavors and the deep gorge beneath. Where was the Kelpie, wondered Setanta.

He lay flat at the gorge's edge, peering down at the demented waters. The gorgeous Kelpie arose from the depths, calming all in front and behind. The waters parted to a smooth surface as he cantered toward the setting sun. Once more, the Kelpie shook his tail in farewell to Setanta. Behind the great sea horse followed his ravenous subjects, hailing their Lord of the Deep. Giant fish as long as nine spears with teeth as long as one. Swords with fish attached, thrusting forward. Fish that flew in the air as they swam in the water. Spouting hillocks of whales, like Old God pissing in the morning. A white testicle with waving willies. Slow fish. Blow fish. Glow fish. And a three-headed monster from a loch called Ness. Grateful for knowledge of the Kelpie, Setanta rolled over on his back. On the eve of a brand new adventure, the first star of the evening winked at him.

After a year of hard labor on the rock, I row away from my island in the ocean. Alone, strong, and steady, I now return from whence I came.

At the request of my order, I have gathered the grapes of my labor. My quills, my vellum, and my legends of Setanta are secure in satchels on my shoulder.

Farewell Setanta, love bright of my heart. My boy beautiful. I leave you on the Isle of Skye, outside the fortress of Scatach the Shadowy One.

And so I leave a world beyond wonder, where ancient romances are burnished by time and telling. It is here I pray to continue the saga of Setanta the Warped One.

So be it.

Mael Moró

www.ingramcontent.com/pod-product-compliance
Lightning Source LLC
Chambersburg PA
CBHW021520240626

47154CB00002B/721